# WHEN IRISH EYES ARE LYING

THE KILTEEGAN BRIDGE SERIES - BOOK 4

JEAN GRAINGER

*To my mother, who taught us how to be a family.*

# FOREWORD

The story so far…

Beautiful Lena O'Sullivan is only seventeen when she falls passionately in love with Malachy Berger. Despite a promise of marriage, Malachy abandons her, and Lena, who is pregnant, goes to Wales to have her baby in secret. There she meets Eli Kogan, a Jewish doctor. They marry and return to Kilteegan Bridge, where Eli raises Lena's baby, Emmet, as his own.

Years later, Malachy, who is still in love with Lena, returns to tell Emmet that he is his 'real' father. Meanwhile, it emerges that Malachy's father, August, murdered Malachy's mother, Hannah, and Lena's father, Paudie, in a fit of jealous rage – even though the two victims were only friends.

As Emmet gets older, he starts to behave with a self-centred arrogance reminiscent of his grandfather, August Berger. An unrelated legal battle has ensured he is the true heir of Kilteegan House, and he complains about Lena's sister Emily and her husband, Blackie, using 'his' sheds for their business and Lena's brother, Jack, for farming 'his' land. He objects to Eli building a surgery in the gatehouse, and even stops talking to Jack and his friend Skipper because he suspects them of being gay. But when Emmet is threatened by local conman Jingo Crean, and Jack, Skipper and Blackie come to his rescue, Emmet finally discovers the importance of true friends and family. And afterwards, when his cousin, Nellie, confides in him that she is pregnant by a married man, he stands by her.

Meanwhile, Lena's widowed mother, who suffers mental ill health but is benefitting from modern medicine, marries historian Klaus Rizzenburg. With Klaus's help, she finds her beloved brother, Ted, who has been missing since the war, and Ted returns to Ireland just in time for him and Maria to claim a substantial joint inheritance from their adoptive mother's estate.

Now read on…

# CHAPTER 1

'She won't tell us who he is or where he comes from or who his family are or anything.' Emily's voice rose in exasperation as she related to Lena her latest argument with her sixteen-year-old daughter, Nellie.

'Don't be too hard on her, Emily,' Lena said sympathetically. She was sitting at her sister's kitchen table, where the windows gave a perfect view up and down the main street of Kilteegan Bridge. Outside the library, Nettie Collins was pasting up a poster advertising a new book, *Salem's Lot* by Stephen King. From the shop below came the sound of Peggy chatting to a customer. But in her mind's eye, Lena was in the past, remembering what it felt like to be a young pregnant girl abandoned by her first love. 'Poor Nellie. She must be heartbroken.'

'I know.' Emily sighed. 'And I promise I'm not being hard on her, but I still wish she would tell us who he is, though she says she can't. She says she's too worried Blackie will kill him and end up in prison.'

'Well, maybe she's right about that.' Lena smiled a little. 'I know Blackie normally wouldn't hurt a fly, but he adores Nellie so much. Anyway, Emily, what good would it do you and Blackie to know who the father is? Are you going to make her marry some ignorant young fella who hasn't got the guts to stick by her in her hour of need?'

'No, of course not.' Lena's older sister looked uncomfortable 'It's just, well, it would be good to know if he's going to make anything difficult in the future, like walking into our shop out of the blue and saying he wants to have a relationship with his son or daughter, just like when Malachy came back into Emmet's life and, well, you know...'

Lena did know. Malachy Berger turning up in her son's life had been confusing and disruptive, though things had settled down since then. At least Emmet now said he knew who his real father was, and that was Lena's beloved husband, Eli, who had taken Emmet into his heart from when he was born.

'Emily, is Nellie still planning to bring up her baby here in Kilteegan Bridge by herself?' she asked tentatively, trying not to let the worry show on her face.

She knew Emily and her husband, Blackie, would do anything for their daughter, but the reality was this was going to create a terrible scandal for them. Monsignor Collins, the local parish priest, would have something to say, no doubt, and the associated shame might even impact the shop. He wouldn't shun them overtly, but he wasn't above making remarks from the altar about loose morals and the people who held them. The Monsignor had tried to stop his parishioners using Eli as their doctor after Eli prescribed Mrs Moriarty the contraceptive pill. The last thing Emily needed was another public row with the priest. She and Blackie had already had a terrible time this year, what with Blackie's dreadful brother, Jingo, turning up and wreaking havoc on their family's reputation yet again.

Emily kept her eyes lowered as she poured them both another cup of tea. 'Well, not exactly. She's decided she doesn't want to be a mother.'

'Oh...' Lena was surprised and puzzled. As far as she knew, Nellie didn't want to have her baby adopted, but if her headstrong niece had changed her mind, why was Emily so worried about the father coming into the shop and claiming his son or daughter? The child would be over in America or something, with a different name, completely untraceable.

'I mean, I think she's right, actually. I wouldn't even want her to be a mother.' Emily was blushing now. 'She's too young to raise a child. She'll only have just turned seventeen when it's born, and she doesn't want to anyway. She doesn't want this baby. She said the father wanted her to go to England to have…' Emily's eyes filled with tears. She couldn't even say the word. 'Anyway, Nellie wouldn't do *that*, sure she couldn't, but the thought of my grandchild being given to strangers, when all Blackie and I ever wanted was another child, it feels so wrong. So you know…' She looked at Lena appealingly. 'We wouldn't even have to go through an adoption process, if Eli would agree to it. So that's what I was going to ask you to ask him?' She stopped, clearly wanting Lena to understand what she was saying without her having to spell it out.

'Ask him what, Emily?' Lena was utterly confused.

Emily took a sip of her tea and looked at Lena over the rim of her cup. 'To ask him to say it's me who's having the baby and not Nellie.'

'What? Wait…' Lena stared at her sister in incredulity. 'You're going to tell everyone the baby is yours and you want Eli to act like it's you that's pregnant, not Nellie?'

Emily's face was full of determination. 'We've all three of us been around it and around it. It's the only way.'

'Blackie is in agreement?' Lena was staggered at the enormity of what her sister was suggesting.

'Well, as against the alternative, yes, that's what he wants.'

'And Nellie is happy to go along with it?'

Her sister nodded firmly. 'She is. It's happened before, Lena, we all know it. There's plenty round here who were reared with their mother as their sister and their granny as their mother. And people sometimes have their suspicions, but they're never able to prove it. I don't think in this case they'll even be suspicious. Everyone knows I've been trying to have another baby forever.'

'But how will you do it?' Lena was still nonplussed.

'We're going to tell everyone that Nellie has a live-in hotel job in

London, and I'll go with her to settle her in. We'll find a nursing home for her to have the baby in. It will have to be soon, before she starts showing. I dread the thought of her going, but it has to be this way, in case the Monsignor or someone else sees her and suspects something. I'm scared of my life of him finding out. And then when I come back, I'll start wearing bumps, getting bigger and bigger as time goes on. I ordered these tight slips for the shop. They're made of a kind of nylon and elastic, so that will hold a bump I'll make from foam in place, and we'll start telling people. Then when the time comes, I'll pretend I have to go into a special nursing home because I've had so many problems with losing babies before – the last one was only two years ago…' Her voice caught briefly on the sadness of that loss, but she rallied and carried on. 'But actually, Blackie and I will go to England to be with Nellie, and afterwards we'll bring the baby home as our own. Nellie will be free to live her life, and Blackie and I will become parents again after all these years.'

There was a hint of joy in Emily's voice, despite the difficulty of the situation. Lena knew the toll miscarriage after miscarriage had taken on her sister, so many times her hopes raised only to have them dashed, most of them early enough, but twice when she was over three months pregnant and they'd already told people. It was a pain her sister bore bravely, but it was there. Blackie felt it too but maybe not the same way. Lena always thought that men became fathers when they saw the baby, but women were mothers from the moment they conceived. A baby was a miracle, a dream come true, and Emily obviously thought her own grandchild being raised as her son or daughter was a great idea. But the reality was that secrets like that, the web of lies it would require, had a horrible power to come back on even the most kindhearted people with the best of intentions. Lena's mind went back to that maternity hospital in Cardiff sixteen years ago, when she thought she could give Emmet up. But when it came to it, she just couldn't. Nellie might just feel the same.

'And what if when she has the baby, she can't give him or her up to you?'

'She says she will, and she is determined, Lena. You know what she's like. She's got her mind made up, and she wants to live her life and not be shackled to a baby without a husband.'

'But, Em, and I don't mean to be horrible or anything, but she doesn't know how she'll feel – she can't. She might be all gung ho for this plan, but so was I, and then I found I just couldn't let him go to strangers.'

'But this baby wouldn't be going to strangers. He or she would be coming home, to their family,' Emily said quietly.

'That's true.' Lena thought briefly about what it might have been like to have Emmet raised by Maria, supposing her unstable mother had been able to cope. Of course, unlike Maria, Emily had proved herself a wonderful mother, both loving and practical.

'Will you support me? Even if you think it's mad?' Emily asked, putting her hand on Lena's.

Lena didn't need to consider that. Her sister had been by her side through thick and thin. She would never turn her back on her. 'Of course I will. I'm just worried, that's all. So Nellie's…I mean, your baby is due around Easter?'

Emily nodded, happier now she knew her sister was backing her.

'Right.' Lena exhaled. 'We'd better get planning then. I'll talk to Eli. I don't know what he'll say, but I'm sure when it comes down to it, he'll want to help.'

'Thanks, Lena. I'd be lost without you. My head is scrambled trying to figure it all out. I feel like I can breathe now I've told you. How's Emmet, by the way?' asked Emily suddenly, 'he seemed a bit stressed when I met him yesterday in the shop.'

Lena was surprised by the abrupt change of subject, but she was always willing to talk about her sixteen-year-old son. 'Well, he's studying like mad, but he's being driven up the wall a bit by his adoring visitors, Isobel Lamkin and a few other local girls have set their caps at him but he's not interested it would seem.'

'The poor boy's in the library trying to study for the Stanford entrance exam. He wants to do well and drives himself on. I'd swear the teacher thinks myself and Eli are right tyrants, but it's all Emmet himself. The other two don't give a fiddler's curse about the books.

But he's determined to get top marks and he's going demented because all these girls keep coming in on top of him. Sarah thinks it's hilarious to keep letting them in even though he's begged her not to.' Lena chuckled a little and looked at Emily, expecting her to laugh as well, but Emily stayed serious.

'Well, if he has a spare moment to himself between the books and the girls, maybe you could ask him…' She stopped again.

Lena wondered what was coming now. 'Ask him what?'

Her sister looked uneasy again. 'You know what I'm saying, about worrying the father of the baby might come into the shop one day and ask to see his baby?'

'Yes, I do, but won't he assume Nellie's done as he wanted her to do, and gone to England to…?' Lena stopped there, not wanting to say the word any more than Emily had.

'That's true, and that's what Nellie says.' Emily nodded. 'But you know the way Emmet looks so like Malachy?'

'Mm. Yes.' Sometimes it surprised her that more people in Kilteegan Bridge didn't realise that Malachy Berger had to be Emmet's biological father. The resemblance between them was so striking, the same alabaster skin and bright-green eyes and thick, rich coppery hair, despite Emmet being taller than Malachy now. She supposed it helped that Malachy had been at boarding school in Dublin as a teenager so wasn't much seen around the town, and he was living in America by the time Emmet was born. But she could see why Emily was worried.

Emily continued. 'Anyway, you know the way Nellie tells Emmet everything, and it was Emmet who told you she was pregnant before Nellie did?'

'Mm,' said Lena again. She thought she knew the way this conversation was going, and what Emily said next only served to prove her right.

'So do you think Emmet might know who the father is?'

Lena didn't answer straight away. It had crossed her mind before that her son might know the truth, but she was sure if he did, Nellie had sworn him to silence, and she hated the idea of forcing her son to choose between lying to his mother or betraying his cousin. 'I don't know, Emily,' she said at last.

'Then do you think you could ask him?'

'Oh, Emily…'

'Please, Lena? I know they're as loyal as dogs to each other, him and Nellie, but I don't even want a name. I just need to be sure that no young man is going to come in on top of me because he's realised how the baby looks like himself and suddenly he's feeling all paternal. I mean, I'm hoping it's some boy who's moved away or something, like Malachy went to America.'

'Can't you ask Nellie that question?'

Emily sighed. 'I could, I suppose, but she just gets so upset if I so much as mention the father. She's so heartbroken about him. And you're going to have to tell Emmet what's happening anyway – he's the only one besides us who knows Nellie is pregnant – so maybe at the same time…'

Before Lena could answer, she heard feet running down the stairs from the bedrooms above, and Nellie appeared. As always, she was done up to the nines, a full face of make-up, hair perfect, although it wasn't one bit necessary for her to paint her face. She was a natural beauty like her mother, her pale waving hair falling just below her shoulder blades and her eyes more indigo than blue.

She hung back at the sight of Lena, shamefaced. 'Oh, hello, Auntie Lena.'

'Hi, Nell, how are you?' Lena smiled warmly. Nellie needed to know she was loved by all her family and that nothing she could do would make a difference to that.

'Has Mam told you?' asked Nellie, with a quick glance at her mother.

'She has.'

'Do you think we're mad?' The poor girl looked suddenly very young and vulnerable, despite her thick mask of make-up.

Lena thought for a moment. Her niece needed the adults around her to be decisive and supportive, not fearful. This situation was scary enough without Nellie thinking all the people she trusted to be in charge were just as worried and uncertain as she was.

'I think if you are sure it's what you want, then your baby will have a wonderful home and a lovely life here with your mam and dad and you'll get yours back.'

Nellie eyed her. Like her grandmother Maria, she had an uncanny knack of reading people's faces.

'You think I won't be able to do it, though?' she asked astutely.

Lena stayed confident. 'I think it will be hard, but people do, and it's not like he or she will be going to strangers.'

Nellie nodded and seemed satisfied. 'Yes, you're right. And I don't hate this baby, Auntie Lena, I truly don't. But I've thought about it a lot, and I don't want to be a mother. And I know you're probably worried I'll change my mind when I see the baby, like you did, and Mam will be in a situation then, but I swear to you, I won't, I just know I won't. I'm not like you. I just can't be a mother, not now, and maybe never. This kid deserves a chance like anyone else, and Mam really wants to give it to them, don't you, Mam?' Then her face fell; clearly a thought had just struck her. 'You're not just saying you want this to get me out of the mess I'm in, are you, Mam? I'm so sorry. I've been so stupid and selfish, letting you and Daddy down…'

Emily jumped to her feet, opening her arms wide. 'Not at all, pet. I really, really do mean what I say. And it's not us who have been let down, it's you, by whoever that stupid boy was.'

'Please don't talk about him, Mam, not ever again,' said Nellie unhappily. And then the headstrong girl, who rarely cried, broke down and had a small sob in her mother's arms.

Emily soothed her and rubbed her back, catching Lena's eye over her daughter's head. And then Lena knew she had to let go of any reservations and talk to Emmet and find out what he knew. There was nothing else to do.

# CHAPTER 2

Lena strolled, deep in thought, up the avenue of Kilteegan House, the chestnut trees rustling above her, dropping their autumn leaves of crimson and gold. Eli was still in his surgery; she could see plenty of heads in there through the converted gatehouse window.

Eli's pale-blue Rover, fully repaired since Emmet crashed it, sat in front of the stone steps that led up to the arched front doorway. The rose bushes on either side of the steps were in the last flush of bloom, and the low sun turned the long windows of the old stone house to a golden copper, not unlike the colour of her oldest son's hair. Despite the time of evening, she could hear the thud of Pádraig kicking a football against the gable end of the stables and the clop of hooves around the lower paddock, where Sarah was schooling Second Chance because Emmet was too busy with the books.

Lena often wondered where Sarah and Emmet got their horsemanship from. Neither she nor Eli were interested, and Pádraig could ride but he preferred football and hurling. Malachy and his mother before him were horse people, being gentry, and Emmet was Malachy's son, but Sarah had also taken to it like a duck to water since she was a tot. Skipper had told Lena that, like Emmet, Sarah had a natural way with horses and could actually do well professionally. At the moment, she was determined to win gold medals at the next Cork Summer Show, in dressage and showjumping with Molly, and in the cross-country on Second Chance.

Lena entered the house quietly, her feet sinking into the deep-pile antique Turkish carpet she'd bought only last week, and opened the door into the library. Emmet looked up from the sofa with an expression of alarm, which quickly turned into a smile at the sight of her. The mahogany side table beside him bore a plate of iced cakes, and a large textbook was open on the table. 'Bloody hell, Mam, I thought you were Isobel and her friends back again. Sarah keeps on letting them in. She thinks it's bloody funny or something.'

'Less of the swearing, please.' Lena smiled as she drew up a chair beside him and sat down. He was in dark-blue jeans and a cream t-shirt, and Lena could see why all of the girls fancied him. He looked just like Malachy did at that age. 'Anyway, I thought you liked Isobel?'

'I did. I do, I suppose, but she keeps acting like me being friendly means I must be madly in love with her, and I'm not, Mam. I never should have danced with her at Billy Costigan's party, I just think she's quite nice, that's all. But it's awkward, and she keeps trying to stop me from working and concentrate all my attention on her, and I feel like an eejit when she drags her friends around to ooh and aah over me.'

'Poor Emmet.' Lena smiled again, reaching to stroke her son's red hair. 'What a bore for you, to be such a heart-throb.'

'Ah don't you start Mam, getting into Stanford is all that matters to me now and I just want to concentrate on that, the competition is fierce so I need every second.'

LENA FELT a pang of sadness at the thought of Emmet leaving Ireland, but she did her best not to let it show. She was going to lose him to America soon enough, and it might be four years before he came home with his engineering degree. She still didn't see why he couldn't take the same degree in Cork, but Malachy had offered to pay Emmet's way through Stanford, and she supposed the draw of one of the world's most famous universities was irresistible.

'They'd be lucky to get you,' Lena said loyally.

'Yeah,' said Emmet with a smile, 'but you're my Mam so forgive me if I don't take your opinion of my chances as unbiased fact.'

She ruffled his hair. 'You will get in, my love. You know you're brilliant. Can I get you anything? A sandwich?'

'God, no.' He indicated the pile of cakes. 'I'm stuffed to the gills with everything the girls keep bringing me. Go on, Mam, have one yourself and save my waistline.'

'I might.' She took a bun with buttercream icing and bit into it. 'Mm...this is delicious. Who made this?'

'The Lamkins' housekeeper, Annie Gallagher.'

'I wonder if she wants a new job?' Lena said lightly. She still hadn't replaced Frances Moriarty as her housekeeper; it seemed almost heartless to do so. But she supposed it would have to be done at some stage, as the house was too big for one person to manage.

'She actually might,' said Emmet seriously. 'The Professor is OK, but Isobel's mam is a bit of a tyrant. She thinks she's a cut above because of being from old Anglo-Irish stock.'

'Ah.' That figured. Lena knew the type, convinced they had a God-given right to boss around the 'peasants'. She suspected the only reason Fiona Lamkin allowed Isobel to socialise with Emmet was because the Kogans lived in Kilteegan House, the largest estate in the area. Probably if Lena and Eli had still been living above the surgery on the main street, Emmet would have been left alone to study in peace, hero or no hero.

'Anyway, Mam, I need to get back to this before the next girly invasion.' Emmet settled against his cushions and turned a page in his textbook of applied trigonometry.

She stood up but didn't leave.

He looked up at her, one eyebrow raised. 'What?'

She hesitated, then took the plunge. 'I haven't told your father this yet, but Emily has a plan about Nellie's baby, and she wanted me to tell you and ask you if…well, if you can see a problem with it.'

He pushed himself into an upright sitting position with his hands and frowned at her, puzzled. 'What plan? And why would she want my opinion? Whatever she and Nellie decide is fine by me, providing Nellie's happy.'

'I know. The thing is, Emmet… Well, your Auntie Emily is going to raise Nellie's baby as her own.'

'She's going to adopt it?' He looked both pleased and impressed. 'That's a great idea. Good for Auntie Em and Blackie.'

'No, I mean…really, as if it's her own.'

He was puzzled, then his face cleared. 'Oh, you mean she's going to pretend…'

'Yes, so Nellie doesn't have to deal with the Monsignor, or people pointing fingers and the child getting a raw deal at school because of being illegitimate or anything like that.'

He nodded. 'Well, if she really wants my opinion, I think that's an even better idea. But I still don't see what this has to do with me, apart from me having to keep my mouth shut, which I would anyway?'

'I know you would, my love. No, it's not that, it's… Well, Emily's worried that if the father is someone who lives close by, in Kilteegan Bridge, they might one day, you know…'

Emmet smiled, a little oddly. 'Claim their son or daughter and it would all come out? Like Malachy did with me?'

'Well, yes.' Her face felt hot. She still remembered her fear that Emmet might abandon her and Eli for his biological father. At least she had been Emmet's real mother, but Emily wouldn't even have that advantage.

'Don't worry, Mam,' said Emmet, still with that odd smile. 'Nothing like that is going to happen.'

'Are you sure?' She hovered by the sofa. 'I don't want to know who this boy is out of nosiness, but you see, Emily is worried someone might come into the shop one day and say, "That's my child," and –'

'Mam.' He cut her off in a loud, firm voice. 'You can tell Auntie Em from me that she has my one hundred percent cast-iron guarantee that won't happen, ever. Hand on heart. Hope to die. As God's my witness or whatever else you want me to say, she can forget that evil man ever existed.'

Lena was almost alarmed by her son's vehemence. 'Goodness, Emmet, you didn't –'

His green eyes flashed. 'Hurt him? No, though I'd have loved to, and he definitely deserved –' He caught himself and flushed. 'Not that I know who he is, of course.'

'Well, obviously not,' said Lena with heavy sarcasm, but he only grinned and waved her away.

'Mam, I have to work. Just tell Auntie Emily not to worry, OK? Seriously.'

As Lena left the library and went in search of her other children for dinner, she wasn't sure what she felt about her conversation with Emmet. Granted, it did sound like this unknown father wouldn't darken Nellie or Emily's door again, ever, and that was a good thing. But she would still have liked to know what her teenage son had done to ensure that happening.

* * *

LATER, after the dinner table was cleared and everything put away, she asked Eli to go for a walk with her around the grounds, past piles of rustling autumn leaves raked together by their gardener, Joseph Murphy, a good-natured settled Traveller who had replaced the late Mr Shanahan.

'So what's the plan, Mrs Kogan?' asked Eli with a wink as they walked along arm in arm.

Lena pretended to be indignant. 'How do you know I have a plan? Such cheek. I might just want to go for an evening stroll with my lovely husband.'

'Out of the earshot of the children? No, my lovely Lena, I'd say there's a plan.'

She smiled. 'Well…' She had another glance around to make doubly sure no one was listening. She could see only autumn trees and hear only the bleating of sheep in Jack's fields. 'Emily and Nellie and Blackie have decided…'

When she finished, Eli stood staring at her in open incredulity. 'For God's sake, why does it have to be this big convoluted secret, Lena?'

She sighed. She remembered Eli overhearing a conversation in the shop one morning when he was buying his paper. Two old biddies were tut-tutting about some young girl 'who'd got herself pregnant'. Her husband had proceeded to shock the parish by loudly explaining to the women, and several other people in the vicinity, that whatever else the girl might have done, she most certainly didn't get herself pregnant, that he could say with one hundred percent medical certainty that some man was involved in the process. He'd even used the word 'sperm' in the shop, and everyone was scandalised.

Being Jewish and German Welsh, he didn't understand the shameful, embarrassing and downright awkward obsession with sex and all matters pertaining to it that dogged the faithful in Ireland.

'Because, Eli, that's just the way it is. Nellie's an unmarried teenage girl, and her life will be ruined if this gets out.'

He sighed, clearly exasperated with the world. 'I can see Nellie is too young to be a mother, of course, and I'd like to have a serious conversation with the boy who got her into this fix if I ever get to meet him, but why can't she have the baby and then Emily raise it without having to go to all sorts of ludicrous lengths to pretend it's her own baby rather than her grandchild? It will come to the same thing, without having to be all secretive about it, and the danger of it all coming out in the future. I know people will talk and gossip, but it will be a five-day wonder and then they'll accept it like they do everything in the end. Surely that's better than telling a gigantic lie like you're planning to do?'

Lena tried to explain. 'It isn't better, unfortunately. I wish it was. I wish Nellie could stay here, have her baby, and Emily would raise it as her grandchild and let Nellie be the girl she is, not the woman and mother fate has decided. But society won't accept it. Maybe Em and Blackie and even Nellie could stand it, but the baby would be seen as illegitimate, and it's a hard thing to bear. It's not the child's fault, of course, but it's how things are.'

'It just seems so unnecessarily complicated.'

'It's not really. It's quite simple. Nellie doesn't want to be a mother, and Em has wanted another child since Nellie was born. It's not a perfect solution, of course it's not, but it's the best we've got with the minimum of hurt.'

'Supposing this boy lives locally and when he sees the baby, he realises –'

'Emmet says that's not going to happen.'

'Emmet?'

'Yes. I think he knows who it is because he's absolutely certain we're never going to hear from him again.'

'For goodness' sake.' Eli strode off across the lawns, shaking his head, with Lena at his side almost trotting to keep up with his long legs. 'You're all of you at it. Can't anyone do anything straight in this country?'

'Now stop that,' said Lena angrily. 'It wasn't so long ago I was in *your* country – I mean Wales – and everyone was telling me my life would be ruined if I kept my baby.'

'Nearly twenty years ago. Times have changed.'

'You might think so, Eli, but for women and girls, change can be very, very slow, and sometimes the new things are very like the old things. They might not stone Nellie in the street these days, but they'll stone her with their words, and the baby too, and whatever they say about sticks and stones, words can break people too, Eli.'

She took his arm and pulled him to face her. 'Please, Eli, I'm begging you, please go along with this. Don't let Nellie down. She loves you and so does Emily.'

He looked absolutely astonished. 'What are you talking about? Who said I was going to let anyone down?'

She felt a rush of relief. 'I thought…'

'Ah, Lena, allow me to have a bit of a rant before I become embroiled in another O'Sullivan conspiracy.' He shook his head at her. 'When have I ever, *ever* said no to you about anything?' And then he grinned and took her by the collar of her coat and kissed her, as leaves spiralled down around them in a gust of air.

# CHAPTER 3

'Urgh, that's so disgusting.' Thirteen-year-old Pádraig was standing in the doorway of the kitchen with his nose wrinkled in disgust. He'd come in on Lena and Eli cuddling and clearly found any intimacy whatsoever between his parents revolting.

'Well, don't watch us then. Don't you have homework or something?' Eli said good-naturedly.

'I've done it, OK?' Pádraig rolled his eyes.

Lena gave him a warning look. 'Less of the cheek, please. And you might not have homework, but Sarah's cleaning the bathroom, and those new football boots of yours won't pay for themselves, so the weeds in the kitchen garden outside need pulling. So off with you.'

Pádraig looked stricken. 'Ah, Mam, now?'

'Well, it's only four in the afternoon, so that gives you' – she checked the watch Doc had given her when she got married – 'two hours until it's dark.'

'Dad! Did you hear this?' Pádraig sought the backup of his more lenient father.

'I did, and as you know, I am on Lena's team, always was, always will be. You won't divide us. She's the boss of this house, and I'm happy with that, and the sooner you accept it, my young bucko, the better.'

'This is so unfair,' Pádraig moaned. 'Oliver Lamkin got the newest ones. He had to get the shop in Cork to order them in from England – they're the ones Franz Beckenbauer wears – and his father just bought them for him, none of this rubbish about having to do jobs.'

'Well, when you've finished the weeding, why don't you stroll up to Professor Lamkin's and ask him if he'd like to adopt you? I'm sure he'd jump at it. After all, you're such a little ray of sunshine,' Lena teased. It was hard to be cross with Pádraig; he was such an endearing child. He was fair like his Dad, with sapphire-blue eyes and a light dusting of freckles across a nose that had been broken in a match last summer and had not healed straight. He wasn't a classically handsome boy like Emmet, but he was charming and funny and an excellent sportsman, and he seemed to be friends with the whole parish. Even though he was still only thirteen, he'd scored the winning point in the under-fourteens county final, putting Kilteegan Bridge in the top four teams in the country, so he was a local celebrity and maybe a bit too adored for Lena's liking.

'Look, come on, Pádraig,' said Eli, opening the back door. 'I'll help you, and the two of us will have it done in no time. Lena, I'll be back in a few minutes to give you a cuddle.' He winked and kissed her neck, to loud retching noises from their youngest son.

A few minutes after they were gone, Emmet shouted from the library at the front of the house. 'Mam! Someone's here!'

'Who is it now?' She walked out of the kitchen and looked through the hall window. A car she didn't recognise was on the gravel with both doors open.

She flung open the door to find Fintan and Vera Slattery, farmers from out the Knockmore direction. Fintan was being half-dragged, half-carried across the threshold by his wife. He was bleeding profusely from his outer thigh, his trouser leg soaked in blood.

Sarah had arrived down the stairs when she heard the commotion, and Lena said loudly and urgently, 'Sarah, go for Dad! He's out in the kitchen garden helping Pádraig with the weeding.'

As Sarah took to her heels, Lena helped Vera lower her husband onto the deep, soft cerulean-blue carpet in the front hallway. He was grey and sweating profusely.

'I'm sorry, Mrs Kogan, it being a Sunday and all, but we had to come. Fintan was cutting down a tree and missed the trunk and sliced his leg instead…' Vera was panting with the effort of carrying him, barely managing to get the words out.

'Don't worry, Mrs Slattery. My husband will be here in a moment. He'll sort this out.'

While Vera cradled Fintan's head, Lena hastily ran for cushions from the library.

Emmet brought a blanket from the couch. 'Take this, Mam.'

Lena grabbed the woollen blanket and turned back to the farmer, whose blood had already soaked through the rug and spread out across the polished teak floor. As he groaned and moved, Lena saw a flash of white bone through the flesh and fought the urge to retch.

Moments later, Eli arrived with Pádraig and Sarah and quickly assessed the situation. 'Well done for getting him on the floor. Pádraig, run down to the surgery and get my bag. Lena, fetch my scissors and a basin and some bandages from my store upstairs. Sarah, can you take Mrs Slattery and make her a cup of tea, please?'

He sounded so calm, so authoritative, that even Vera Slattery, normally an opinionated woman, obeyed him without question and walked trancelike behind Sarah to the kitchen. As Lena ran up the stairs, she heard her husband in the library instructing Emmet. 'Call an ambulance and then the Monsignor and use your authoritative voice – get him to hurry.' Then Eli came back out of the library and closed the door behind him.

As soon as she arrived back downstairs with the bandages, Eli set to work, dressing the area and applying pressure to the wound. 'Right then, let's take a look here. Don't worry, Fintan, you'll be grand. We'll get you patched up now. There's an ambulance on the way, but we'll stop the bleeding in the meantime.' The blood continued to ooze and pulse through the bandage, soaking it in seconds.

'Place your hands there, Lena.' He pointed to where Fintan's leg met his pelvis. 'Press down, hard, as hard as you can. Good woman. Don't worry about hurting him. That's great, you're doing fine.'

As Lena pressed down, fighting waves of nausea, Eli wrapped more bandages even tighter around Fintan's thigh and elevated the farmer's leg, using the cushions and the blanket she had brought in from the library.

Pádraig arrived back in record time, and after sending him into the library to stay with Emmet, Eli took out a syringe and a test tube. Fintan, who had been drifting in and out of consciousness, groaned loudly again. 'Right so, Fintan, you're fine now. This is going to help with the pain, and all you need to do now is stay still, try not to move, breathe in and out. That's it, in and out, nice deep breaths.' Eli's voice was soothing; clearly he didn't want to give any indication that Fintan's ragged breathing was a cause of concern. 'Good man. Stay awake now, there's a good man. What in the name of all that's holy were you doing?'

'Tree…' was all his patient could manage.

'He was using an axe and missed,' whispered Lena.

'Well, Fintan, I hope you've enough firewood cut for the winter, my friend, because you'll be out of action for the next two months and they'll have to wait on you hand and foot.' Eli smiled, and though Fintan didn't return it, Lena noticed that the farmer did relax a little.

Eli took his temperature and his pulse. 'Good man. The ambulance won't be long now, and they'll get you into hospital and patched up in no time. Don't you worry about a thing. Keep pressing, Lena, as hard as you can.' He prattled on encouragingly, checking Fintan's vital signs and giving positive updates to the patient while all the time keeping an eye on the wound. 'Now then, that's the bleeding nearly stopped, so you'll be fine. Keep pressing, Lena, you're doing great.'

A car pulled up, and the Monsignor hurried in through the open front door in his black robes. He took in the scene and, without a word, got on his knees on the bloodied carpet and gave the last rites to the half-conscious man. Lena was glad to see Monsignor Collins had more humility now, finally prepared to get blood on his trousers. She knew from her husband how the priest had used Mrs

Moriarty's favourite cushion to keep his knees clean beside her deathbed.

In the distance a siren sounded, wailing up the country lanes, and Eli brightened. 'Here's the ambulance coming now. Lena, go quick into the kitchen and tell Mrs Slattery. I'm sure they'll allow her to go with Fintan here.'

But Vera had already reappeared in response to the wail of the siren. 'I'll not be going with him,' she announced angrily.

Lena stared at her in surprise, wondering if the woman was in shock.

The big priest heaved himself to his feet, and she assumed Monsignor Collins was going to say a few characteristically sharp words about a woman's place being at her husband's side, but for some reason, he never looked at her.

'May the Lord watch over you, Fintan.' He nodded at them. 'Dr Kogan, Mrs Kogan.' And then he headed out the door back to his car without a word.

Eli was also staring at Vera, clearly thinking the same thing as Lena, that the woman was in shock. 'He'll be fine, Mrs Slattery, don't worry. They'll patch him up right as rain. Now here come the lads.'

The priest drove off in his car as the ambulance came to a halt, religion giving way to science as the paramedics came running in through the open front door with a stretcher. They had a few words with Eli, he gave them the medical vitals, and then they set about carrying Fintan out to the ambulance. To Lena's relief, Vera followed. But she only stood at the back doors of the vehicle, her hands on her wide hips.

'You were told, but you wouldn't listen! You knew better, and now see? Good luck to you. You'll need it, God knows,' she roared. And then she got into her car and drove away down the avenue of Kilteegan House, leaving the ambulance and her husband behind. Lena looked in amazement at Eli, who just shrugged.

The cool but dry afternoon had given way to heavy misting rain, and the sky had darkened. The clocks had just gone back, so it was getting dark now by 5 p.m.

'Nothing is ever as it seems,' he said. 'That's the first thing you learn in this business. Now I guess the next thing is to get this hallway washed down.'

'Oh, yes.' Lena looked in disappointment at her lovely Persian rug. She'd seen it at an antique fair, and it was more money than they could afford, but she'd loved it so much, she'd bought it anyway. Now, only a week later...

'We can get it cleaned,' Eli said, noting her expression.

'I suppose so.' She sighed. 'Though could you roll it up for now and take it out to the tack room? I can't look at it covered in Fintan Slattery's blood. Maybe Mam will have some ideas on what to do with it.'

'I'll take care of it now anyway. Have you some baking soda?'

She nodded. 'In the larder.'

'Right, a paste of baking soda and water on the stain before it dries will make it easier to get cleaned afterwards.'

'Aren't you a marvel?' she asked with a weak smile.

'Oh, I am. You're the luckiest woman on earth to be married to me.' He grinned and took the rug up and went.

'Sarah and Pádraig.' Her two youngest children had reappeared in the hall. 'You've both been wonderful, so no more weeding or cleaning for you. Off you go now and do what you like.'

Lena brought the phone back into the hall, then fetched Emmet a clean blanket from the hot press and tucked it in over his legs because the room felt cold to her. 'Well done for getting the Monsignor to come so fast,' she said. 'He's not usually that quick off the mark.'

'I just said we had a patient bleeding to death,' said Emmet. 'Probably it reminded him of Mrs Moriarty.'

'Poor Frances, such a tragedy.' Lena still missed her gentle housekeeper, who had been so badly let down by Dr White. The Kellstown doctor had since been struck off, not for letting a pregnant woman die unnecessarily but for self-prescribing drugs. He was a pity really and was in a treatment centre in County Tipperary. Eli went to visit him now and again.

She went out to the scullery to fetch a bucket, soap and rags, and for the next fifteen minutes, she and her husband worked together in the hallway, cleaning the floor, the door handles and everything else that got splattered, and then she ran upstairs to change her clothes. Coming back down, she checked herself in the hall mirror and found a last spot of blood on her nose. 'The perks of being a doctor's wife, I suppose.' She grimaced ruefully as she rubbed it off.

'It's a roller coaster, all right,' Eli said, standing behind her, smiling at her in the mirror. His clothes were also soaked in Fintan's blood. 'Now let me go and get a bath myself. I think this shirt and trousers might have to go in the bin. We'll have a drink by the fire, will we, after such an eventful day?'

'Joseph Murphy already set the fire in the small sitting room, so I'll put a match to it. It's after getting very cold all of a sudden, isn't it?' Lena shuddered, feeling cold to her bones.

'It is, but also that was a shocking thing to see, and that makes people feel cold.' Eli peeled off his bloodied shirt as he walked up the stairs.

Lena went into the kitchen to fetch a glass of fresh apple juice and brought it to Emmet who was studying as usual. 'I think I'm just getting why you don't want to follow your father into medicine.' She smiled as she made room for the glass on the side table.

He smiled back at her. 'Seriously, Mam, I'd know he'd love it if I did, and it's not that I'm afraid of blood or don't want to help people, but being a doctor never stops, does it?'

'I know. He's never really off duty. It's a huge responsibility.'

'So is building bridges that don't fall down, but at least engineering is a bit more nine to five,' agreed Emmet, turning back to his textbooks.

She moved on into the sitting room, an inner sanctum she had created for herself and Eli where they could retreat from the hustle and bustle of their always busy house. It was decorated with chintz sofas, woollen throws and a silk rug on the pitch-pine floorboards, and it overlooked the orchard and the huge old apple tree where Lena remembered her daddy lifting her and Malachy up onto the low branches when she was little. It gave her comfort to see it bloom and give fruit year after year; it was as if the sweet red apples were a gift from her father.

She knelt to light the fire. The dry twigs immediately crackled in the grate, the flames licking around the applewood logs they stored in one of the stables behind the house.

'Well, you look less gruesome.' She smiled, looking over her shoulder as her husband entered the room. His blond hair was combed back from his high forehead, and she noticed it was receding a little. They were both getting older, but she didn't care to try to stop the hands of time. She looked her age, thirty-five, and Eli was forty. He was wearing a collared t-shirt with the crest of his rugby club back in Cardiff on it and a pair of old corduroy trousers. He was in his socks; he never bothered with slippers, frequently going barefoot.

He poured them each a small whiskey, adding a drop of water to release the flavour, then sat down beside her on the sofa before the fire, one arm around her shoulder.

'What did you make of that then?' she asked.

'Which bit? Fintan Slattery almost chopping his leg off, or his missus saying she didn't want to go with him in the ambulance? Or Monsignor Collins scuttling off without saying anything to her?' He shook his head, bemused. 'Where to start?'

'It was all very strange,' Lena agreed. 'She's a bit...I don't know... She has a reputation for being a bit odd, though, doesn't she? Vera, I mean?'

'Has she? I don't think I've ever met her before, or heard anything about her. Fintan came to me a while back, nothing bad, just a bit of gout, but her, never.'

Lena furrowed her brow. 'I'll ask Emily what she knows about it – she finds out about everything from her customers. She's not a mad gossip herself, not like Maureen Parker from the dress shop, but she gets to hear people talk.'

# CHAPTER 4

Lena had discovered a lot of information about Vera Slattery from Emily. The strange woman and her husband had been the main topic of conversation all week in Better Buy Farm and Home Stores, which was what Emily and Blackie's shop was called these days instead of Crean's Hardware.

'So, Eli, listen to me. This is what Emily heard in the shop. Vera is one of the Kellys from Inchicrohan, and people used to say that old Madge Kelly, her mother, was a witch.'

'Really,' murmured Eli, without even lifting his eyes from the Sunday newspaper that he was reading while propped up against his pillows in the bed. Lena had decided to let her hard-working husband have a lie-in instead of going to Sunday Mass, and she had brought up a tray of tea and freshly baked scones and jam for their breakfast.

Now she was ready for a good chat with her husband because the children were leaving her in peace for once. Emmet was downstairs studying already and getting Pádraig to run around for him, fetching this and that, which Pádraig was still young enough to enjoy doing for his adored big brother. And Sarah had walked into Kilteegan Bridge to see Nellie, saying she wanted to spend as much time with her cousin as possible before Nellie disappeared off to her new job as a hotel receptionist in London, which Sarah thought very exciting.

'Yes, well, I can see you rolling your eyes, and I know Madge probably wasn't a witch as such,' Lena said patiently as she stood at the side table in her ivory dressing gown, pouring out the tea and buttering scones. 'All the same, people used to go to her, and her mother before her and all the Kelly women, going way back. They were known around for having the knowledge, and even though it's more modern times now, people still put great store by the old beliefs.'

This time, Eli looked up at her curiously over his glasses. 'What do you mean, "the knowledge"?'

'Well, just that they know things, like they know about the fairies, and they use the old cures and can hear the banshee, things like that.'

'I'm sorry, what? Fairies, banshees? Are you serious?' Eli laid down the newspaper. 'I thought that was all in children's storybooks, leprechauns and the like. Are you telling me people around here actually believe that stuff?'

'They definitely do.'

'I've never seen that…' he said, half to himself.

'Well, you have seen it. You just haven't realised what you were seeing because it's so far from your own culture growing up. You know the hawthorn tree in the middle of the top field of our farm? Don't you think it would be easier for Jack on the tractor to chop it down? The old horse wouldn't go near the tree, so there was no point in getting rid of it when it was Susie pulling the plough, but the tractor doesn't care. So if the tree was gone, Jack could plough the field easily then. But he doesn't because it's a fairy tree, and no farmer would dare touch one of those for fear of upsetting the Good People.'

'The Good People?' Eli looked amused and intrigued.

'That's what they're known as, or the people of the sídhe, sheeogs, and they have their ways and we shouldn't antagonise them. People believe that they can bring terrible misfortune down upon a person or a family if you offend them, so even the most levelheaded person around here wouldn't dream of it.'

'And does that include my levelheaded wife?' he teased.

'It certainly does.' After getting back into bed with her tea, and balancing a plate of buttered scones on Eli's legs, she snuggled against him. She loved relaxing in this gleaming brass bedstead, with its gorgeous feather mattress and heaps of pillows, its starched Egyptian cotton sheets, warm layers of Foxford blankets and the patchwork counterpane. 'If you cross the Good People, they could take a healthy baby and replace it with a changeling, one of their own, or destroy crops, or make it so the animals give no milk. And maybe you think it's a load of nonsense, but my dad, Lord have mercy on him, would always leave the beestings out in a bucket for them, or if he got a bottle of poitín, he'd always set a glass on the wall of the byre for the *púcaí*, the ghosts, and a more practical man you'd not meet.'

'And he never cut that tree either?' Eli asked, astonished.

'No, and he never would. There's all manner of superstitions here. Remember when the babies were small and we'd meet an old person who would put a coin in their little fist and then place it under the mattress? That's called to hansel a baby, to protect them from poverty.'

'I knew people had funny customs, but I didn't think they actually believed in it all.' Eli sipped his tea and took a bite of his scone, slathered in butter from Jack's cows and jam made from the patch of raspberries in Maria's garden, the one thing she grew these days apart from flowers. As he set the cup down again, he grimaced and massaged the knuckles of his left hand.

'Is it still bothering you?' Lena asked. Eli had a touch of arthritis in his finger joints from an old injury he'd sustained while playing rugby in his teens.

'It is,' he said, grimacing again. 'I've tried a variety of the new creams on offer, but nothing seems to get rid of it. Arthritis is so hard to treat. Maybe I should go to this Madge woman.'

'She's dead now, I'm afraid, bad luck. But she was good, you know. Blackie told me that once, when he was only a young fella, three or four, Peggy took him to Madge. Dick wouldn't allow her to go to Doc because she had a black eye, and he said he'd give her another one to match it if she went squealing to the doctor. Blackie had whooping cough.' Her contempt for Blackie's father, Dick Crean rang in every word she spoke. 'But anyway, Peggy brought him to Madge, and she told her to slice up a turnip and cover the slices with brown sugar, and once the turnip gave up its juices and mixed with the sugar, to give him three spoons of it each day. Then Madge took Blackie outside and passed him under the belly of an old donkey three times. And Peggy swears by that Sunday, Blackie was fine.'

Eli was grinning from ear to ear. 'Well, we'll have to get a donkey in, Lena, and have him tethered outside the surgery. Or do you think Ollie will do?' Ollie was Emmet's old pony from when he was seven, a Shetland who now spent happy days in the orchard eating the windfalls and sometimes the apples straight off the trees if the branches bent low enough.

'Don't mock, Eli. I had an interesting experience with Madge myself once. I knew her a little bit, though I never knew till now that Vera Slattery was her daughter.'

'Don't tell me – she sold you a love potion and that's how you got me? I always wondered how it could have been love at first sight…'

Lena laughed. 'No, something different. It happened when I was above in the churchyard visiting Daddy and Doc. It was when we were still living in Doc's little house above the surgery. Remember we were looking for the keys for his big old desk? There was a small locked drawer at the back of it, and when we went to move it, something was rattling inside. So my nose was getting the better of me, but we searched high up and low down and no trace of the key.'

'I remember, but then it turned up.'

Lena smiled. 'It did. In the pocket of Doc's fishing jacket, which was hanging inside the door of the scullery. And the only reason I knew to look there was as I was coming out of the cemetery that day, I met old Madge Kelly, who was coming in. She was still alive then, though she was ninety if she was a day. And she stopped me, and she said, "I don't know what this is about, but Doc says to tell you it's in the pocket of the coat hanging on the door."'

Eli's eyes twinkled. 'And how come you never said how you found it?'

'Era, I thought you'd just say it was a load of old rubbish, being a scientific man. I searched every door for a coat, but there was nothing, and only that night in bed I thought of the scullery. I crept down, there and then in the middle of the night, and lo and behold, there was his old green fishing jacket with all the pockets, and inside one was the key of the drawer.'

'And you're sure Madge Kelly had no idea the key was missing?'

'None whatsoever. But I'm so glad she helped me find it. The rattle in that drawer was this hinged silver frame I keep here on my side of the bed, the picture of me as a kid on one side and Mike on the other. Though it was only later I realised who the boy was. I actually thought it was a picture of Doc as a young boy, he and Mike look so alike.'

Lena's godfather, Doc, had fathered a child for a woman called Anthea O'Halloran when her husband, Michael, who was Doc's best friend since college, had discovered he was infertile and asked Doc for help. Doc had remained in his biological son's life as his godfather, but he'd never told anyone the secret of Mike's parentage, and Lena had only found out when she went to stay with the widowed Anthea in Dublin.

'Oh, Eli, I forgot to say, Anthea told me in her last letter that Mike's started practising medicine again. They were finally able to get him one of those new electrified wheelchairs. He's able to get around properly by himself for the first time since he broke his back, so he went back to college for a while to update his skills and now he's back working as a GP. Just doing locum work, but it's a start.'

But Eli was still thinking about Madge, not Mike. 'I expect Madge knew Doc, and he could have told her where it was before, and she guessed you might want it,' he mused. 'I mean, any key is useful.'

Lena considered this possibility. 'Well, it's true Madge was a patient of his. I remember from when I was his receptionist, he liked her. They used to spend a long time in the surgery together when she came in, just chatting.'

'So the healer went to a normal doctor for her own illnesses,' said Eli with a grin.

'Oh, she always gave modern medicine its due. They had a harmonious relationship, Madge and Doc.'

'And how about him? Did Doc have any time for "the knowledge", as you call it?'

Lena shrugged. 'Well, he didn't disbelieve that sort of thing, put it that way. He'd seen too much over the years. I remember him telling me one time about a farm, up the side of Knocknasheega, where the husband killed his wife with a shovel. He threw himself in the lake then and drowned. Rumour was she was sleeping with a neighbour's son – she was decades younger than the husband, a made match, you know? But anyway, no animal will pass that house. You can't drive cattle past it, no horse, no pony and trap, nothing. Daddy used to know a man who had a goat herd further up the mountain, and on the day he was going to the mart, he'd have to drive the herd about three miles out of his way because the animals wouldn't pass the house. So everyone knows the place is cursed because of the terrible things that happened there.'

Lena sipped her tea as Eli waited for her to continue, his mouth turned up at the edges.

'But anyway, it was a nice bit of land, only four acres and a cottage but looking down the valley on the lake to the east and towards the ocean on the west. So this auctioneer came out from Clonakilty one day with a prospective buyer, a couple from America who wanted to retire back here. Well, several people made it their business to warn them, tell them not to buy it, but they laughed and went ahead anyway.'

'And what happened?' Eli smiled. 'I'm assuming they didn't live happily ever after?'

Lena wagged her finger at him. 'You might scoff, but she got cancer and was dead within six months and the husband was gored by a neighbour's bull, left paralysed, and he died the following year. It's been empty since and will be allowed to go derelict.'

'That's terrible, but it could just be a coincidence,' Eli said reasonably.

'It could.' Lena nodded.

'But you wouldn't walk up there?'

'Not a hope.' She smiled and took a big bite of her own warm scone, licking the jam and butter off her lips.

# CHAPTER 5

Jack and Skipper were making plans for their trip to the USA and Molly and May were all excitement at the opportunities for young farmers in New Zealand. The intrepid twins had attended a seminar back in September where they were told the New Zealand government was offering incentives for farmers to emigrate there.

The O'Sullivan sisters, Jack and Skipper and their mother had met for lunch at the West Cork Hotel in Skibbereen to celebrate Maria's birthday and though the twins were in high spirits, Maria was very cast down by the prospect of the departure of her youngest children.

Lena pulled up a gilt and crimson chair next to her mother's while the twins had gone to the bathroom. Even now, they still did every single thing together. 'I know you'll miss them desperately, Mam, we all will, but it was too good an opportunity to give up. Imagine my little sisters, farming in New Zealand?' Lena still found the idea amazing, even though she knew the twins had been so self-sufficient out of necessity all their lives, their father being killed before they were born. The years of their babyhood and childhood were traumatic and hard. Still, they had found strength in each other, so much so it seemed they didn't really need anyone else.

Skipper grinned as he took a seat on Maria's other side. 'I don't reckon New Zealand realises what kinda deal they're gettin' with Molly and May O'Sullivan. I know the twins say it's just for five years, but I wouldn't be surprised if that pair owned the whole of the South Island by then. I know they weren't much for the book learnin', but they're as sharp as a steel trap.'

'I know.' Maria smiled sadly. 'I'll just miss them. But you're right – it's a wonderful opportunity. You here from Montana, Eli from Germany via Wales, Klaus from Germany, Ted coming back home soon after decades in Australia and now the twins in Greymouth, New Zealand – we must be the most international family in the village,' she mused.

'We're certainly the most interesting anyway.' Lena grinned. 'Especially Molly and May. They march to the beat of their own drum and always did.'

Maria nodded. 'I can't imagine them being on the other side of the world, but I'm so proud of them as well, and I'm lucky to have them. I was in such a very bad way when they were born, and, Emily, you stepped in to care for them, and Lena and Jack, and Deirdre Madden raised them as well is the truth, once they were old enough to run across the fields to her house and play with her daughter, Lucy.'

'Ah, Mam, they always knew you loved them, and that means as much as everything else put together,' said Lena tenderly.

Klaus nodded. 'They are remarkable young ladies now, and I've seen how they are with you. They adore you, Maria.'

'Like we all do,' added Emily kindly.

'I know that,' said Maria, 'and I'm grateful. I never had that sort of love between me and the woman who reared me. In fact, maybe even without the manic depression, I wouldn't have known how to be a good enough mother.' She spoke quite matter-of-factly. There was no self-pity in her, but she'd had a lot of time with psychiatrists to be quite introspective.

'Oh, you would, Maria. It's intuitive, and you have it,' Klaus assured her as the twins returned.

Maria smiled, raising her glass of lemonade. 'So let's have a toast to my two brave young girls, and may they arrive safely at the ends of the earth and have all the success they deserve, and then come home.'

'To Molly and May,' chorused the rest of her family.

* * *

'Did you know the Maddens were so miserable about Molly and May leaving, they offered to sell them the farm?' Jack asked Skipper, setting a bottle of beer down beside him. 'May told me this morning. I didn't like to mention it in front of Mam – she feels a bit ashamed about Deirdre having had to do so much of the twins' parenting.'

'That's sure is somethin', offering to sell land.' Skipper was lying on the sofa, naked from the waist up, rubbing poitín into his bruised right shoulder. 'I suppose Bill and Deirdre ain't gettin' no younger, and Lucy's not gonna leave her big city job to come home, so they ain't got too much choice. But it sure is hard, to sell it out of the family.'

'I think they regard the twins as family,' said Jack. He plumped down on the sofa beside Skipper with his own bottle of beer but shot back to his feet when the sudden movement of the cushions made Skipper groan aloud. 'Are you all right? Is your arm still that sore?'

'It sure is. That silver mare damn near broke it. Thank the Lord for Bill's moonshine. He swears he only makes it for medicinal reasons, and I ain't askin' no questions.'

'Quite right. Ask no questions, you'll be told no lies. Skip, are you sure it's enough, though? I thought that mare looked mad when they took her out. I don't like a horse that rolls their eyes like that. The driver told me that was the third box they had to find – she kicked out the other two. You should have waited till I came back from the mart. I'd have helped.'

'I'm just glad Sarah wasn't here. She'd have laughed her head off seeing me dragged around the arena.' Skipper winced as he continued to rub in the poitín.

'One of them has to be the one to beat even you, Skip.' Jack perched carefully on the arm of the sofa so as not to rock the couch.

'Here, let me do that.' Jack rubbed the alcohol gently to his shoulder as his life partner groaned in pain.

Skipper was rapidly becoming famous in Ireland as the man you went to if you had an untameable horse. He had a way, learnt from watching the wild mustangs in the Rocky Mountains, of communicating with horses in such a manner that he never hurt or intimidated them but made them want to please him. It was a joy to watch. But this silver mare from Carlow was like nothing they'd ever seen; she was beyond furious all the time, like she was possessed.

'I dunno, maybe I'm just gettin' old. Time to get me an old rockin' chair and a pipe and bore the kids with stories about when I was young and strong.'

Jack laughed. 'You're only in your thirties, so no, you're not getting away with that one. There's too much to do around the farm, especially now the twins will be leaving and Emmet's out of action with his exams. I know you have Sarah, and she's brilliant with the horses, but it will be a couple of years before we can rope Pádraig into the heavy work.'

Skipper laughed but winced again at the same time. 'Don't drive me too hard now, Jackie-boy, I might end up running off to San Francisco and just lying around smoking pot to the end of my days. I hear it's almost as great for sore muscles as Bill's miracle cure.'

Jack sat in silence looking down at the face of the man he'd loved for about fifteen years, and he wondered if Skipper was really joking or if this was a case of 'many a true word spoken in jest'.

Skipper had a friend called Carlos, who wrote and told them how the Port of San Francisco had become home to a huge gay community They planned to visit him when they went over there on holidays. Carlos explained that men who were expelled from the navy for being homosexual often decided to stay among people like themselves rather than going back to wherever they came from and facing persecution. There were more gay people in San Francisco than anywhere else in America, and while Jack was looking forward to the trip, he knew it would be a strange experience to feel like he and Skipper could be a couple without causing comment. Jack had thought his whole early life that there was something wrong with him, something unnatural. His family never spoke of it, and he doubted either of his parents had even an idea such people as he existed. The girls and Eli and Blackie seemed to know now, and treated Skipper and him as a couple, though they didn't talk about it, and that made him feel a bit more normal. But he could never envision himself being like the men Carlos described in San Francisco, being openly demonstrative with their partners. He just wasn't like that. Jack was a quiet, private man, and he felt no need to walk down the street holding hands with Skipper.

He was happy the way it was, farming their land, sharing their lives in quiet companionship. No, not even that, Jack thought with a smile. Sharing their lives in love.

But maybe Skipper felt differently? And it wasn't only that. Jack knew how excited Skipper was to see his brother, Wyatt, again in Montana, and Wyatt's wife, Laurie Lee, and their girls.

'I know you were willing to come here to live with me, but you gave up a lot, your friends, your family, didn't you?' he asked. 'I have mine all around me, and I hope you think of them as family too, but still…maybe you'd like to go back to America?'

Skipper looked puzzled as he nursed his arm.

'But we *are* going, on vacation.'

'THAT'S TRUE WE ARE, but you could stay on, if you wanted to, and I'd come back here and take care of everything and wait for you to come back to me, praying the bright lights don't seduce you forever and leave me here broken-hearted.' He laughed like he didn't mind at all, but Skipper didn't join in.

Instead he turned, painfully and gazed into Jack's eyes. Long seconds passed and neither man spoke.

'Jack O'Sullivan, that ain't never gonna happen,' Skipper drawled sincerely, 'cause I ain't never livin' anywhere without you. And I know you're being generous, sayin' I should stay there, but I don't want that, so I won't. Thanks but no. It's us two or nothin'. So poor Delores Kavanagh will have to go on breaking her heart over you.'

'Ah, stop...' complained Jack. Delores was the very pretty woman who ran the accounts office in the mart, and she had an eye for Jack, always dropping very unsubtle hints about them going on a date.

'You want to be careful, Jack. I've heard she's even been down the holy well tying a ribbon to that there old hawthorn bush.'

'She'd be better off asking the fairies for a hot January or a pink cow.'

'Poor girl. Maybe she should start makin' cow eyes at Fergal Deasy instead. He's crazy about her.' Skipper took a sneaky swig from the poitín, then sat up on the sofa, with a grimace. 'Damn this shoulder.'

'You should have gone down to Eli earlier. He might have been able to do something with it.' Jack hated to see him in pain, and it must have been bad because Skipper never complained.

'It'll be OK. This moonshine is powerful stuff, and by tomorrow I'll be fine. If not, I'll go down to Eli, though, I promise. Or maybe Vera Slattery. What was it went on between her and Fintan, do you know?'

Jack shook his head as he got off the arm of the sofa and crouched to damp down the range for the night. 'She won't say it out loud, but according to Imelda in the café, who heard it from her boyfriend, Con Hurley, who sometimes works up at the Slatterys', Fintan was trying to chop down a fairy tree. He said all that talk of the Good People was just old *piseógs*. Vera told him not to do it, but he wouldn't listen. He missed the trunk with the hatchet and went straight through his leg, and now he's above in the hospital with pins and stitches and the whole shebang.'

'No kiddin'?' Skipper was shocked. He might be American born, but he had been in Ireland almost half his life by now and had learnt a long time ago that no farmer ever took such a gamble with the fairies. There might be some people who were brave enough these modern days to dismiss the old knowledge as nonsense, but even for the likes of them to cut down a hawthorn tree, well, that would be like spitting in the eye of fate, and whatever happened next, no one would have any sympathy or kindness for you.

'Which reminds me,' said Jack, closing the firebox door. 'I'd better set a glass of that poitín on the wall of the byre, for the fairies, like Dad always did when he came by a bottle. In fact, I'll put out two, and a slice of apple pie, and then maybe they'll give you a hand with the silver mare.'

'Jackie-boy,' said Skipper, grinning as he stood up and headed for the stairs and bed, supporting his right elbow with his left hand, 'that's one hell of an idea, 'cause somethin' sure as hell has to be done with her or she'll be going right back where she came from and I'll have to admit defeat for the first time in my life.'

Outside, under a clear dark-blue sky pricked with stars, Jack breathed in the grassy smell of home, the scent of beasts that rustled and snorted sleepily in the fields and stables and the salt tang of the Atlantic that muttered softly in the distance. The silver mare was still kicking angrily at the door of its stall; he'd had to back the tractor-trailer up against it earlier to stop the mad creature from breaking out. Now he placed two small glasses of the fiery alcohol side by side on the wall outside the byre, and a large slice of pie, and stood for a while looking in the direction of the dark fairy fort, the ancient ring of stone and hawthorn in the top field that Susie the old horse would never go near, nor any of the three sheepdogs. And nor, for that matter, Jack himself.

With a murmur of thanks to the Good People, he went off to follow Skipper to bed.

# CHAPTER 6

'But I would happily move to America to be with you...' Lena heard Isobel Lamkin say as Lena walked past the door of the library, her footsteps muffled by the rug that Maria had managed to restore to its former glory, thanks to Eli's quick thinking with the baking soda. Lena knew she shouldn't eavesdrop, but she couldn't help stopping to listen for a moment while rearranging the family photographs in their silver frames on the walnut side table. Through the half-open door, she could see Emmet on his feet by the fireplace, his arm resting on the mantel.

'Sure, don't your parents want you to go to the girls' school in the Alps or something?' he said, frowning. 'And then art college?'

'Yes, but I mean after that...'

'Isobel, in four or five years' time, you'll have forgotten me entirely.'

'Emmet, don't say that, we're going to be together forever aren't we?' And Isobel came suddenly into view, wrapping her arms around Emmet's neck. He sighed, then laughed and kissed the besotted girl. So, Lena thought, it wasn't quite the one-sided love story Emmet liked to pretend it was.

Lena carried on into the kitchen and checked the joint of lamb in the oven, which she'd put in three hours earlier for their Sunday dinner. Her new housekeeper, Annie Gallagher, a rosy-cheeked woman who'd raised eight children of her own, had been delighted to come and work for Lena. Annie liked her Sundays off as she was a devout Catholic, and Lena had no problem giving them to her. Snobby Fiona Lamkin had always insisted on having poor Annie prepare their Sunday roast and serve it up as soon as the Lamkins returned from the Protestant church, which meant Annie had to go to first Mass where there was no choir, which, as she confided to Lena, 'just wasn't the same'.

Annie, cutely enough, engineered a big falling out with the Lamkins – well, with Mrs Lamkin specifically – and got herself fired, so no blame could be cast on Lena for poaching her. One of the first things Annie had done for Lena was make several jars of wonderful mint jelly from the mint in the kitchen garden, which would go beautifully with the lamb. The roast potatoes on the bottom shelf were also crisping up nicely.

As she basted the joint, Lena kept splashing herself with the hot juices and had to drop the spoon and lick her fingers. In her mind, she was still stuck in the conversation she'd just overheard. What did Isobel mean about going out to see Emmet in America *after* she'd been to finishing school and art college? How long was Emmet intending to stay in California? Was his degree going to take longer than three years? He hadn't warned her about that.

Bad enough her son had turned up his nose at University College Cork, which was a wonderful university with a long tradition of academic excellence and a prestigious list of alumni. Emmet's own step-grandfather, Klaus, taught history there. America was so far away, and she still couldn't see how the degree that Emmet would get there would be any better than one here in Ireland.

She remembered the years when she was growing up in the '50s, when politicians lamented that Irish boys and girls were raised for export like cattle. But it was different now. The economy was booming. De Valera was gone, Lemass had dragged the Irish economy by the scruff of the neck into the new century with T.K. Whitaker by his side, and of course, everyone here loved Jack Lynch, a Corkman and a hurler to boot, universally liked and admired. He and his party were in opposition right now, but they'd be back on top soon, everyone was sure. And yet, when the mothers of Ireland were heaving great sighs of relief that Boston or Birmingham wasn't claiming their children, here was her precious boy determined to leave her for America.

When she'd suggested Cork instead, Emmet had lapsed into his old arrogance. 'Mam, come on, it's Stanford, California. So many notable people graduated from there, presidents even. You don't think an engineering degree from one of the finest schools in the US would be better than one from University College Cork? Nobody internationally will even have heard of Cork. It would be so much better for my career, and not only would I get a quality education, but I'd make all the right connections. You can't honestly say that would happen in Cork, nice and all as it is.'

'Well, I suppose it would depend on what connections you wanted to make,' Lena had said, feeling very hurt. 'And why do you need international recognition? I mean, if you get a degree here, and set up in business or go to work for someone else, then surely the connections you make here will be enough?'

But he'd just laughed at her and gone back to his books.

Now Eli came through the back door into the kitchen, with carrots, garden peas and the head of summer cabbage she'd sent him out to collect from the glasshouse. There wasn't much left – it was right at the end of the harvest season – and soon she would have to pick the last of the cabbage and pickle it the way Klaus had shown her. Like Eli, her stepfather still had a taste for German foods, and both he and her husband loved sauerkraut with frankfurters, though they complained the ones she bought in tins in Ireland were nothing like the proper German ones.

'You want me to peel these?' Eli asked, placing the earthy vegetables on the table.

'Yes please.' She smiled at him as she closed the oven. It was always a pleasure, the way Eli enjoyed helping her in the kitchen. So many men thought it beneath them to perform domestic tasks, but Eli had been well-brought-up by his mother, Sarah.

As her husband set about the carrots, she chopped the cabbage, but her mind was still on the scene in the library. She opened her mouth to tell Eli about it but then closed it again. Maybe she'd misheard or misunderstood.

'I forgot to tell you, by the way,' said Eli cheerfully. 'Jimmy Piper came into the surgery yesterday and said the date is set for the wedding.'

'Wedding?' she asked absently.

'Jimmy's wedding to Mrs Weldon. Surely you remember? He asked me to be his best man?'

'Oh…' Lena made a big effort to pull her concentration away from Emmet to her husband, who was grinning at her. 'Of course. Jimmy. The leather worker. He made you that lovely medical bag, didn't he?'

'He did indeed. It was a thank you present for suggesting he clean himself up and take Mrs Weldon to the dance, and when one thing led to another, well, there you have it.'

'But…' She wrinkled her forehead. 'Wasn't there some sort of problem stopping them getting married?'

'There was indeed, because Mr Weldon, or should I say Reverend Weldon, is still very much alive.'

'*Reverend* Weldon? No, Eli, that's not –'

'Possible for a Catholic priest to marry? You're right, but a short while into their loveless marriage, didn't Mr Weldon skip off to England, change coats and become a Protestant vicar.'

'No…' She was enthralled.

'So off went Jimmy and Mrs Weldon to Monsignor Collins, seeking an annulment of her first marriage, which had never been consummated –'

'Eli.' Lena glanced nervously towards the kitchen doorway in case any of the children came in and overheard.

Eli rolled his eyes humorously at her primness, but it was a habit of privacy that Kilteegan Bridge had bred into her, and it still made her uncomfortable if he talked about sex in front of the children.

'Anyway, whatever, they sought an annulment on *certain grounds*, but the Monsignor was having none of it, wouldn't even listen. Jimmy thinks it was because he and Mrs Weldon walked out of the church at Mrs Moriarty's funeral.'

'Mm, that wouldn't endear him to them, that's for sure.' At the infamous funeral, the Monsignor had started talking about how God had forgiven Frances Moriarty her terrible sin because she'd repented and stopped taking the pill, and though she'd then bled to death from a miscarriage, just as Eli had warned she would if she got pregnant again, that somehow meant she'd gone straight to heaven. Half the congregation had walked out in disgust, and Jimmy and Mrs Weldon had been at the head of the queue. 'So how are they able to get married then, without an annulment?'

'Well, like I said, he was against it at first, but then they explained Mr Weldon had become a Protestant vicar and he completely changed his tune. He fired off a letter to the archbishop, and because he's a Monsignor, it was all fast-tracked, so the annulment was granted and the wedding is set for next summer.'

Lena laughed so much she nearly forgot about Emmet, but then she was distracted by voices in the hall. Isobel was leaving, and moments later Emmet appeared into the kitchen. 'Mm, that smells good,' he announced, sniffing the air.

'Hi,' Lena said a little stiffly, no longer laughing, and although Emmet didn't notice her change of mood, Eli shot his wife an enquiring look, his eyebrows raised.

'That was Isobel,' added Emmet unnecessarily, settling into a seat at the table. He started 'helpfully' shelling the garden peas, although Lena noticed more were going into his mouth than into the bowl. 'She keeps pestering me about coming to visit me in America.'

'While you're at college?' asked Lena quietly. 'I thought she was going to school in Switzerland? And don't forget, her dad's a professor. He'll want her to go to college as well maybe. I know she was talking about art school.'

'Yeah, I know, I said she'd soon forget me. But she's still on about coming after we've both finished our education.' Emmet threw it out there carelessly, his mouth crammed with peas, avoiding his mother's eyes.

'Well, won't you be back in Ireland by then anyway?' Lena's throat felt tight. She didn't want to ask the question as she thought the answer might break her heart, but she knew it had to be asked or otherwise there would be nothing but sleepless nights ahead of her. 'Aren't you planning to come home after your degree?'

There was an awkward silence in the kitchen. She stopped chopping cabbage. Emmet stopped eating peas. Only Eli calmly carried on peeling the carrots.

'Look, Mam…' There was a long pause.

'Look, Mam, what?' she asked sadly.

'It's just…well…Ireland is fine for you. This is where you feel happiest. And it will always be my home obviously, but I have bigger plans than designing small little houses in Kilteegan Bridge or even bigger ones in Cork. I want to design huge buildings, like opera houses and bridges spanning mighty rivers and even airports, things that get noticed, things that would not happen here.'

'We do have those things in Ireland, Emmet,' Eli said mildly as he threw another carrot with a splash into the pan of cold water beside him. 'And I think as the years go on, we'll be getting a lot more of them. The railway network desperately needs updating, and there will have to be more and better roads as more people get cars.'

Emmet turned to him, pleadingly. 'Look, I'm not saying that's not true, but can't you see the huge opportunity this is? I can't believe you'd stand in my way, Dad. Come on, you of all people. You have a degree, you understand about education. You went to University in Cardiff and worked in Wales before coming here. You can see how much better it would be to have a career outside Ireland?'

The inherent insult that Emmet's degree-less mother would have no clue about such matters, nor any dreams of her own, was not lost on Eli. He put his knife down and looked hard at his son. 'Emmet, your mother is the most intelligent person I know, and if you've anyone to thank for that brain you've got, it's her. If she'd had the chance to go to university, she'd knock both of us into a cocked hat, I can assure you, so do not forget that.'

Emmet winced. 'Sorry, Mam. I didn't mean to sound superior. It's just, well, Malachy has this thriving engineering firm, which I could maybe slot straight into after college if I do well enough, so I'd get a great start and be able to move on to any other company from there, maybe even New York –'

'So you're telling me you want to emigrate to America, is that it?' Lena failed to keep the tremor from her voice. 'For good, not just for university?'

Emmet's face gave him away. 'Well, not for good...' he said, but she could see the future in his gaze, his dreams of glory. The bright lights of California were luring her boy away from her.

'Emmet, tell me the truth.' She locked her eyes with his. She and her son had always shared a special bond. Sarah and Pádraig teased her about it and Eli put up with it though he didn't like it, but they had a different connection to any she had with anyone else. When the whole world frustrated and puzzled him, he came to her and she soothed his worries.

Her son sighed. 'I love you, Mam, and Dad and everyone here, you know I do, but...I want something else, something beyond here. Have you never felt that way?'

She had, of course. Back when she'd been in love with Malachy, she'd had such plans, and Malachy had been like her, eager to travel. She was going to train as a nurse, and he would be an engineer, and they were going to take off around the world for endless adventures... And then there was Emmet, and the dreams ended. She could hardly say that to her son; it would sound too much as if she regretted having him. She didn't. She had a wonderful life here in Kilteegan Bridge, and she loved her husband and all her children.

She thought deeply about what to say to him, while Emmet watched her anxiously and Eli with a quiet interest, clearly not wanting to interfere any further but silently urging her to say the right thing. She steeled herself. 'You know, Emmet, my godfather, Doc, always used to tell me about this woman – she was a widow out towards Ballydehob. She had two daughters and never let them out of her sight, no dances, no boyfriends, no jobs even. She kept them close, terrified they'd leave her. And she was a bit of a hypochondriac too, the same woman, so Doc was always being called, and when he was there, he'd always ask after the girls. She'd moan about how they were always getting notions to go here and there, but she never allowed it.'

Emmet said nothing, his green eyes doubtful.

'And Doc, who was a great observer of human life – a country GP means you see it all – he used to say that those girls would escape one day, whether she liked it or not, and they'd never come back for fear of getting caught in her web again. Best to let children go, let them live their lives and hope they come back, but if you hold on too tight, they'll get away anyway but that will be that.'

'So you don't mind?' Emmet asked, his eyes shining now.

'Well, I'm not saying I don't mind, but at the same time, it's your life, Emmet. Though I and your father will have to talk to Malachy about your plans.'

'He's been very respectful, Mam. I swear, every time we talk about it, he says you and Dad have to agree and he won't do anything without your approval. And' – Emmet turned to Eli then – 'he knows it's not like we're going to become father and son after all this time. He might be my biological father, but you're my dad and he knows that.'

Eli smiled and tousled Emmet's copper curls. 'I know that, but thanks for saying it.'

'So will I write, ask him to telephone you?' He couldn't keep the enthusiasm from his voice.

'Do that.' Lena sighed. Deep down, she'd always known this day was coming, in some form. Malachy Berger had stayed in Emmet's life since he reappeared when Emmet was seven; he'd had him over for visits, wrote often and sent him money. He was careful every Christmas to pick lovely gifts for the whole family, if a bit too extravagant for Lena's liking, and she knew he meant well.

Eli was mostly fine with Malachy Berger's role in her life, and the fact that he was Emmet's biological father, though he always maintained that Malachy had never really got over Lena, that he always held a torch for her, which she didn't believe but she couldn't persuade her husband otherwise.

As she went back to slicing the cabbage and Emmet to eating the peas, Sarah burst in, her boots and jodhpurs splattered with mud, wearing an old jumper of Eli's.

'Hi, family. How long's dinner going to be?' she said. 'I'm starving.' At fourteen, Sarah was slender and strong, the image of Lena though much taller, and like Emmet she ate like a docker.

'I thought you were having Sunday lunch at Maggie's after the hunt?' Lena asked in surprise.

'I did, but honestly, her mam thinks because Maggie eats like a little bird, I do too. What she gave me wouldn't feed a sparrow. And she was telling me – you know Maggie's mam is obsessed with looking young, and she's always taking mad potions and rubbing stuff on herself – she told me I shouldn't laugh so much 'cause I'll get crow's feet and then I'll have to have an operation to fix them.'

Lena laughed, shaking her head. Lizzie Spillane was a bit daft. Trooping up to communion at Mass each Sunday with a painted face, wearing clothes more appropriate for her daughter. Emmet had said she was like the rich women in Los Angeles, who were always trying to fix themselves with surgery and ended up looking like startled dolls.

But Eli laid his knife down once more, looking even more serious this time. 'Don't pay her any attention, Sarah. Birth, death, even the degeneration of our bodies and our faces over time is all part of the living process. And I think it's beautiful. People who try to subvert it, risk operations even, for their version of the perfect body or face, to be forever twenty-one, I don't understand it. We should be proud of our scars and lines and grey hairs. They show we've lived, that we've survived.'

As a child of the Holocaust, Eli embraced life with a fervour others didn't. He knew what a privilege it was, and so he sucked the marrow from every second. Lena loved it about him.

'All right, all right, Dad. Keep your receding hair on.' Sarah laughed, one of her long legs thrown over the back of a chair as she ate dry breakfast cereal from the box she'd taken down from the shelf. She was a greyhound breed, just like her father. 'You better not let Betty Halpin hear you, or she'll go out of business. Touching up the grey roots of the parish is her speciality, and the things she does with sticky tape are miraculous apparently.'

'Well, she can do what she likes, but she'll be keeping her hands off my girls anyway. When you have such natural beauty as you and your mother have, there's no need of tweaking.' He went back to the potatoes, and Lena gave Sarah a conspiratorial wink. Little did Eli know that for a few years now, Betty had been covering up Lena's grey hairs, plucking her eyebrows and waxing her legs. But sticky tape? That was a new one on her.

'So Isobel wasn't out today, we hacked over to Colcodrum castle,' remarked Sarah, looking pointedly at Emmet, 'according to Jenny Lehane it was because she knew you weren't going.'

'I doubt that,' her older brother said casually, pinging a pea into the bowl.

'I hear things are going great between you. Aren't you glad I kept letting her into the house when you didn't want me to?'

'Yeah, well, stop letting her in, all right? I mean it, Sarah.'

'I also hear you've invited her to move to America just to be with you.'

'I have not.' He was getting red in the face now. Sarah could always push his buttons and did so mercilessly.

'You're a hopeless liar, Emmet. Tell the truth now. And everyone's been told what a great kisser you are…'

Emmet glowered at her, his face flaming. 'Shut-up Sarah, you've such a big mouth, and Isobel and I aren't going out...'

'Not what I heard. I heard wedding bells… Oi!' She laughed and ducked as Emmet hurled a handful of empty pea pods at her head in fury.

# CHAPTER 7

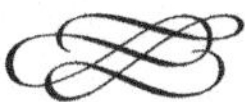

Emily and Nellie stood in silence as the English woman in the beige blouse and beige skirt and beige stockings explained that Nightingale House was a nursing and convalescent home, not exclusively for girls in her position but also for women who 'just needed a nice rest' and that it might be best, for Nellie's own sake, to 'pop a ring on' and have a story in case anyone asked.

They followed her down a corridor that was painted cream, with a lime-green rail and skirting boards, and Emily briefly wondered who on earth thought lime green would be a good colour but dismissed it. She realised she was clinging to the handle of the handbag Lena had bought her for the Christmas just gone, her grip deathlike.

The woman, whose name she'd forgotten, opened a door to a small room with a single bed, a locker, a sink and a wardrobe. It was clean and bright. The home was over five floors and they were on the fourth, so the view was over the River Thames and the seemingly infinite sprawl of London.

How on earth millions of people could live in such close proximity to each other, Emily had no idea. It was her first time out of Ireland. She'd been pregnant with Nellie when Lena got married to Eli in

Cardiff, so she couldn't go, and since then there had been no reason to leave the island. Last night, she and Nellie had stayed in a very nice hotel called the Piccadilly for a treat, and it astonished her how people were out and about till late in the evening, shopping or just hurrying from one place to another. Kilteegan Bridge was nearly dead at this time of year after the excesses of Christmas.

Blackie had never travelled either. He'd been going to come with them, but in the end, she told him not to. He was not angry at Nellie or ashamed or any of the things other fathers might be, but he was heartbroken for his baby girl. Emily doubted he'd be able to leave her here. It would take every ounce of resolve she had herself, but she would do it for Nellie, for her darling daughter.

'So, Ellen, this is your room, and further down the corridor, there is the common room. There's a television and a radio and some books and magazines, things of that nature, should you wish to have some company.' The woman smiled, but the warmth never reached her eyes.

Eli had researched rest homes and asked his medical friends, and this place was purported to be nice. It was private and expensive, but she and Blackie paid the fee willingly. Blackie especially didn't care. Nellie was his pride and joy, and if it was up to him, she'd have stayed in Kilteegan Bridge and he'd have dealt with anyone who had anything to say about it, but neither Emily nor Nellie wanted that. So he would pay for the best care, and he would take the child in as his own son or daughter. There was nothing he wouldn't do for his girl.

'You'll attend the clinic once a week,' the woman was saying, 'just to ensure all is going as it should with your baby. And when your time comes, you will be delivered here, either by Dr Grosvenor if there are complications, or if not – and you are young and healthy, so I'm sure there won't be – by one of our midwives.'

Emily glanced at her daughter. She was ashen and looked even younger than her sixteen years. Her signature look of kohled eyes and pink lips and cheeks, all framed with beach-blond wavy hair, was nowhere to be seen today. Her hair was in a ponytail, and she wore no make-up. Her bump was just visible now, she was lucky she wasn't big, and winter clothes made covering up easier. Emily longed to wrap her in her arms, beg her to come home, tell her they would face everyone themselves, but that wasn't a sensible option, she knew.

'Visiting hours are two to four daily and two to six on weekends, and there is a telephone in the corridor downstairs. Please don't hog it, though, as we have a lot of people wanting to use it and only one line. If you can keep calls to just a minute or two, twice a week, that would be preferable.'

Nellie just nodded meekly.

'Thank you…she will,' Emily managed.

'So, Ellen, I'll give you some time to unpack. Supper is in the dining room at six on the dot, and Mrs Crean, if you have any questions, you can find me at the reception desk.'

The woman left in a blur of beige, and Emily was left standing in the centre of the small room, wondering what she should do or say to make this less awful for her daughter.

'Will I tell them you don't go by Ellen?' she asked, leading Nellie to the bed and sitting beside her.

Her daughter shook her head. 'I'll be Ellen here. Nothing about this is really me. I'll be Nellie again when it's over.'

'All right, pet, whatever you want.' Emily rubbed her back and knew they were both trying desperately not to cry.

'I'm glad Daddy didn't come. He'd never stick her plummy accent and the "supper on the dot of six".' Nellie did a perfect imitation of the woman.

Emily smiled. Blackie had no time for notions, and Nellie was right – he'd have hated this place and seen the woman, whatever her name or title was, as overly bossy and superior.

'It's not too bad, though, is it?' she asked hopefully, glancing around. The walls were papered with a small blue floral print and the single bed was made like a hospital bed, with an extra sky-blue woollen blanket folded at the end of it. The wardrobe and locker were white Formica.

Over the bed was a handmade embroidery piece, framed. Someone had painstakingly embroidered the words.

*A wise child brings joy to the father, a foolish child brings grief to the mother.*

*Proverbs 10:1*

Both women read it together.

'Well, we know which one I am, don't we?' Nellie said dolefully.

'I've no idea what *lúdramán* embroidered that, or what other plonker saw fit to put it up, but that's going in the drawer anyway for starters.' Emily took the offending piece down and put it in the wardrobe drawer. Then she turned and placed her hands on her daughter's shoulders.

'Now you listen here to me, Nellie Angela Crean. You are not foolish nor are you the cause of any of our grief. Your father and I love you, and we're proud of you, and this will pass and you'll be fine. If I knew who the boy was, I swear to you, I'd choke the last breath out of him. But we are where we are, and we'll have to get on with it. I wish I could stay with you, be with you through this, but for the plan to work, I need to be at home.'

'Will it work, Mam? Really? Maybe it's stupid…' Nellie's fear was written all over her face.

'It will if you want it to work. But if now or at any point in the future you decide you want to keep the baby, then of course that's what you must do. You know what your dad said…'

Nellie nodded, her eyes bright with tears. Blackie Crean was like most Irish men, uncomfortable discussing emotions, but as Nellie was leaving, he had hugged her so tightly she could hardly breathe and told her that no matter what she decided, no matter what the outcome, that baby would be as welcome as the flowers of May in their home, and if he was to be that little boy or girl's father, then so be it, but he was happy to be a granda also, and to hell with what anyone had to say about it.

'I can't keep it, Mam, I just can't. It wouldn't be fair to him or her. I'm not ready to be a mother, nowhere near it, and I know I'd resent the kid and that's not fair – it's not their fault.'

Emily nodded. 'Then we'll go with the plan.' She smiled encouragingly. 'As soon as I'm back in Kilteegan Bridge, I'll head into Maureen's Fashions with a fine bump under my skirt, looking at the baby clothes, so believe me, within a few days, everyone will be treating me like a queen and not letting me lift anything heavy.'

Nellie laughed a little at that, then hiccupped, and tears came into her eyes again. 'I'm sorry I've brought this all on you, Mam. But I couldn't get rid of it – I knew that from the start. And the idea of a stranger raising it... I mean, what if they were horrible? Or if nobody adopted them and they ended up in an orphanage? The guilt would eat away at me.'

Emily pulled her daughter to her, wrapping her arms around her and kissing her head. 'Well, you won't have that. Nellie, don't be daft. I don't want you to think it's a burden to me. I always wanted a brother or sister for you, so if it's what you want, this baby will be that. Please God, he or she will be born safe and sound, and I'll be here with you. Your Uncle Eli will tell everyone he's sent me away for bed rest in Dublin because of my troubles in the past, and we can all travel back by boat with the baby, and –'

'I was thinking, Mam, that it might be better if I don't come back with you right away? It will be a bit suspicious that I'm gone working in England, then I turn up just when you've had a baby.'

Emily was startled. 'But, love, you'll just have given birth. Where else would you go? And no one will think it's strange you've come home to see your baby brother or sister. We'll just say you came over to see me in Dublin and then decided to stay to help out.'

'Well, I know, but don't you think it would be best for everyone if I stay here in London? Maybe I can find a flat and a bit of a job here for a while?'

Emily looked at Nellie in terror as a horrible thought struck her. Was she about to gain a new son or daughter but lose her beloved child in the process? 'My love, I need to say something.' She spoke slowly, her daughter's hand in hers. 'I'm doing this willingly, and with an open heart. I'll love this baby like my own, I promise, but if I thought that meant you didn't want to come back, because the child would be there, then that would kill me. You're my girl. For so long you were the only child I had, and if I thought that bringing this baby into our lives as my son or daughter meant you felt you couldn't come back to Kilteegan Bridge, then...' Her voice choked on the emotion of it all, and hot tears spilled from her eyes.

'I'll always be your daughter, Mam, and I'll never forget what you're doing for me. But I feel like I need to stay away for a while –'

'No, Nellie, just no. You're only sixteen. I won't let you suddenly be one of those children that sends a Christmas card but never comes home for years and years. So, no. Kilteegan Bridge is your home, it's where you belong, and no silly mistake or stupid young boy is going to drive you away from me. Now, will I help you to unpack, settle you in?' She tried to infuse her voice with bright, capable enthusiasm, the total opposite of how she felt.

Nellie didn't try to argue about staying in England; hopefully it was just a whim. Instead, she gave Emily a huge hug and said, 'I don't think you've time, Mam. The boat leaves at five in the morning, and you need to get the coach from Paddington at five o'clock to Fishguard. It's quarter past three now, so maybe if they can get you a taxi from here to Paddington station, it will be easier on you.' Nellie swallowed. 'I can't believe you're going to do what we just did, only backwards, on your own.'

The boat over from Dublin had been a horrible rough crossing, and they had both felt so nauseous, but there was hardly time to steady themselves before they were bundled onto a coach that seemed to take an age to get to London.

'I'll be fine, love. Don't be worrying about me. You're the one to look after now.'

'I'll be fine too, Mam. They seem nice, and this place isn't too bad.' Nellie glanced around the small room. 'I'll put up a few pictures and put the blanket Nana crocheted for me on the bed, and I didn't forget Winky.' She pulled a one-eyed elephant that looked like he'd been in the wars out of her bag. Nellie had slept with Winky every night since she was tiny; Doc had given it to her as a present when she was christened.

Seeing her daughter's childhood toy nearly started Emily off crying again, but she blinked back the tears. She would not cry. There was enough time for that on the bus back to the ferry. Right now, Nellie needed her to be strong.

'Go on, Mam, please. I'll be fine,' Nellie assured her, but Emily was under no illusion. This was going to be awful.

# CHAPTER 8

Maria wished she could hurry the builders along. Her brother, Ted, was enjoying being back in Cork, but he was missing his Australian family. The workmen were still renovating the house on Wellington Road. They were putting in proper plumbing and central heating and a new kitchen, but they were also under instructions to retain all the original Georgian features, so it was slow work.

She and Ted had been at the property almost every day since he'd arrived, doing their best to get the garden in order before Gwenda and the girls arrived. Maria was pruning the roses and the overgrown box hedges while Ted was digging up flower beds and planting snowdrop, crocus, daffodil and iris bulbs so that the flowers would come up in succeeding waves of colour.

In Maria's unhappy childhood memories, this house was a dark, cold mausoleum. Their mother, Irene, had been cold and cruel, and neither of them had been surprised to discover that she wasn't their biological mother after all; they were the children of George Hannigan's mistress, who had died of TB. George had convinced Irene to take the children in, and she did but resented every day of it, to the point of trying to get Maria locked up in an asylum and telling Ted his sister was dead. She'd even tried to leave their father's many properties, bank bonds and shares to the Redemptorist mission, but thankfully Ted had arrived home just in time to claim his and Maria's joint inheritance.

'Do you think Gwenda and the girls will mind living in the city?' she asked Ted as she slashed back an overhanging branch of laurel. 'After living on a huge ranch all their lives?'

Ted stopped digging and straightened his back. 'Well, we'll see how it goes. It's impossible to buy farmland around here – people always just pass it down through their own family – or I might have thought about that as an alternative. But this garden is wonderfully big and will be beautiful, the girls will love it, and there's a riding stable nearby. It's not the same as having your own horses on your own land, but right now they're living in a rented three-bed in a suburb, and this is a million times better.'

The Australian drought of '65 to '68 had broken Ted's family's finances, and though they'd done their level best to cling on to the ranch where Gwenda had been raised, the bank had foreclosed on them a year ago and his family had had to abandon the land and move into the little town of Morrirset, three hours north of Sydney.

Sophie and Annamaria were, according to their father, trying their very best to put a brave face on their reduced circumstances, but it was difficult. The idea of coming to Ireland had got them smiling again, so Ted was hoping to move his family over as soon as he had the house fit for them to live in.

'Anyway, it's not like the countryside isn't all around,' added Maria. 'They can spend as much time as they want on the farm. Jack and Skipper will have plenty for them to do especially after the twins go, and Skipper will surely let them help out with the horses.'

Maria was eager to make Ted's Australian family feel welcome and satisfied in Ireland. Her brother's years in exile had melted away from him when he came home after nearly forty years away, but she knew it would be harder for his wife and girls, and she was determined to make this move a happy one for them as well.

Maria's own house where she lived with Klaus, and where Ted was staying for now, was lovely, but it was a new build, all whites and creams and beiges, with large windows overlooking a perfectly manicured lawn. It suited her and Klaus, simple, clean, no clutter. An odd pop of colour with a vase of flowers or a painting they both liked, but generally serene. This house on Wellington Road with its huge garden would be more suitable for active children, and once she and Ted had finished renovating it, it would make a warm and welcoming family home. She was already running up curtains on her Singer sewing machine and picking out paints and measuring for carpets.

'There'll be plenty of cousins to make them feel at home in Ireland as well. They're a little bit younger but that won't matter I'm sure, they're all into horses.'

'I don't want to put your family to any trouble. You've all been so welcoming already,' Ted said.

'It won't be any trouble. They'll be delighted.' She was delighted herself, almost dancing from rose bush to rose bush. It felt so good to have her brother back in her life. The decades of longing for his presence had disappeared like smoke, and she could talk to Ted in a way she couldn't to others.

'So how have you been of late?' Ted asked, and she knew he was referring to her mental health. She suffered from manic depression, and sometimes when she was very happy, like she was now, she could tell her family were anxious about what might happen next. Not so long ago, happiness like this would grow and grow until the rosy bubble got too big and burst and nothing but blackness would remain, a void of horror. But lithium had made a great difference.

It was a relief to have the truth about her illness out in the open. Eli had convinced her to talk about it, though it still embarrassed her a bit, but he'd explained her illness was no more her fault than it was Doc's fault for getting cancer; it was just the luck of the draw. She had got a tough hand to play, but as he was always telling her, even in the bad times, she had a family who loved her and who would do anything for her, and secrets and pretending nothing was wrong were just adding more stress to everyone. So now she accepted that there were times when she was unwell, times when the world looked black and dark, but that she'd come out of it again.

She smiled at her older brother, who had stood up for her all through her childhood every time Irene Hannigan threatened to lock her peculiar daughter up in a psychiatric institution for the rest of her life.

'All right. So much better than I used to be. I take this new drug and it really helps. I haven't needed to go to St Catherine's for ages, but if I do, they will put me back on track again. It's not an easy life, and I don't know how Klaus puts up with it, or the children, but they do.'

'Because they love you, and it's not your fault,' Ted said gently.

'That's what Eli says all the time.' She nodded. 'I've been lucky. Some of the people I've met in hospital over the years, the things they endured were just awful. But Paudie was so loving and patient, and now Klaus is the same, and having Doc and then Eli as my doctors in Kilteegan Bridge...well, I've had the best of care.'

'I'm glad. I only knew Paudie briefly, but he seemed like a lovely man, and Klaus is a gentleman.'

It was wonderful to be able to talk about her past with him like this, openly and honestly. 'Paudie O'Sullivan was a very special man, and a wonderful father too. Honestly, I wasn't fit to be a parent when the kids were little, and he did it all. That's why his death was so hard. We didn't just miss him, we needed him, more than anyone ever knew. And when I was bad – and there were very bad times, when I felt like I was in a railway tunnel except there was no light at any end, and the darkness would just envelop me, pulling me away from everyone and everything, when even my little children couldn't reach me – Paudie was there. Sometimes just a shadow, or a presence, but I could feel him. And, Ted, I accused him of being unfaithful to me, I hurt him, I hit him, I threw things, and I would wail and scream – you remember how it was when I was young – but he never faltered, never once. He loved me, you see, the broken bird I was.'

Ted came over and took her hand. 'I often wonder if our parents –

well, you know, our father and Irene – had got you better care when you were a child…'

'There was nothing they could have done.' Despite everything, Maria was certain of that. 'They could have been kinder, undoubtedly, to you too, but medically there was nothing. Doc, God rest his soul, tried everything on me, and the doctors in St Catherine's are wonderful too, but until recently, there was no chance of making me better.'

'Me going missing can't have helped, though. I'm sorry, Maria. I should have tried harder, dug deeper. I've spent so many wasted years not knowing you.' He was sad and she knew it.

'You were doing wonderful work in the war, and then when you wrote, Irene told you I'd died, and why wouldn't you believe her? I thought you were dead as well. But we've done all right, Ted, for the children of that pair of oddballs. You should be so proud of the part you played in winning the war, and now you have Gwenda and the girls, and you're home. I'd say that was a victory.'

He squeezed her hand again. 'I think so too, and your children are wonderful. I'm so looking forward to getting to know them properly, and Klaus as well, of course. I'm just sorry I didn't get to know Paudie properly, I really liked him when we met that one time.'

Maria nodded. 'Klaus and Paudie are so different in so many ways. Paudie was a big personality, and a big man, as you remember. He was solid and reliable, and oh, Ted, he was funny. He could make us all laugh till the tears flowed. Everyone knew him, and he was so loved. The outpouring of grief when he died, it was overwhelming actually. It was as if all these other people had a piece of him too and were as devastated to lose him as we were. I was lost, totally and completely lost without him. You'd been my rock when I was young, the person I clung to who made me feel safe, and then Paudie did that, so losing him to that murderer…' – she paused and shuddered – 'and having no idea where you were, well, it wasn't easy.'

'I can't even imagine it, Maria.'

'But I managed, some kind of way. Lena and Emily and Jack held me up, and Bill and Deirdre Madden raised the twins. They all put up with a lot, and it never occurred to me in a million years that I'd have another man. But when Klaus came to visit me in St Catherine's, saying he was a friend of Lena's and that he just thought he'd pop in to say hello, well, I was astonished and a bit suspicious, if I'm honest.'

Ted returned her grin.

'But he was genuine, and for some reason, he liked me. He's been through a lot, an awful lot actually, but he'd never go on about it. He was in the German army and served in France and later on the Eastern Front. He wasn't a Nazi – he despised Hitler – but he feels very guilty about having any involvement at all. Then the Russians took him captive, and he was kept in a gulag for eight years, and though he survived, it also changed him, he says. He's not like Paudie in most respects. He's quiet and academic, he likes being alone, and he's contemplative, I suppose, but he and I get along very well. We like the same things, nature, walking, music. He's a great cook and loves food. Being deprived for so long has had an impact on him, and now when he eats, he appreciates every crumb and leaves nothing on the plate.'

'He shows no signs of eating much,' Ted said lightly.

'No, he's so thin, not like Paudie, who was such a big strong man. But the main thing is Klaus is just as loving and patient as Paudie was. He says when I have bad episodes that he knows the sun will shine again, and that he'll be there for me when it does. I don't feel pressure to get better quickly. He doesn't mind if I stay in bed all day, barely eat. He doesn't fuss or cluck around me. He goes to his study and checks in with me from time to time, but he leaves me alone, knowing it just has to pass. He's protective without being stifling, and he knows how much the human spirit can withstand, much more than we imagine, so he knows I'll be all right in the end.'

'And when it passes?'

She smiled. 'When it does, when I get up, he brings me a bunch of flowers and some Swiss chocolate from the market and we dance in the kitchen, slowly, just a waltz or something like that, maybe to some Strauss. I feel his arms around me and the beating of his heart, and that gives me comfort and peace.'

'So is it true love?' Ted asked.

Maria nodded. 'Yes, it is. Not the kind of love I had for Paudie. It's different, but then so am I. I'm older, calmer, and we've both been through a lot. We give each other peace, I think.'

'Was he married before? Has he children?'

'No, and no children, but he's very close to mine.'

'He seems like a decent man, despite having fought on the German side. Hitler was the devil incarnate, of course, and he surrounded himself with demons, but there were ordinary German soldiers caught up in the whole disaster as well. I suppose we have to remember that.'

Ted had spent the war as a British agent, constantly risking his life by feeding false information to the Germans, right up to the Normandy invasion, when he was instrumental in assuring the German military command that the Allies were planning to land in Calais. After that, the British had smuggled him off to Australia to keep him safe from revenge, and there he had met Gwenda and settled down.

'How do you feel when you look back on it all?' Maria asked.

Ted laughed and returned to the mundane task of digging the flower beds and planting his bulbs. 'Honestly, sometimes I wonder who that man was, who did those things during the war. I don't recognise him most of the time.'

# CHAPTER 9

Eli tried not to grimace as Fintan Slattery showed him the weeping scar on his leg, still livid and sore. Pus oozed from the original site of the stitches, and the smell was putrid.

'Right, Mr Slattery,' he said, putting on some latex gloves. 'Let's see what's going on here. You've taken the last full course of antibiotics I prescribed and used the ointment every day?'

'I did.' The man winced as Eli inspected his leg by the light from the tiny window, set deep in the stone wall of the old farmhouse. The axe had cut clean through to the bone at the time. The bone had been pinned and the wound stitched up, and after two weeks of treatment in the hospital, his leg had seemed to be on the mend. Yet as soon as Fintan was sent home, the oozing started again and the wound became reinfected.

Every two weeks, Eli had cleaned it thoroughly, dressed it and warned Fintan not to get it wet or dirty, and three times now he had put Fintan on a very strong course of antibiotics to kill the infection. The last time he'd cleaned the wound was only ten days ago, and today it was worse if anything.

'I don't know what in the name of God I'll do. I need to get back to the farm, and I can't put my foot under me, Dr Kogan. And the pain, especially at night, I do be roaring.'

Fintan was like many of his patients, a tough West Cork farmer, not given to complaining or being too precious about themselves, so the fact that he was saying he was so unwell, admitting he was in terrible pain, meant it was probably much worse than he was even letting on. Eli was at a loss as to what to do. The consultant Fintan had seen at the hospital had telephoned him back this morning. Eli had contacted him for some advice, but the other man had nothing to offer. They'd run blood tests, checked for any sinister bacterial infection going on that would impede healing, but apart from this terrible wound, it seemed the man was fine.

'I'm going to write you a prescription for stronger painkillers – you can't drink alcohol when you're on them, mind – and a sleeping tablet to help you at night and a new antibiotic. It's different to the others you've tried, and it might just work. Also, Fintan, now the wound is clean again, maybe don't try to manage it yourself? I don't know why the infection keeps returning, but I think we should try having Mrs Slattery unwind the bandage and spray it with this antiseptic spray every second day.'

'I'm going out of my mind here, Doctor, so I'll take whatever potions you have. But my missus, well, like I've told you before, she's not going to help me, so there's no point in talking to her, Doctor. And if you don't mind, I'd still rather you didn't ask her.'

Fintan had been insistent on leaving Vera out of his treatment plan ever since she'd refused to go in the ambulance with him, but Eli had had enough of this domestic argument. Vera clearly just didn't understand the seriousness of her husband's situation. The only other possibility was that she was squeamish, but that was very unlikely. Farmer's wives were always up to their elbows in birthing sheep or slaughtering calves or wringing the necks of unfortunate chickens, so they were used to blood. 'I'm sure she will help you,' he soothed the sick man, 'so I'll see her before I go and explain what's to be done – it's not complicated. I'll pop back in a few days anyway to check on you, and of course in the meantime, if you need me, just ring the surgery.'

Fintan leant back against the pillows, his face a mask of pain, muttering something about it all being a waste of time.

In the kitchen peeling potatoes was Vera. Lena had warned him that Vera was a bit peculiar and came from a line of psychics or fortune-tellers or some such, but he had no time for such fanciful notions. Surely she'd help the man she was married to for what must be fifty years in his hour of need.

'Mrs Slattery, I wonder if I could have a word, please?' he asked tentatively as he pushed the kitchen door open.

'You can of course, Dr Kogan. Come in.' She seemed welcoming enough.

'I was just in with Fintan, as you know, and his leg is still very bad. To be honest, I'm at a loss as to why nothing is working but –'

'I'll tell you, will I?' she said conversationally as she gathered the potato peels into a bucket, presumably to feed the hens.

Eli set his leather medical bag on the table and riffled through it for his prescription pad. 'If you have an idea, I'm all ears,' he said courteously.

'You know what he was doing when it happened, do you?' She had iron-grey curls and small dark eyes that seemed to never miss anything.

'He was chopping wood?'

'Indeed. And he wasn't just chopping wood then,' she said, sliding the potatoes into a saucepan of boiling water on the range, a big old monstrosity in the middle of the back wall, a basket of turf beside it. 'He was chopping at the hawthorn, the one above in *pairc na sídhe*.' She glanced sideways at him to see if he understood her.

'Sorry, my Irish isn't very good,' he apologised, and she nodded, politely forgiving him for being foreign.

'Yes, I hear the Welsh is very different, more like Cornish or Breton. *Pairc na sídhe* means the field of the fairies, the Good People. The hawthorn is their tree, and woe betide anyone who'd try to harm it. Fintan wanted to plough it because he's greedy. The old horse would never have let him go near it – she had more sense than my husband ever did – but them tractors are soulless beasts. Anyway, I told him, as if he didn't know himself, that the Good People wouldn't like it and he'd be made to pay, but he knew better.' She wiped her hands on her apron. 'He swung at that tree, and my husband has been chopping trees since he was a *garsún* – he's well able. But the Good People made sure he missed and cut clean through his own leg instead. 'Tis why it won't heal either, no matter what you or any doctor does.'

Eli was nonplussed. The matter-of-fact manner in which she delivered her prognosis left no room for response; she didn't seem to expect one either.

'Um...well...' He felt at a complete loss. 'If you could unwrap his bandages every second day, I've given him –'

'I'm telling you, Doctor, it will do no good. He'll have to make reparations to the Good People, and even then...' She shrugged.

'And how would he go about doing that, do you think?' he asked warily.

She turned from her work then and faced him, a knowing smile playing on her lips. 'You've no time for the knowledge – I can see it in you, Dr Kogan. You're a good man and a good doctor, I'm not saying you're not, but in the heel of the hunt, you think this is a load of old rubbish. But mark my words, that leg of his won't heal, no matter what you do.'

He stood looking at her, and she back at him, until he sighed and gave up. 'Well, will you do one thing for your husband, Mrs Slattery, that I don't think will offend your beliefs?'

'Oh, my beliefs aren't offended by anything, Dr Kogan. I'm a practical person no more than yourself. I just know what will or won't work, that's all, and I don't like to waste my time.'

He ploughed on. 'So if you could get these prescriptions from the chemist. One of them is a very strong painkiller, and there's a sleeping tablet and some new antibiotics.' He wrote out the medications on the yellow pad, slowly because his arthritis was bad today and he was having difficulty holding the pad steady with his left hand.

She walked towards him then, and when he held out the prescription, she took it, but she also took his left hand in her own, turning it over and examining the knuckles. 'You should take that off until it's healed.' She tapped his wedding ring. 'The fairies aren't fond of them.'

She let his hand go and went back to the range, moved the basket of turf and grabbed what he thought was empty air at first but turned out to be a spider's web. She rubbed her hands together, rolling the wisps of web into a soft clump, and then stood before him again, waiting for him to take off his ring. When he did, reluctantly putting it in his pocket, she took his hand and rolled the grey stickiness over his skin. She said nothing by way of explanation. Eli didn't want to offend this woman – he wanted her on his side for Fintan's sake – so he complied.

As he stood there, she went to a galvanised bucket inside the back door and dipped a glass milk bottle into it to fill it. Then she took a piece of waxed paper that had wrapped the bread from the baker's and twisted it to make a cork for the bottle.

'That's water from the holy well. They say 'tis Saint Bridget blessed that well, but 'twas there long before her time. All the same, it will work. I'll put the good wish on it for you, ask them to cure you. Wash your hands in this, no soap, every morning and evening, and that pain in your knuckles will be gone.'

Eli took the bottle with a smile. 'Are we going to be business rivals, Mrs Slattery?'

'Not a bit of it, Doctor. You have your way and I have mine. Sometimes your way is best, other times mine is, but we're not against each other. Sure aren't we both trying only to help?'

'But you won't help poor Fintan?' he asked gently.

She sighed and shook her head. ''Tisn't that I won't. 'Tis that I can't. He offended them, you see, the Good People, and there's no cure for that. I haven't it, and you haven't it either.'

Eli tried once more. 'Since we're in the same business, will you try anyway, just unwrap the bandage and spray it with the antiseptic every second day?'

''Tis a waste of time, I'm afraid, Dr Kogan, but sure if Fintan thinks it will help, it might cheer him up a bit anyway.'

Pleased with this small victory at least, Eli bade her goodbye and left, putting the bottle of water she gave him in the passenger footwell of his car. He didn't want to offend her, but spiders' webs and holy water were not scientifically sound and therefore were meaningless to him.

# CHAPTER 10

Skipper watched in utter astonishment as Gwenda directed Fifteen and Sixteen, the two young border collies, with a series of whistles and commands to round up the sheep. Jack was grinning broadly, watching from the top of a slight rise. Their grandmother, Thirteen, once belonged to Paudie ,had died in her sleep after a long and happy life and her daughter, Fourteen had given birth to this pair who were keen as mustard for sheep work. Fourteen now lay next to Jack in the damp grass, her head on her arthritic paws, her tufted eyebrows twitching as she followed the action.

'Come by,' Gwenda commanded. The two young collies instantly moved around the sheep in a clockwise direction.

'Fifteen, stand.' The dog stayed on his feet but continued to watch the herd.

'Away to me, Sixteen.' Sixteen changed direction, all the time keeping an eye on the sheep, which were totally in the two sheepdogs' control.

Ted's wife kept the dogs moving and pausing until the sheep were herded into a tight woolly circle in the bottom corner of the field. She was a broad, rangy woman, with skin like burnished leather from years of exposure to the harsh Australian sun, and her hair, once red, was now streaked with golds and greys and tied up in a messy knot on top of her head. She was dressed like a man, with a jacket that smelled, not unpleasantly, of wax and animals, and under that a hand-knit sweater and corduroy trousers tucked into wellington boots.

Finally she nodded and said, 'That'll do.'

Like a switch was turned off, both young dogs returned up the hill to Gwenda's side, and even Fourteen heaved herself to her arthritic feet and staggered over, flopping down at the Australian woman's feet.

'How come you managed to train the dogs so fast? You've only had them for a couple hours.' Skipper pushed back his Stetson and scratched his head in awe. He'd spent the afternoon with Lena's daughter, Sarah, and Ted and Gwenda's daughters, while the three girls jumped and raced the silver mare, which had become, if not sweet and docile, then certainly less homicidal since Jack's midnight offering to the fairies. Meanwhile, Gwenda had gone off to the sheep field with Jack and Ted...and now this.

'My wife came fourth in the National Sheep Dog Trails, Open competition, with a score of eighty-four. She's one of the finest sheep women in the country,' Ted explained proudly. He was leaning on the gate of the field, beaming with pride.

'Blokes don't rate women much at this sort of thing, but my old man had no son and he had to pass it on to someone, so I learnt,' explained Gwenda, patting the dogs. 'And I'm happy to pass it on to you two blokes if you like.'

'I'm up for it,' said Jack instantly, 'if you can spare the time. I've never seen anything like it.'

'I've all the time in the world to spare now, mate, now the ranch is gone. My old man had a station – no disrespect, but it was probably the size of this county – so I had to step up. Mostly sheep but a few hundred head of cattle, and now it's all gone.' Though in general she gave the impression that not much would faze her, a shadow of sheer grief crossed Gwenda's face.

'Ted told me about it, and I'm sorry to hear that,' said Jack gently. The idea of losing land was a visceral fear in Ireland, stemming right back to the Famine when millions died after English landlords threw so many Catholic peasants off their fields and left them to starve by the roadside. 'It sounds as if it was a fine property.'

'Reckon it was once, but the drought years of '65 right up to '68 broke us. In '66 we had bushfires that destroyed a third of our land, then the drought was unrelenting, and then at the end of '68, flooding. By then we'd borrowed to stay in business and couldn't pay back the bank, so they foreclosed. We held on till last year, but it was no good. We had to let it go. The station had been given as a land grant to my great-grandfather, for services rendered to the new colony, and it was in our family until that day.'

She wiped her strong hand across her eyes, and Jack felt intense empathy for her. Like him, it was clear the land and the farm were in her blood. He could see how much it hurt her to be the generation to lose it.

'This is a beautiful farm you have here, Jack, with views all the way to the sea. You're so lucky,' said Gwenda, clearly trying to be cheerful again.

'We love how green everything is around here,' agreed Annamaria, who had come with her sister, Sophie, and Skipper and Sarah, to watch her mother's show. She was a good-looking girl, red-haired, big and of an athletic build like her mother, while Sophie was more like Ted and Maria, slim with pale hair and bright-blue eyes. 'We're fighting drought all the time back at home, so seeing so much grass is amazing.'

'It is,' Sophie agreed. 'It's beautiful in Australia, but here is lovely too, just in a different way, I reckon. Like home is dusty and the earth is red, and it's so hot too – in the summer it's too hot to do much at all. But here is so green, although it's freezing today.' She was huddled up in a thick coat and gloves, still acclimatising to the drop in temperature.

'The summer will come soon, and then you'll see how nice it can be,' said Sarah, determined to defend her country's uncertain weather.

'Skipper's a magician with horses, Mum.' Annamaria chatted away as the party strode back towards the farmhouse, the collies at their heels. 'I mean, as good as you with the sheepdogs almost. He can soothe them. People bring him animals from all over the country, ones that they can't manage, and he has them eating out of his hand. And he let me jump Silverspeed, and he let Sophie race her round the sand track.'

'They're both of them amazing, seriously, Uncle Jack,' said Sarah, who had been astonished and humbled by her new cousins' amazing horsemanship.

'Looks like we have some wondrous people in our family, when it comes to four-legged creatures anyway,' Jack said with a chuckle. 'Now how about a tour of the rest of the place?'

The three girls peeled off back towards the stables with Skipper, but Gwenda and Ted followed Jack all over the farm as he showed them proudly the herd of Friesians, happily munching grass, the pens where they kept the Tamworth pigs and the large henhouse that was now on wheels.

'This is some operation you've got here. I never realised when Maria married Paudie that the place was so big or so diverse,' Ted said in admiration as they leant on a gate and looked down a valley of rich ploughed earth under the clear-blue sky.

'It wasn't really. In my father's time, it was half the size and mostly a dairy farm, but Lena and Eli allow us to use the land of Kilteegan House, so we've been able to expand and diversify into different things. We try to use natural fertilisers and feed, no chemicals if we can avoid it at all. It's a bit more labour-intensive, but the rewards are wonderful.'

'Fascinating. DDT was a wonder and a curse, I suppose.' Ted sighed.

'Rachel Carson was a huge influence in getting its use restricted. Did you read *Silent Spring*, Jack?' Gwenda asked in her Australian twang.

'I devoured it,' Jack said, delighted to connect with a fellow fan of Carson. 'In fact, it was what brought me to America. I was in touch with a rancher in Montana, a man called Chuck Frawley, and a fan of Carson's ideas. He knew she was correct about the toxicity of synthetic pesticides. His mother was Chippewa, and he understood the land in the way native people do, and he was interested in what I'd learnt from the Travelling people here. I spent a summer in Montana learning from him, and we shared what we knew. And that's where I met Skipper, who came back to work here and hasn't left yet.'

'Maria tells me he's like part of the furniture now.' Gwenda smiled.

'He's that, all right,' Jack agreed. 'Sure, I don't know what I'd do without him around the farm. It's as much his as mine now.'

'Sounds like you two complement each other well then, different skills and that?'

Jack smiled. 'We sure do.'

* * *

LATER, a delicious dinner was eaten at Lena's, everyone was there except Nellie. The conversation was in full flow, but Blackie and Emily were very quiet.

'Lena?' Maria asked as she carried the dishes into the scullery, the room off the kitchen where the washing up happened. It was Sunday, so it was Annie Gallagher's day off, and everyone else had left. Lena's own children had scattered to the four corners of the house, and Eli had gone back to the farm with Jack to try out that weird cure Vera Slattery had given him on Fourteen's joints.

'My arthritis is gone, but supposing that's just a placebo effect?' he'd said to Lena. 'I'm not going to pretend my hand isn't better, because it is, but I'd rather try it out on an animal who doesn't know what's happening, and then we can see for ourselves whether the dog improves or not.'

'Well, you'll be hard put to find cobwebs up at Jack's farm.' Lena had laughed. 'Though the twins' little house has plenty. They kept it clean, but they could never keep on top of the spiders – it's the height of the ceiling.' She was impressed with her husband's willingness to investigate Vera's cure, but he'd explained it was simply the scientific method – if something worked, don't dismiss it, just test it again and again, and if it keeps on working, then that's good. It wasn't even necessary to know why. Nobody had discovered yet why aspirin, which came from willow bark, worked as a painkiller.

Now Lena, up to the elbows in suds in the deep Belfast sink, turned and smiled at her mother. 'Yes, Mam?'

'What's going on with Nellie?' asked Maria. 'I know you say she's gone for a job, but something is wrong. I know you used to not tell me things, but I'm all right now – I can manage. And honestly the worrying and imagining all sorts can't be as bad as the truth.'

'Nothing, Mam. She's just got a new job.'

'Ah, Lena love, I know you're trying to protect me, but please, just tell me.' Maria closed the door to the kitchen so nobody could hear. 'Blackie and Em were like a wet weekend out there today, and they've gone off without hardly saying a word.'

'Sure, Mam, they've lost their lovely daughter to London, and they hate it.' Lena scrubbed the saucepan where she'd accidentally burnt the base making custard. She was distracted these days; there was so much on her mind.

Maria sighed as she set the dirty plates down beside the sink and picked up a tea towel. She seemed to accept Lena's explanation. 'Well, they shouldn't feel so down about it. I know they probably think she's too young, and she is only a girl, but Emily said it's a live-in position and the hotel will keep an eye on her. Nellie will get on fine. She doesn't like school, so it's for the best she goes to work, and she's very sociable, so she'll love being a receptionist. And won't she be back here in six months, having got plenty of experience and ready to apply for the same job in the Bandon hotel instead of being a kitchen maid – isn't that the plan?'

Lena felt a pang thinking of her little niece over in England in a nursing home. 'It is. And you're right, Mam – it's definitely for the best.'

Maria looked thoughtful. 'I don't know, though, Lena. I still feel there's something more than Nellie getting a job that's troubling them, Em hasn't been herself in recent weeks, I know maybe it's the pregnancy but she should be over the moon, they were trying for so long. You're sure there's nothing wrong?'

Lena stopped scrubbing and contemplated her mother, who was drying dishes. She had aged so gracefully over the years, her skin remarkably smooth and her eyes clear. Her figure had never changed, and though her blond hair had more silver in it, it made her look even more ethereal somehow. She still dressed in a slightly offbeat way, long flowing skirts and silk tops, but she'd always managed to stay just the right side of alternative to remain elegant.

'You're so beautiful, Mam.'

Maria smiled brightly. 'Now I know you're hiding something from me.'

'I mean it!'

'Maybe you do, but you're also trying to change the subject.'

Lena laughed. Her mother was so intuitive, it was impossible to fob her off once she sensed you were holding something back.

'I'm not Mam honestly, I think she's just a bit worried, you know, that the baby will be alright. She's older and well you hear of higher numbers of babies born with problems to older mothers and I think she's just terrified. Not really allowing herself to be excited in case something is wrong.'

'But sure she's as fit as a trout, she'll be fine.' Maria exclaimed, relieved that was all it was.

The whole place was fascinated at Emily's news and nobody as far as Lena knew had made any connection between Nellie leaving and Emily's pregnancy. Whenever they were asked about their daughter they responded brightly that it was a wonderful opportunity, a chance to move up in the hotel business, live-in accommodation right in the centre of London, the hotel owners a couple in their sixties who would look out for her. They regaled customers how she was loving life, letters, phone calls all confirming how much fun she was having.

'And you promise me that's all it is?' Maria persisted, still not convinced.

'That's all Mam, she misses Nellie and she's worried about the new baby, that's it.'

. . .

Behind her, Maria sighed softly. 'I wish you girls trusted me enough to tell me things like this sooner. I mean, I know it's not your fault, that it's mine for being so useless...'

Lena dropped the scrubber and went to hug her mother. 'Oh, Mam, don't be daft. It's just normal nerves and she didn't want to worry you. She feels like it's very risky even though Eli has said over and over that she's fine and the baby is fine too but remember when she found out? She actually thought she'd started the change early. She never in a million years thought she was expecting. She feels silly being so worried so she only told me.'

Maria looked both pleased and indignant. 'Well, it's hardly roaring it from the rooftops telling her own mother, is it?'

'I know, but everyone is so happy for them, it feels wrong to her to be so apprehensive.'

Smiling again, Maria stood up and kissed Lena on the cheek, then tucked a stray strand of hair behind her ear. 'I love how ye all look out for each other, maybe being a terrible mother made ye that way, but I know that even when I'm gone you'll always be there for each other.'

'You weren't, you were sick,' Lena said reassuringly, 'but yes, we are all close, and you and Daddy made us like that.'

After her mother had left the scullery, a sad smile on her face, Lena slumped down on the three-legged stool Maria had vacated and sat with her cheeks pressed between her palms, thinking about all the little lies that would get spun around it as time went on.

Poor Em and Blackie. What a strain it was for them. She could only imagine the trauma of knowing their precious young daughter was left in London all alone, facing the prospect of giving birth in a strange country surrounded by strangers. The thought of it made her own heart quail, let alone Em and Blackie. So much was changing in the family. Kilteegan Bridge was a wonderful place to rear children, but it was so hard to keep them close and safe as they grew older. Emmet was going to be leaving sooner even than she had imagined. Stanford held interviews in May, so he was going to go to those and then take exams in America and stay for the summer while he found his feet rather than wait in Kilteegan Bridge until the term started as she had hoped. 'Sure, it only means going a couple of months earlier than planned, Mam,' he'd said, like it was nothing at all, when to her, all her remaining days with him were the most precious time in the world.

Malachy had written to explain it all at great length, assuring her that Emmet would be well looked after, that his education would be exceptional, his prospects wonderful, and that basically he had every intention of bringing Emmet into the business if that was what Emmet wished. She knew Malachy was telling her all this in the interests of honesty and openness, but every word of that letter was like a blow to her heart. She was losing her son to America; that was all there was to it. The son and heir to a wealthy man, a dazzling education in one of the United States' most prestigious universities, a brilliant business to walk into – it was Emmet's deepest heart's desire. How could she stand in the way of it, even if it meant breaking her own?

She remembered seeing a painting in the art gallery in Cork years ago while on a school trip, of a mother in a shawl holding onto her son as he emigrated. She had vowed at the age of fourteen never to be like that; she'd let her children fly and live their own lives. Fourteen-year-old Lena had no idea how hard that was in reality, but she had to pretend to be happy for Emmet. He was now seventeen and could go without her consent just as easily, and if that happened, she might never again see him.

She finished tidying the scullery, then made herself a cup of tea in the kitchen and on impulse made one for Emmet too; he used to love having a cup of tea with her when he was little. She took a packet of chocolate biscuits that Gwenda had brought from Australia called Tim Tams, which were apparently the best the biscuit world had to offer. Balancing the cups, she knocked on his door.

'Come in,' he called. He was lying on his bed with a book beside him.

'I brought you a cuppa, and one of Auntie Gwenda's amazing chocolate biscuits,' she said, smiling at the sight of him.

'Is everything all right?' he asked in surprise.

'Of course. Why wouldn't it be?' She raised an eyebrow.

He shrugged and smiled. 'You don't visit me here with cups of tea and chocolate biscuits for no reason, so there's something on your mind.' There was no acrimony in the words, and he took his tea gratefully, moving over to allow her to sit on the bed beside him.

'No, it's more like I was feeling a bit sad, thinking about you leaving, and wondering what it will be like not to have you in the house, or even in the country. And so I thought I'd spend some time with you when I could – is that so awful?'

'No, and I'm a bit sad too, but I'm excited as well.' His green eyes smiled into hers. His copper curls were Brylcremed back from his forehead, and he looked so like his father, it took her breath away sometimes. He was the age she had been when she fell in love with Malachy. Both of them had been just kids, but the love felt real at the time, and who knew – it might have lasted if it wasn't for August Berger poisoning the well. But then she would never have met Eli, or had Sarah or Pádraig, and that didn't bear thinking about.

'Of course you are, and everything will work out. Often the best things come out of what seem to us...well, to me, I mean...to be the end of the world.'

'You think me going to America is the end of the world?' He looked genuinely surprised. 'I'll be back loads, Mam. I have to see you and Dad and Sarah and Pádraig.'

That sentence gave Lena the warm glow she longed for. Her boy wasn't rejecting his life here in Kilteegan Bridge; he was simply spreading his wings. She should support him in that and not take it personally. It wasn't like years ago when all a parent could expect was an occasional letter or a card at Christmas. Emmet would, if he did as Malachy planned, be a wealthy man. Planes crossed the skies, and who knew what the future held? Maybe she and Eli would be visiting him in California one day.

'Well, darling, I'll be sad to see you go, and we'll all miss you terribly, but it's an exciting time and a wonderful opportunity for you, so go with all my love and my blessing.'

His green eyes shone gratefully. 'Thanks, Mam. It's not forever, and I'll be home, but I do really want to go.'

'I know you do, pet.' She sat beside him, drinking her cup of tea and feeling happier than she had for a long time.

'Were you talking to Auntie Emily today?' he asked after a while, breaking a piece off a chocolate biscuit without putting it in his mouth.

She turned her head to look at him. 'Not yet, I'll pop in later. Are you worried about your cousin?'

'Of course I am. Nellie's my best friend, always was, always will be. I'm planning to see her in London when I'm on my way to the States next month. I'm going to ask Malachy to book a flight with a stopover, so I can keep her company for a few days.'

'That's wonderful. She'll love that. And try not to be too worried. Auntie Em has made sure she's in a really nice place where they'll be kind to her until the baby is born, and she'll have the best possible care until she comes home again.'

'That's fine, but it's still horrible she's having to hide away and pretend nothing has happened to her, like it's her fault instead of that...' His voice trailed off.

'I know, it is the boy's fault as much as hers. People always forget that,' agreed Lena.

'It's entirely his fault, and I wish I'd bashed his head in,' Emmet said darkly.

Lena felt a stab of fright. 'But she wasn't forced, she *did* say that?'

Without answering her directly, Emmet said, 'I tried to talk her out of it, but she just laughed at me and said I was like something from a Jane Austen novel, and that he loved her and she loved him. It was all lies, though, and I knew it too. I should have put a stop to it earlier whether she liked it or not.'

'I'm sure you did all you could,' Lena said, wanting to reassure and comfort him while still wishing she knew who he was talking about. 'She's headstrong, our Nellie, but hopefully not too much damage has been done. She's a tough one. I'd say it will take more than this boy to break her spirit.'

'I don't know, Mam.' Emmet sighed, breaking off another piece of the Tim Tam but still not eating it. 'I know she comes over like that, but I think he has really hurt her, deep down, more even than she's letting on.'

Lena thought about the last time she'd seen Nellie, wearing full make-up but definitely more subdued than usual behind the mask. 'Yes, it's very hard to have your heart broken by your first love.'

There was a long pause while she swirled around the last of her tea in her cup, and then Emmet said softly, 'Is that what happened to you, Mam?'

She glanced at him, shocked. 'Oh…what? Goodness, Emmet, no. Well, I mean, yes, of course, I did think I loved your father, but we were only children like Nellie. We didn't know what love really was.'

'You think sixteen is too young to know what love is?' he asked, with what seemed like genuine interest.

Lena felt bad then. She would have hated when she was sixteen for anyone to tell her she was too young for love, and of course she was still so young when she'd married her beloved Eli. 'Well, I'm sure Isobel Lamkin is a great girl, and I know she's mad about you.'

He laughed. 'Don't worry, Mam. She likes showing me off to her friends, but that's as far as it goes with her, I think. And I think she's nice enough, but I'm too young to be serious about anybody, I know that, and I'm going away, so there's no point. I have so much to do, Mam. So many dreams. So many new experiences to have…' With his thoughts on the future, he finally popped one of the pieces of the Australian Tim Tam into his mouth, and his green eyes flew open in delight. 'Talking of new experiences, Mam, this has got to be the best chocolate biscuit I've ever tasted!'

# CHAPTER 11

'So yeah, there's all sorts of wild things going on in America right now, hippies, the summer of love, people who don't get married but just kind of live together, and there's all the music and everything.' Emmet was sitting in the chair by Nellie's bed, flipping through the letters Malachy had sent him over the last year, looking for pieces of description to amuse her. 'This is funny. He was in a gas station on the way to a building site and he saw a bunch of women, well loads of them actually in a place called Oakland and they told him they were there for the Covenant of the Goddess, turns out they were from an organisation called Wicca and they were all witches. Maybe we should tell Miss Slattery about them? She might join?'

Nellie lay propped up by pillows on the nursing home bed, her eyes fixed on her cousin. She was only half-listening to the bits he was reading out, just luxuriating in his presence.

Life was so boring for her here, sitting and lying about all day long, and she'd been missing her family so much. She'd actually cried when Emmet came in the door – 'Surprise!' – with a present of Barry's tea and Kimberley biscuits, explaining he was stopping over in London for a few days on his way to New York.

She was already dreading him going again. She knew she was

lucky to be here and not in one of Ireland's cruel mother-and-baby homes. She had a private room, most of the staff were kind, and she was well taken care of, but she was only allowed to telephone home for a couple of minutes two times a week, and there was only one phone on her floor, and there was always a queue, plus it cost so much money.

Not that there was much to say to her parents anyway; nothing here ever changed. She spent most days in her room reading the books Lena sent her from the Kilteegan House library or watching television in the communal lounge, and the time was passing so slowly, all the while waiting for this terrible scary thing at the end. Her dad had sent her a five-thousand-piece jigsaw of Salisbury Cathedral for her birthday – he and she had always loved doing puzzles together – and a nice nurse had found her a big tray to do it on, but it was dull work without her father helping her and she'd given up a quarter of the way through.

Also her abdomen was so distended, she found it hard to settle the tray on the bed in front of her, or even sit at the desk with it. She still had four weeks to go, but she was very uncomfortable already, finding it difficult to sleep at night. The doctor told her that the pains in her sides were normal at this stage; it was from her ligaments stretching, her body preparing to give birth.

She didn't know whether she wanted this baby to hurry up, or whether she wished it wouldn't come at all. The matron, who had no children of her own, said childbirth was painless if you relaxed, but she'd heard horror stories of labour from the other girls. One, a girl from somewhere called Scarborough, was in here having her second child; the first was given up for adoption and she cried over him a lot. This one too would go the same way. She told them the reality, the pain, the pressure, the tearing, and Nellie could hardly breathe for fear of it. That girl, Sylvia was her name, only ever had one visitor, her father, and he was a stern-looking man. Some of the girls spoke of their boyfriends, how they wished they could tell them where they were but their families forbade it. They all seemed to think that if the fathers of their babies knew, they'd rescue them like a princess in a tower. Nellie, young as she was, felt she was under no such illusion. Not for her and probably not for them either. Men had fun, and women paid the price. That phrase, 'left carrying the baby', was no longer just a meaningless phrase she'd overheard.

The counsellor, a nice softly spoken woman, had asked her about her own baby's father and if she felt she would like to contact him. She gave an adamant refusal, and that seemed to be the right answer. She was doing her best to forget him, the forty-six-year-old married man who got her pregnant. She tried to tell herself he wasn't worth a second of her time, that she didn't want to know if he thought of her, wondered about his child, ever felt regret. He'd written to her saying he was never going to see her again, so he obviously couldn't love her the way she still loved him; she'd got it all wrong. She hated him, she insisted to herself, and it was true that at the moment, the entire species was in her bad books. Life was so easy for boys and men. They could do as they pleased, and society even secretly applauded them for it. A boy who had sex with lots of girls was admired, whereas a girl who did it was a dirty hussy and soiled goods.

It wasn't fair, but it was how it was, and Nellie felt it deeply. She didn't tell anyone, but she felt very dirty inside. The baby even felt dirty to her, a flag of her shame and stupidity and weakness. She didn't know how she was ever going to even look at the child after it was born and not feel rotten and wicked. The worst of it was, she still loved the child's father even more than she hated him, and that made her feel disgusted at herself, like she hadn't really repented of her sin.

Emmet had stopped reading passages out of Malachy's letters and was looking at her anxiously, so she tried to relax and smile. 'Tell me more about California,' she said. 'It sounds so wonderful.'

'Are you sure?' He was frowning. 'Don't you want to talk about you for a bit? I mean, how do you feel? I hope the whole pregnancy isn't too sore or worrying. I'm sorry if that's not the right thing to say – I don't really know much about it.'

'It's absolutely fine. All the girls say it's a breeze. I can't wait to get it over with and have Mam take this baby away with her to Kilteegan Bridge.'

She suppressed a wince. All day long she'd been having pains on and off. She'd told the sister in charge, who said it was normal, just the body getting ready and that there was nothing to worry about.

'Oh, all right. But aren't you going to go home at the same time as them?' He looked puzzled. 'I thought the story was that Auntie Emily was going to say she's going to a nursing home in Dublin for "bed rest" and you were going to come over from London to see her, then you would help her bring the baby back home?'

'Mm...yeah. Though I did say to Mam that maybe I should stay here in London for a while, but she wasn't keen. She seemed to think I would never come home again if I did that.' She added bitterly, 'She probably thinks if I'm left alone, I'll go and fall for someone else unsuitable and then she'll be left holding a second baby.'

Emmet smiled. 'No, of course she doesn't think that. I'm sure she just thinks you're awfully young to be looking after yourself.'

'I'm seventeen now.'

'Even so, alone in London...'

'Well, you can't talk. You've only just turned seventeen and you're already escaping to America,' she said, with a flash of the old tempestuous Nellie.

'That's not the same, Nell. I'll be living with Malachy in his house.'

'Tell me about his house. Tell me everything.' She jumped at the chance to get off the subject of herself, and he hesitated but then relented. The achy dragging pains made it hard to focus on what he was saying, but on the subject of California, he had a lot to tell her, and she didn't need to contribute or answer questions.

'It's an amazing house in a place called Palo Alto. Everywhere there has Spanish-sounding names, and there are loads of people from Mexico working there too, so you hear Spanish spoken a lot. My bedroom has its own bathroom and a balcony overlooking the garden, and there are steps up to the new swimming pool on the roof. Imagine, our very own pool! I haven't seen it yet, but Malachy says it's something called an infinity pool, so when you're in it, it feels like you're swimming in the sky. There's a cool architect in the States called John Lautner – he came up with the design in the early 1960s, and he did Malachy's pool. You know the vanishing-edge pool in that James Bond movie *Diamonds Are Forever*? Lautner did that one too.'

'I wish I could swim in it,' breathed Nellie, fascinated.

Emmet warmed to her enthusiasm. 'There are trees in the garden, lemons, oranges, plums, and on the back wall are grapes. These two men called Jorge and Miguel, they look after the garden and the pool and any maintenance that needs doing, and there's an elderly housekeeper called Juanita who loves making cakes. If you came over, you could just lie by the pool getting a suntan. It's warm all year round there, no ice or snow or sideways rain like we get in Kilteegan Bridge...'

Nellie listened with starry eyes. 'Oh God, I'd love to live there. Will you have to move out when you start college?'

'No, not at all. The Stanford campus is only a short drive away. I could even walk or cycle, but Malachy is going to give me a present of a convertible sports car as soon as I arrive – he says he's bought it already. It's a royal-blue Corvette, with navy-blue upholstery and a white leather roof, so I can drive around with the top down and the sun on my face. Honestly, Nell, I feel like pinching myself. I just can't believe this is going to be my life now. You'll have to come and visit. Maybe in the autumn? Malachy would pay for your flight, no problem at all. He's already said if I want any friends or family to visit, he'll stand them tickets. He can put them down as a business expense, so he doesn't mind at all.'

'A business expense?' Nellie was a bit shocked. Her parents' insistence on honesty, especially when doing business, was deeply embedded in her soul, even if she was a bit wild at times.

'I'm going to be his business partner, he says.' Emmet grinned. 'So keeping me happy in America is a legitimate expense, or so says his accountant, and I'm hardly going to argue with that, am I? So when will you come?'

She felt her heart lift. It was like someone had come into her dull, hard existence and promised her she *could* go to the ball, just like in *Cinderella*. 'What about in a few weeks? I could fly right from London after...you know.'

'Oh.' He looked confused. 'I mean, that would be great with me, but what would your mam say?'

'I don't know, Emmet, but please be on my side over this. I can't go back to Kilteegan Bridge right away, I just can't. I need to be away from this baby. It reminds me of so many awful things, the things I shouldn't have done... Can you understand? I don't want to leave Ireland forever, but I need a bit of space to get over all this, to get my head clear.'

The pain was getting stronger now, but she dismissed it. She couldn't tell Emmet, because he'd insist on calling the nurse and she'd be cross because she'd already told Nellie today that it was nothing.

He looked doubtful but nodded. 'Well, if you're sure, I'll talk to Malachy. I'm sure he'd have no problem.'

'Don't say about the baby!'

'Of course I won't, Nellie. That's your secret, not mine.'

She beamed and reached out her arms to hug him but then doubled over with a cry. A terrible pain had just hit her full in the abdomen.

'Nellie, what's the matter?' Emmet was on his feet in panic.

'Oh, Emmet, it hurts so much! Oh, oh, oh...'

In a flash he was heading for the door. 'I'm getting the nurse!'

'Oh, oh! Be quick. Don't let them send you away...'

'I won't, Nellie,' he promised fervently. 'I'll be straight back.'

# CHAPTER 12

Blackie sat bolt upright.

'What?' Emily was startled from her sleep. 'What is it?'

'I don't know, a dream, I think...'

Her husband was sweating, she realised, as she put her hand up to his neck. 'What about?' she asked, sitting up herself.

'Nellie. She was calling me, just calling me, but I couldn't reach her. I was almost there, almost seeing her but not quite, and she was getting more and more distressed.'

'It's just a dream, love. She's fine. She's being well cared for.' Emily tried to soothe him. Her poor husband had gone very grey in the last couple of months, and there were deep lines furrowing his brow that had never been there before. 'Remember I called the matron yesterday, and she said Nellie was fine. And Emmet must be there by now – Nellie will have been delighted to see him...'

Blackie turned to her with tears in his eyes. 'But that's it. Emmet's gone to see her, but I haven't. I know you think that's for the best, but I...I need to see her too, Em, I need to...' The tears that had remained unshed since hearing of Nellie's pregnancy fell now, and Emily was dismayed to see her big tough husband sobbing like a child.

'It's all right, love, it's all right.' She cradled him in her arms and let him cry.

'She's just a child, Em, just a baby herself. How could we have let this happen to her? Our precious little girl. How can that…that scumbag…walk the roads, as if he'd never done a thing wrong, and our baby girl is over there on her own, terrified and needing us…'

Emily made a sudden decision. She'd always been the one who made the plans, who decided what to stock, what to charge, where to place it. It had been her idea to buy the other shops, to get Peggy a cottage of her own. And sometimes she didn't include Blackie enough, she knew, but he was happy to always follow her lead. Now, though, she realised that this time she'd left him out too much. 'We'll go, Blackie, the two of us. We'll go tomorrow evening. I'll book cabins so we can sleep on the boat, and your mother can mind the shop. Peggy can tell everyone I took ill in the night and Eli said I had to go to the nursing home early for the month of bed rest.'

'Can we do that?' her husband asked, wiping his eyes on his pyjama sleeve, and her heart melted for him. He'd been stoic and strong and kind through the whole thing; she was so proud of him. More men in his position would be full of recriminations, revenge, shame. Many would have packed their daughter off to one of those dreaded mother-and-baby homes where they took the baby away as soon as it was born. But not her Blackie. He just wanted his daughter in his arms, and she realised trying to do this without him was a folly. She needed him, Nellie needed him, and he needed to be with Nellie.

'Of course we can go. And I'll ask Eli to tell everyone who asks that there's no danger to me or anything but to keep up the idea that I needed to go to Dublin earlier in case I gave birth a bit too soon, and that you had to come with me and stay in a hotel. Nellie is due in the next three or four weeks anyway, so it won't be for long, and Lena will get Sarah to help your mother after school if she needs it.'

'I love you, Em,' said Blackie simply as he lay back on the pillows, and she stroked his forehead softly as he began to drift off.

The phone rang in the shop, and he jerked awake again, sprang out of bed and rushed downstairs in his bare feet, while Emily glanced in alarm at the bedside alarm clock. It was ten to three. Who was ringing them at this hour? She got up and started getting dressed in case it was some sort of emergency, strapping on the hard foam bump beneath her clothes. She would be glad to be rid of this cursed thing in the next few weeks. The number of people who touched her pregnant belly was truly astonishing. It never upset her when she was expecting Nellie, but this time, fearful of being found out, she wanted to scream at them to leave her alone.

She could hear Blackie's voice downstairs, promising to be there as soon as he could, so she'd made the right decision, getting dressed. Before she could get her shoes on, he'd reappeared in the bedroom, looking very scared yet somehow excited.

'What time can we get the boat?'

'The boat?'

'It's Nellie. She's fine, but that was Emmet. He says he'd have called earlier, but the doctor said it was some other sort of contractions she was having, bracks something...'

'Braxton Hicks. Remember I had them with Nellie? You get them in the third trimester. If that's all it is, we can still go tomorrow.' Emily, relieved, was already removing her shoes.

'No, don't get undressed again,' gasped Blackie. 'It wasn't brackie whatyamacallit. They were real contractions, and she's dilated two inches or something, whatever that means. They've taken her into the labour ward now, and they made Emmet leave even though she wanted him to stay, and he had to go back to his lodging house to call us, so that was an hour ago...'

Emily's heart raced, but she managed with a huge effort to stay calm. 'Right. If we hurry, we can catch the early boat.' If they left now, they'd be at the dock in Cork by five, and she knew from Lena and Eli's frequent trips that a ship to Wales sailed at six or seven. The train from Fishguard to London would surely have them in London in twenty-four hours from now, or not much more than that, please God...

She pulled the suitcase off the top of the wardrobe, rapidly filling it with clothes for herself and Blackie, while her husband dressed in record time, then fetched the carpet bag of baby things they'd packed weeks ago from under Nellie's bed. Within fifteen minutes they were in the car, leaving a note for Peggy on the counter.

*Dear Peggy, I'm having some mild contractions, probably Braxton Hicks. Can you believe a male doctor 'discovered' Braxton Hicks contractions? Ha, ha. Anyway, we're off to see Eli, and I wouldn't be surprised if he wants to send me to the Dublin nursing home early – nothing to worry about, just as a precaution. Blackie might stay with me for a while, depending on what's happening. Tell Lena to get Sarah to help you with the shop. She's on her Easter holidays from Monday, and she can afford to take a bit of time away from the horses. Tell her we'll pay her properly. Love, E x*

Peggy was like the tomb when it came to a secret. Being married to that scoundrel Dick Crean for years meant she knew how to keep her mouth shut, and her loyalty to Blackie, Emily and her darling Nellie was absolute. But Nellie had been very strong about not wanting her grandmother to know the truth about the pregnancy. She'd said Peggy had had enough scandal in her life and she didn't want to be the one to bring more trouble and worry down on her head.

As Blackie started up the Ford Anglia, Emily remarked sadly, 'I feel like all I do is tell lies.'

'I know, love, and we're about to live our lives as a lie, but what choice have we?' Blackie said as he drove away down the deserted street of the village, not a soul about.

Emily sighed, gazing out of the window as the houses dwindled away. They'd lived all of their years in Kilteegan Bridge, her and Blackie, and had no plans to ever leave. Their families, their business, their history, it was all here, but sometimes the idea of starting again, going somewhere new, filled her with such longing.

'No choice whatsoever,' she agreed.

They made the boat with time to spare, parking the car in the port car park and boarding the boat. Blackie settled them at a Formica-covered table in the lounge, stashing the suitcase and carpet bag underneath it, and fetched two cups of tea and two limp-looking ham sandwiches from the canteen hatch.

'I've never left Ireland before,' he remarked with a small smile as he settled down opposite Emily and the crew made the *Celtic Dawn* ready for sea. 'What a way to start.'

Emily reached over and placed her hand on his. 'I had never been until I went with Nellie.'

'I did think about it once, but I was too afraid of running into my father's "other wife" and kids.' Blackie laughed bitterly. 'England wasn't far enough away for me when it came to him.'

'Well, I suppose we shouldn't speak ill of the dead,' Emily said, though not with much conviction.

Blackie felt no such compunction. 'If he's not below roasting away with the bad lad for all eternity, then it's all nonsense, the stuff they teach us.' He stirred some milk into her tea and opened her sandwich for her. He was always doing things like that, little gestures of kindness all day long. She could never imagine having anyone else.

'But then, you know, Em,' he added, looking lost again, like after his terrible dream, 'you'd wonder, wouldn't you, all the rules and the judging the priest tells us about, especially that Monsignor Collins – he's mad for the hellfire. Our Nellie, she'd be a sinner in God's eyes, and you and me too for telling a load of lies on her behalf. That's what the Monsignor would tell us if he knew anything about it. It seems wrong to me that humans are more forgiving than God, but they are if the Monsignor has this right. Real people know life just happens, or people are born a certain way, or in a time and place where they can't help things going wrong. But according to the Monsignor, God's made of sterner stuff and His judging goes on all the same. Do you think he's right? That we are all three of us sinners and destined for hell?'

Emily's heart went out to her big handsome husband. His dark eyes were shadowed, and he looked so tired. Blackie was a simple man in the best sense of the word. He loved his family, he was great fun, he worked so hard for them all, he was honest and loyal and a decent human being. He'd had a hard start in life, but he made the best of it, and he always said that marrying Emily was the making of him. Everyone agreed with him about that and thought he'd got the better bargain, but she knew better. After years of her mother's erratic behaviour, her father's attention being given to her and then his death when she was sixteen, Blackie Crean was her rock. He was solid and dependable and never changed. She loved him more every passing year. She knew that each child they lost through miscarriage broke his heart a little bit more, but he adored his daughter. In many ways, she realised now, what had happened to Nellie was harder on him than on her. He saw his place in the world as being Nellie's protector and strongly felt that he'd failed her, and now he seemed to think God might fail her as well.

'Nellie isn't a sinner, Blackie, and God understands we're human beings and that we do what we can and sometimes we get it wrong.' This time, Emily blazed with conviction. She'd had a lot of time to think about this in the early hours when she couldn't sleep for worrying about her daughter. 'If God is our father and He loves us, and that's what the priest tells us, then He will forgive us and love us anyway. You forgive Nellie and love her anyway, don't you? You can see she was just a child, led astray by someone who maybe should have known better himself, but either way, she's ours and we love her and we'd never abandon her, and I don't think God will abandon us either.'

He took her hand and held it warmly. 'You've the right answer for everything, Em. 'Twas a lucky day for me the day you took leave of your senses and married me.'

She took a sip of her tea as the foghorn blared to indicate they were pulling away from the quay. 'I had all my senses then, Mr Crean, and I have all of my senses now. You're a wonderful husband and a wonderful father, and you will be doing it all over again, please God, in a few weeks.'

Something like a smile passed over his craggy face for the first time in months, and Emily felt herself relax a little. Maybe this was going to be all right after all. Nellie would have the baby safely and all would be well. She and Blackie would bring them both home, happy to be back in Kilteegan Bridge and ready to start their lives again.

'Hard to imagine, isn't it?' she said. 'Like, we only thought about poor Nellie and the whole thing as a crisis, but now that we're here, on the boat, well, we'll be coming back in a short while with a baby, a little boy or a little girl that's going to be ours. It might sound a bit daft, but I haven't really thought about that side of it. Changing nappies and feeding bottles and reading stories.'

A spark of enthusiasm lit in Blackie's tired eyes. 'I know, and I'm really looking forward to it, Em, I have to admit. Like, when Nellie was small, we thought we'd have a tribe of them – that was the plan. And I often think if I'd known she'd be our one and only, that I'd have paid more attention...'

Emily pealed with laughter at this, and the family sitting beside them glanced over. 'Paid more attention to Nellie? Are you serious? You never let her out of your sight, remember? I used to have to send you back down to the shop all the time because you'd be dreaming up reasons to come up, but it was just to see her. And when she was older, you took her to and from school, her dancing classes, you went to all her football matches. Blackie, you got more out of fatherhood than anyone I've ever seen, and now we get to do that all again.'

He grinned ruefully.

'Remember how I used to murder you for waking her up because you were convinced she wasn't breathing? Holding a mirror up to her little nose to see if it would fog up?' Emily reminded him.

'I suppose I was a bit obsessed with her, all right. Still am, truth be told...' A spasm of anxiety crossed his careworn face. 'And I'm still so worried for her, Em. I remember hearing you having Nellie, and you were older and bigger and stronger, and when I think of her having to go through all of that... Like, will she even be able to...'

'It will be fine,' she soothed him again. 'I know it must look terrifying, and it's no picnic, I can assure you, but women's bodies are amazing and nature knows what to do. The mother is kind of swept away by the whole thing, to be honest. It's like you are there but the power of nature just takes over. Nellie is young and strong, and her baby will be fine and so will she, and she'll love it as soon as she looks at it and forget all the pain.'

'And if that's true, if she loves it so much at first sight, what if she can't bear to give him or her up, even to us?'

Emily kept her expression cheerful, even though Blackie had voiced the one thing she was secretly most worried about. 'Well then, I don't know… Honestly, love, I don't. We've told everyone I'm pregnant, so Nellie turning up with a baby and us without one would be the talk of the place. Our lies would be exposed, and we'd never be able to show our faces again. But seriously, I don't think that's going to happen. Nellie's quite adamant she doesn't want to be a mother, and remember, she's a very strong personality.'

'And what about later, like in years to come and she changes her mind then?'

Emily looked at him. Blackie was such a good man, but he was not a risk-taker. If it was up to him, the shop would look exactly as it did when she was a child, dark and dingy, with him and his mother working themselves to the bone for a tiny profit. She'd made him trust her, let her change the business, and their lives. But that old tendency to worry, to resist change, was always there. She resented it sometimes, being the one who had to make the decisions, who had to reassure him they were doing the right thing. Sometimes she wished he was more decisive when she was worried herself, but she also knew that if she sounded anything less than confident now, he would be cut completely adrift.

'Blackie, none of us can tell the future, so we need to take her at her word, I suppose. Nellie says she wants us to raise the baby, and we will. She says she doesn't want to be a mother to this child, and if that changes at some stage down the line, then we'll deal with it then.' She held his gaze. 'This will be all right, love, I promise.'

Trusting her, as he always did, he just nodded.

Emily said a silent prayer she was right.

# CHAPTER 13

They sat in the café across the street from the nursing home, sipping English tea that tasted weaker than they were used to and eating delicious toasted crumpets. Blackie was trying to focus on the newspaper, Emmet was supposed to be writing an essay on quantum physics, and Emily was knitting bootees and a matinee coat in lemon so either a boy or girl could wear it.

Nellie had been in labour for thirty-six hours now, and the matron had told Emily ten minutes ago that her waters had finally broken so progress might start to speed up. Emily had begged to be allowed in, but that request was refused. The matron was insistent that they would be told when the baby arrived and could visit immediately, but until then, the home had a strict policy of no visitors in the labour ward.

She'd had Nellie in the same way, with just a midwife in the room like everyone did back then, but the thought of their child in such pain, on her own, made Emily nauseous, and she'd shed a few tears as she made her way back across the road to the café.

'Here is a fresh pot of tea.'

Emily glanced up from her knitting to smile at Marissa, the Greek lady who ran the café with her Italian husband, Pietro. In the hours the three of them had been sitting there, they and the couple had become very friendly. Emily, who had discarded her bump as soon as they were out of Ireland, didn't even have to explain why they were there; the two of them had seen it all before.

'Her waters have broken,' Emily said, and Marissa nodded.

'Not long now,' she said in her heavily accented English. 'I will say a prayer for your girl and her baby.'

Marissa was heavy-set, with dark features and dark hair on her face, and Pietro was almost entirely hairless and tiny. They were as united as any pair could be. They ran their little café together, both doing everything as far as Emily could see, and their raucous laughter and fiery fights had been heard coming from the kitchen ever since the café opened at five thirty that morning, when she and Blackie, who had been standing with their bags in the rain outside the locked door of the nursing home, stumbled gratefully in.

The first thing Emily had done was borrow their phone to ring Lena, for which the couple refused to take money, and at seven, she'd rung Emmet, who was staying at a hotel nearby; he'd joined them an hour later.

'Here is gelato. I make it today. Here only in summer people eat this, but that is not good. Gelato is for all of year, any time, because we need some happy all of year.' Pietro presented them with three stainless steel bowls filled with chocolate ice cream. His bald head and drooping eyebrows made him look like a sad puppy, but he belied it with his good humour. 'No money. It is for friendship.'

'Thank you, Pietro, thank you. That's wonderful,' Emily said, accepting his gift, though eating ice cream on a cold London morning was the very last thing she wanted to do. She'd always heard Londoners were a bit rude and thought themselves too busy and important for idle chat, but since she'd got here, she felt she'd been treated to nothing but kindness. The taxi driver who had brought them to the nursing home from the railway station was full of fun and chatter despite the ungodly hour, the lady who ran the boarding house the nursing home recommended had been so kind, knowing the reason for their visit and expressing her best wishes for Nellie and the baby and brushing aside their apologies for arriving so early, and now this couple.

London was a sprawling city with loads of people, but she was beginning to realise that just as in Ireland, each one of those people was an individual, with a story, their own challenges and victories. London was just more colourful about it.

By six that morning, workmen had started to come into the café for breakfast, and over the next couple of hours, the street outside had filled up with cars and pedestrians. Emily had been astounded to see so many different types of people. A group of Hasidic Jews in black suits, tall hats and ringlets had gone walking by, laughing together, and the man who delivered the post to Marissa at seven was an unsmiling Sikh who wore an orange turban. Everywhere she looked there were different faces, different stories.

Blackie poured her another cup of tea from the pot Marissa had brought them. Emily didn't really want it, but it was something to do. She ate her chocolate ice cream, which was surprisingly delicious and tasted of real chocolate. The day was dragging on and on. They were afraid to leave the café in case the news came. The matron had promised to call the café when it was all over, and Emily jumped every time the telephone behind the counter rang, but it was never the nursing home.

They sat there all day, regularly assured by either Marissa or Pietro that they were welcome to rest there, but each minute felt like an hour. Food came and went, tea was endless, and the conversation between them began and died on their lips within moments. The three of them, the three people in the world who loved Nellie the most, were each lost in their fears for what the girl must be enduring.

The café closed at six, and at ten past the hour, the last of the other customers left and Marissa placed the closed sign on the door.

'I'm sorry, Marissa, we'll go,' Emily said. They could go and sit in the pub on the corner, the Queen's Arms, she supposed.

'No, stay of course. We live upstairs. Come.'

Emily looked at Blackie, and he shrugged slightly. 'We don't want to intrude. You've had a long day…'

'No, please, is better you come upstairs. Is warmer and more comfortable. We have television,' Pietro announced with a broad grin. 'Do you know *Fawlty Towers*? No? Come, we will watch, very funny.' Pietro ushered them upstairs. 'This man is crazy, own hotel, always making big mistake, very funny.'

They settled Emily and Blackie on the sofa in their flat over the café, and Emmet, despite his protests, in the only armchair. Marissa sat on a chair brought up from the café, and Pietro took a footstool. The couple clearly lived in this one room; the two doors off it were a bedroom and a bathroom, and for a kitchen, they used the café. The living room was simply decorated but warm and cosy.

*Fawlty Towers* wasn't on until seven thirty, so they watched the rest of the six o'clock news. A gang of six robbers had stolen sixteen million dollars from bookies in Australia. Some sort of soap opera followed, then finally the promised comedy, which was set in Torquay in England.

The antics of Basil Fawlty and his wife, Sybil, would have normally made Emily laugh out loud – she could see it was very funny – but it was hard to think about anything except Nellie. By the time the credits rolled, she felt so agitated, she murmured to Blackie, 'I know they said they'd let us know, but…'

Blackie and Emmet stood immediately, as if they'd been only waiting for her to say the word. 'Let's go,' said Blackie.

'Marissa, Pietro, thank you so much for your hospitality – we will never forget it. We are going to go over and see. They told us to wait, but it's been so long and we need some idea of how our daughter is.'

Marissa nodded. 'I know, is worry. She will be fine. They are good there, always the babies are fine from there, but go, and…' She dug in her pocket for something. 'Take.' She gave them a door key. 'We will go to bed now, up very early, and if you need, come back, wait here.' She gestured to the sofa. 'Is OK.' She smiled, and though by nobody's standards could she be called a beautiful woman, in that moment Emily knew she was seeing pure goodness.

'Is OK.' She smiled at Emmet. 'Is baby, is good. You are good boy, is all OK.'

They realised Marissa thought Emmet was the baby's father, but nobody wanted to try to explain, so he just smiled.

'Thank you, Marissa.' Emily had tears of gratitude in her eyes as she took the key.

'Make drinks or coffee in café. Is OK.' Pietro placed his hand on the small of his wife's back. '*Tantissimi auguri*!'

Marissa tutted and gently pushed him. 'Always Italian. He never leave Napoli is truth.'

'*Grazie mille*,' Blackie replied, and all four of them looked at him, astonished.

He chuckled at the expressions on their faces. 'It's the only Italian I know, but there was a travelling salesman who used to come into the shop years ago, shoelaces and safety pins, that kind of thing, and he was from Modena. Every time we gave him an order, he used to say *grazie mille*, so I just guessed.'

When Marissa let the three of them out into the dark street, Emily was amazed to find it was as busy as daytime, cars and pedestrians everywhere, and she wondered where on earth everyone was going. The air was heavy with the smells of diesel and coal smoke and several other odours she couldn't recognise. Surely the working day was over; would they all not want to be at home, having their dinners and watching Basil Fawlty? She longed for one breath of clean Kilteegan Bridge air.

Blackie held her hand as they crossed the road separating the nursing home from the café. The door to the home was closed but not yet locked for the night, so they pushed it open and hurried inside out of the biting wind and the beginnings of a sleety rain.

Inside was the rotunda where she had met the matron that morning. It had black and white tiles on the floor and a reception desk of dark wood, with a frosted glass screen all around it, obscuring the view of who might be inside. Despite the late hour, there was still a figure behind it, so Emily knocked gently on the glass. For what seemed like ages, nobody responded, and then one of the panels opened to reveal a man in what looked like a police uniform. Emily assumed he was a night porter or a security man or something. He had an unkempt mop of grey curls and a very elaborate moustache.

'Yes?' he asked imperiously.

'I…I wonder if I could speak to the matron again, please?' Emily realised she sounded intimidated and tried to pull herself together.

'The matron has gone off duty,' he said in a bored voice, one eye on the small television in the corner of the office. There were crumbs down his shirtfront.

'Well, is there anyone…' She still lacked confidence, even to her own ears.

'Can't help you. You'll have to leave. I'm just about to lock up.' He went to close the glass screen.

Blackie placed his hand square on the counter, in the way of the screen. 'Our daughter has been in labour for nearly forty-eight hours, and we want to know how she is. Now you can call someone to give us information about Ellen Crean, or I'll go looking for her myself.' Unlike Emily's, his voice held no hesitation.

The man looked at Blackie's determined face and then down at his huge hand and clearly decided he'd better sound more helpful. 'One minute. Wait over there.' He went to close the screen once more, but Blackie didn't remove his hand.

'We'll wait here,' he said.

The man sized him up again, the annoyance evident on his face, but he realised he'd have to do as he was asked and reluctantly lifted the phone receiver and dialled.

'I've people here inquiring about an Ellen Crean. They're Irish,' he added, and Emily heard the contempt there. They'd all heard the stories of how English people treated the Irish, how there were signs on doors of boarding houses that read 'no dogs, no blacks, no Irish'. There were always a few, she supposed…

The surly man listened for a moment, then put down the receiver. 'Someone will be down shortly, so please' – he glanced at Blackie's hand once more – 'take a seat over there.'

Blackie locked eyes with him, never saying a word, but slowly withdrew his hand and led Emily gently to a bench against the wall where Emmet was already sitting, keeping out of the way. The man's shadow moved behind the frosted glass, and there was the sound of a bolt being shot; he was locking himself in, as if the uncouth Irish people were planning to attack him.

'What a horrible man,' Emily whispered, as Blackie rolled his eyes.

Within a few minutes a nurse appeared, and she spoke in the accent of the north of Ireland. 'Mr and Mrs Crean?'

Blackie was already on his feet, his voice shaking. 'How is she? Is she all right?'

The red-haired girl smiled, and her blue eyes twinkled. 'Right as rain and has just fifteen minutes ago given birth to a healthy baby boy. Would you like to go and see him? He's in the nursery now, and your daughter will be back in her room shortly. I'm sorry, but parents only,' she added to Emmet. 'I'm sure she'll be happy to see you tomorrow.'

'Oh…' Emily looked at Emmet, disappointed for him after he'd been waiting all day, but he seemed perfectly content to stay where he was.

'It's fine by me. I just wanted to be sure she's all right, and the baby too. I'll wait for you here.'

'Thanks for everything, Emmet.' Emily hugged him tightly, and he hugged her back, then winked and gave a thumb's up to Blackie.

'How did it go? Is she all right?' Emily asked as she followed the nurse through several doors into the bowels of the building, Blackie beside her.

'She's fine, Mrs Crean. Very tired of course and a little bit sore, but that's to be expected. She'll be fine, and the baby is a little wee dote, so he is. You are all from Cork, I take it?' she added, making conversation as they walked.

'Yes, West Cork.'

'I'm from Omagh, County Tyrone, but I'm over here four years now. I suppose Charles was rude?'

'I'm sorry, Charles?' Emily asked.

'On the front desk? His wife was Irish, ran off and left him – can't blame her – and he hates us all as a result. Don't take it personally.' She grinned and pushed through double swing doors. They entered a ward where cots were lined up against the walls on both sides, the boys wrapped in blue blankets, the girls in pink.

'Rita, which is Baby Crean?' she asked another nurse, who was busy trying to get some drops into an infant's mouth. A younger nurse was soothing another baby on her shoulder by rubbing its back.

'Second from the bottom, left-hand side,' Rita replied in a Cockney accent.

'I'm Jenny, by the way,' the nurse said as she led them through the ward.

'Emily and Blackie,' Emily said automatically, but she was no longer paying any attention to the chatty nurse. This was it, the moment they would meet the child who would be theirs, their son.

The simple little crib was painted white, with tubular bars and a small mattress. The baby was swaddled in a blue blanket. 'Would you like to hold your little grandson, Mrs Crean?'

Emily swallowed but couldn't speak. Jenny took the baby from the crib and placed him in Emily's arms. He never stirred, sleeping peacefully. He was perfect, with a big head of dark hair. Blackie looked down in astonishment and gently stroked the baby's cheek with his finger.

'He's had a bottle and is all nice and comfy, so I'll leave you three to get acquainted and I'll see if Ellen is back in her room. Once she's settled, I'll come and find you. There's a little room at the end there. You might be more comfortable if you'd like to take him down there.'

Jenny led them to a small room with a couch and an armchair and a bunch of plastic flowers on a small coffee table. 'Can I get you a cup of tea?' she asked kindly.

'No...no, thanks, we're fine,' Emily whispered. She didn't want to put her son down for a moment, and anyway she'd drunk enough tea that day to last her a lifetime.

'Ellen will need a bath and some medication and so on, so it will be a few minutes before she's able for visitors. Is that all right?'

Emily simply nodded; she couldn't take her eyes off the baby.

Once Jenny left them alone, Emily unwrapped him a little from the blanket, freeing his little arms. He was dressed in a snow-white Babygro and had been bathed. Blackie placed his finger by the baby's, and the infant's little fist opened and gripped it. Blackie gazed at Emily, and the tears ran down his face, just as they had when he'd woken up two nights ago dreaming that his daughter was calling to him from somewhere far away.

'He's so beautiful,' he croaked.

'He really is,' Emily said, still unable to take her eyes off the little pink face.

'I wonder what Nellie will call him?'

'I asked her ages ago, and she said we were to choose.'

'What do you think?' Blackie asked quietly. The window to the outside was bubble glass, so they couldn't see out, but a streetlight shone outside. It felt as if they and this baby were the only three people in the world.

Emily watched as the little boy yawned, his toothless tiny rosebud mouth opening and closing, before he settled back into her arms.

'What about Aidan?' she said softly.

Blackie beamed. It was the name on his birth certificate, but he'd been known as Blackie since he was a child. Almost nobody knew his real name, and nobody, not even his mother, ever used it.

'Aidan Crean,' Blackie said with a smile.

Emily kissed the downy head. 'Well, Aidan Crean you are, named after your daddy.'

'We're doing the right thing, aren't we, Em?' Blackie asked, the baby's tiny perfect fingers still curled around his.

'We are, love,' Emily said, with more certainty than she'd felt since this whole thing began.

The nurse arrived back a while later and took them down to Nellie's private room. She looked tired and wan, sitting up in bed when they arrived, and she refused to take Aidan from Emily when she offered him, just pointing to the armchair beside the bed for her to sit there with the baby. But she seemed delighted to see her father.

'Daddy.' She reached her arms out to Blackie, who wrapped her in his embrace and rubbed her back. She cried quietly into his shoulder as he soothed her.

'Shh, pet, it's all right. You're all right now, don't worry...'

'It was horrible, Daddy,' she sobbed. 'I thought I was going to die. And it went on and on...and it....it was awful.'

'You poor girl. It's all right, Nell, love, it's over now and you're all right and we're here.' Blackie's voice was gruff with emotion.

Emily felt a wave of murderous rage for the boy who had put her darling daughter through this ordeal, but then she looked down at the beautiful baby in her arms and reminded herself that without that unknown man, Aidan wouldn't be here.

'I know, darling. Labour is very hard, but I promise you'll forget it. I had a very hard time with you, but I forgot it instantly when you...' She stopped. She'd been about to say 'when you were put in my arms'.

Nellie turned a tear-stained face to her. 'Is he all right?' she asked. 'They said he was a boy before they took him away.'

'He's absolutely fine and he's beautiful. We thought we'd call him Aidan.'

Her daughter nodded indifferently. 'That's nice.'

'Would you like to hold him, Nell?'

'No!' Her lovely girl recoiled in horror. 'I don't, and please don't make me. I don't want to look at him. I will, sometime, when I come home in a few months, but not now. I can't look at him now. Will you take him away, Mam?'

'Nobody is going to make you do anything, love,' Blackie hastily reassured her. 'You don't have to hold him if you don't want to.'

Emily knew Nellie didn't want to talk about it, but she had to have this conversation. 'Nellie, you don't have to hold him of course, but is the reason because it's so hard to let him go, that you're afraid you'll want to keep him if you do look at him?'

Nellie didn't answer. Two big fat tears rolled down her cheeks.

Emily's heart quailed. 'You can tell us the truth, love. We won't be cross or anything. We just need to know how you feel. You're our child too.'

Nellie shuddered. 'I don't want to see him because I don't want him,' she managed, her voice catching on the words. 'And I don't want to look into his eyes and for him to see that I don't want him. I don't know if this makes me a bad person or not, but I haven't changed my mind, Mam. I don't want to be his mother, and I never want to be. I'll be his big sister, sometime, after I've got over all of this...' She waved her hand around the room. 'But nothing has changed. He's yours and Daddy's.'

'All right, love, if that's what you want. He'll be our son and you our daughter and we'll love you both till our last breath.' Blackie held Nellie's hand solemnly. 'I promise you that, Nel.'

'Thanks, Daddy.' She lay back on the pillows and her eyes closed.

'So you get some rest, love. We'll be back to see you in the morning, all right?' Emily kissed her forehead. 'I'll give the baby back to Jenny for now, and then we'll come and see you both tomorrow.'

'All right...' Nellie murmured, drifting off. 'But ask Emmet to tell you about California.'

# CHAPTER 14

The people who ran the tiny boarding house in Lambeth that Emily and Blackie had booked into, Suncroft, were made up of one family, the Jones family from Kingston, Jamaica.

Emily had known Father Otawe, of course, and seen pictures in the church magazine of Africans on the missions, but she found it amazing to see a whole family of Black people in real life.

Candice, the mother, had long hair in tight braids that hung down her back like shiny black ropes, and she was strong and lithe with long limbs. She was a great cook and had a huge pot of stew waiting for them when they all arrived exhausted that evening.

Jada, Candice's daughter, was about Nellie's age, and she sang as she waited on their table. She at least did appear to help her mother, but Candice's husband and son weren't much use, Emily noted. Jada's brother, Kimona, seemed to resent having to work in the hotel and did everything his mother asked him to do with a thunderous look of fury on his handsome scowling face.

As for the husband, Egbert, he was purely for decoration, it would seem. He had an enormous halo of hair that stood at least four inches from his head, and he wore the most outrageous clothes. He reminded Emily of a peacock, with his indigo-blue silk shirts, open to almost his navel, and tight denim jeans that flared out at the ends over beaten-up tennis shoes.

Neither he nor Candice looked old enough to be parents to two almost adults, but Candice explained that they'd married at sixteen. Her family had been horrified – Egbert wasn't who they had in mind – so they ran away to England. An uncle of Candice's had gone over after the war, when there was an influx of West Africans to London, and had made a good life, and when they arrived, he'd set them up with jobs in this small hotel. It was a Mrs Hawes who'd owned it but she got Parkinson's disease five years ago, so Candice more or less ran it by herself now.

Emily wondered if the talkative Candice didn't regret her decision to run off with the handsome young waster Egbert, and thought that she should have listened to her parents and escaped all this hard work, but life was never easy, was it? No matter what the background, or the place, people were messy and situations were complicated and everyone just muddled through as best they could.

Emmet had checked out of his hotel and come to stay with them at Suncroft.

'So Nellie said to ask you about California?' said Emily as soon as they had the dining room to themselves. 'Was there something else you've forgotten to tell us? Do you need me to take a message to Lena for you about something?'

Emmet paused with his fork halfway to his mouth. 'Oh… She didn't say what it was about?'

'No, just to ask you?'

'Oh, all right. I'd rather she'd said it to you herself, but…well, she wants to come to California for a holiday.'

Emily smiled at him encouragingly, wondering why he looked so alarmed. 'That's a lovely idea. When are you thinking she might come? Next summer maybe?'

He blushed, looking guilty. 'Er…well, it's this summer she wants to come really. As soon as she's got out of the nursing home actually. I mean' – he hurried on, clearly seeing the hurt and confusion in his aunt's face – 'she does want to come back to Ireland, but this way she says she can have a rest and recover a bit first.'

'But that's ridiculous! She's in no fit state...' Blackie began, and Emmet coloured.

'I'm sorry, Uncle Blackie. It was Nellie's idea. I think she just can't face going back and being around the baby all the time just yet...'

'I wish you'd said something to us about this earlier, Emmet.' Emily couldn't help the note of accusation in her voice, even though she knew she shouldn't blame him. Nellie had clearly put him up to this, and he was just being loyal to his cousin.

'I'm sorry. I thought she might change her mind, and nothing's been decided. I haven't even asked Malachy yet. I wasn't going to until Nellie checked with you.'

'Oh, in that case.' Emily breathed again. 'Please don't mention it to him.'

Candice came in at that point with a plate of cakes, little tarts with spiced coconut inside that she told them were called *gizzada*. They were too sweet for Emily's taste, but Blackie and Emmet started eating them, even on top of their huge dinner.

Halfway through his second tart, Emmet said suddenly, 'Look, to be honest, Auntie Em, I know you're against the idea of her coming with me, but Nellie was saying she really doesn't want to go back to Kilteegan Bridge right away after...you know. She was talking about staying in England and getting a job or something, but I said I thought that was a bad idea, her being by herself, so then she suggested California. And I do think if she's going to do anything, that's the better idea. She can relax and recover by the pool, the weather will be sunny, and nobody will know her or anything about her. And Malachy's house is so much nicer than some old bedsit. And Malachy and I could look after her. Just for the summer, and then we'll send her home.'

'Emmet, I really don't think...' She just couldn't allow the idea. She couldn't bear the thought of Nellie being so far away, so soon, so young. She didn't know how Lena could bear it with Emmet. She turned to her husband, surprised he'd been silent until now. 'Blackie?'

Blackie was eating his way through his third tart, but he swallowed and wiped his mouth with a napkin. To her surprise he seemed to have warmed to the idea.

'Maybe we should think about it, Emily. See what Malachy Berger has to say on the subject. I mean, Nellie will need some time to get over this, to get back to being herself again, being a carefree young girl. And little Aidan needs to settle with us, and we need to get used to being parents of a little one again. So if Nellie thinks she needs some time, maybe it's a good idea, like Emmet says. I prefer the thought of her over there with Emmet and Malachy than here on her own.'

'But, Blackie…' she protested weakly.

Blackie touched her hand with a look of deep compassion. 'I know, love, and I feel the same way as you – how can we allow it? But when I saw her today, Em, I saw such pain. How can the poor child live in the same house as us if she can't even bear to look at poor little Aidan? And you know what Kilteegan Bridge is like. Someone would be bound to spot something and put two and two together. It's too risky. So maybe she does need some space away from us and the baby, to forget all the heartbreak and sorrow and pain that poor innocent child has brought to her. I love my son. I'm going to love him as much as I love my daughter, and I want his relationship with his sister to be happy and normal. I don't want him to grow up feeling like she hates him. I had a terrible relationship with my own brother because my father taught him to despise me. Nellie and Aidan deserve a chance to love each other properly, as sister and brother, so when we're gone, they will always have each other.'

'Oh…' Emily shook her head, speechless. Her throat was tight with unshed tears.

'Will you think about it, Em?' he asked gently.

'I don't know.'

'Ask Malachy to telephone us here, Emmet, as soon as you get to California and you've spoken to him. If he thinks it's a good idea,' said Blackie, holding Emily's hand under the table while he looked at his nephew, 'we can discuss it then. We'll be staying here for the next ten days while Nellie recovers, with Candice and Egbert.' As Emily mopped her eyes with her napkin, he made an attempt at humour. 'Maybe Egbert will teach me to sing some of his songs. That will go down a treat in the Donkey's Ears back in Kilteegan Bridge.'

Emmet laughed and even Emily smiled.

When they'd arrived at the hotel that evening, Egbert had been sitting on the stairs playing his guitar, and when Blackie asked him what kind of music he was playing, his face had split into a huge grin and he'd replied in his sing-song way. 'Reggae, mon. Da music of da people.' It was the most endearing accent, and Emily thought she could listen to it all day, which was exactly the same thing that Marissa had said to her about the Irish accent when they'd stumbled into her café at five thirty that morning – which now felt like it had happened in a different life.

# CHAPTER 15

Eli was at a loss. Every single ointment, antibiotic and disinfectant had failed spectacularly, and Fintan Slattery was in terrible pain. He was bed-bound and being kept only barely comfortable by the strong painkillers he was on, which Eli knew he couldn't take long-term without doing further damage to his poor body.

He left the bedroom and went to the top of the stairs. 'Mrs Slattery,' he called down to the kitchen. 'Help us, please.'

A few moments later, Vera came clumping up the stairs into the bedroom. As he beckoned her to her husband's bedside, she put her hand over her mouth and gagged. He didn't blame her. Fintan's leg, free of its bandage now, looked terrible and smelled worse.

'I give up,' he said, standing beside her. 'We've tried everything. The hospital are stumped. I'm stumped. I asked Dr Burke to have a look to see if he could suggest anything, but he had no ideas either.'

Fintan lay back on his pillow, staring at the ceiling.

'I know, Dr Kogan, and it won't improve either,' Vera said, not entirely without compassion.

'Is there nothing you can tell me? I know I might not have seemed very…' – he paused, trying to find the right word –'convinced, I suppose, when you told me why you think Fintan's leg won't heal after the accident, but I'm not claiming to be God or invincible or infallible. I'm all out of ideas and I desperately want to help your husband, so if you have anything to offer, I'm all ears.'

'You might be, but is he?' She pointed at her husband.

'Ah, Vera, stop it, will you?' Fintan groaned.

'See what I mean, Doctor? Fifty years of marriage and he still doesn't believe I have the knowledge. People of this parish have been coming to us Kelly women for cures, for healing, for insights into the future for generations, but my husband, much as I love him, dismisses it as old hocus-pocus. I don't care, I never have. I know what I know, and he can believe what he likes, but he wouldn't listen to me. I told him time and again not to touch the tree – neighbours too. Even people who put no stock at all by the old ways would not dare to chop at a fairy tree, but not my bucko here. He's bigger and stronger and he wouldn't be told. He knew better. And so now here we are.'

Eli glanced at Fintan, whose face had aged so much in the months since the accident. 'Supposing your husband was to agree to do something, take something or whatever it is you suggest, is there something you could do?'

Vera shrugged. 'I honestly don't know. A fairy curse is hard to lift, and when you offend the Good People so grievously, well, there are consequences.'

'Clearly,' Eli replied darkly. 'But we are where we are, and as I said, I've tried everything I can think of. I consulted with former colleagues in Wales, and the consultant at the hospital here, and none of us have any ideas.'

'Why would you? You haven't the knowledge, and it's not good to pretend you do if you don't. My grandmother had a story about a woman who thought she had the knowledge – this is going back years and years ago now. She said that her child had been taken by the Good People and had been replaced by a changeling, a thin, cranky child that would not thrive and ate all the time and was never full or satisfied. My grandmother called to look at the child. A boy it was, and the fairies were more inclined to take boy children – it was why they dressed boys as girls long ago, grew their hair long, and why all christening robes today are dresses, for boys *and* girls. It's a throwback to that time. But anyway, the mother was ready to place the child on a fire, the belief at the time being that the changeling would go up the chimney and the real child would return, but my grandmother stopped her. She knew it was no changeling. The child was sickening for something, and so she made up a tincture of herbs and did a blessing, a healing of the child, and he was fine.'

Eli couldn't understand what this had to do with Fintan's leg. Vera almost seemed to be saying that she thought the whole fairy thing was nonsense herself.

'The point is,' Vera said with purpose, 'it wasn't a changeling child. Such a thing was used as an excuse for a child that was sick – it was how ignorant people made sense of things – and my grandmother knew the difference as all we Kelly women do. We're not after people's money under false pretences. But that's not to say the fairies don't exist, and that they don't jealously guard what is theirs, for they do.'

'And is there anything that can be done to lift a curse?' Eli couldn't believe these words were coming out of his mouth, and he'd dread to think of the reaction if any of his medical colleagues heard him, but he had no options.

'Do you want to hear this?' she asked her husband.

'Will it get me back to work?' he asked sourly. 'I'm having to get contractors in to set my barley, so I'll have nothing out of it by the time I pays them, but I've no choice lying here bedridden for no sensible reason known to man or God...'

'Ah, forget it. I know you're trying your best, Doctor, but as usual, Fintan Slattery knows better.' She turned to go.

'Vera,' he called to her from the bed. 'Look, I'm sorry, all right. I shouldn't have tried to cut the tree. You were right and I was wrong.'

Vera pealed with laughter. 'Well, by the Lord Hokey, we should have recorded that, an admission of guilt from the great Farmer Slattery.'

'I mean it, Vera. I know I used to say things, that it was a load of auld rubbish, but look at me. Not a doctor in the place can help, I can't work, I can't even get out of bed, you're minding me like I'm an infant, and there's no explanation that makes a hair of sense that anyone can give me, so…'

'Maybe I'm right? Is that what you're trying to say?' She stood in front of him, her hands on her ample hips.

'I'm starting to think it's the only explanation, especially since the doctor here seems to think it too. Sure how would I know better than him? So please, Vera, for the love of God, do something if you can.'

She looked from her husband to Eli and thought for a moment. 'There's one day a year it is permitted to touch a fairy tree, the festival of Bealtaine, the first of May. 'Twas the tradition long ago for a bride to marry on that day, and for luck she might carry some flowers from the hawthorn tree. If he were to go there, on that day, with an offering, a gift, and a promise delivered wholeheartedly that he would never again attempt such foolishness, that he would protect the land in that field for the Good People and not plant it or plough it or graze animals there, it might be enough. But I've never seen it happen before, so I don't honestly know.'

'What kind of a gift?' Eli wondered.

'Well, legend tells that fairies can't produce food. They can cast a glamour on our food, re-create the smell and sight of it, but cannot take the nutritional value of it, so food offerings are best. Butter, beer, bread, cheese.'

Fintan didn't scoff as once he might have, Eli noted. Instead he said, 'So if I bring those things to the tree, and promise to protect it and never use the land near it again, allow it to fallow, I'll be cured?'

'You might be.' Vera was noncommittal. 'Fairies are vindictive, Fintan, or they can be, at least, if they are vexed, and I fear you have sorely vexed them, so they would enjoy you being a source of teasing over the field.'

'I'll do it,' he said decisively. 'The first of May is this Saturday. I'll do it and I'll mean it, because I can't live like this and that's for sure.'

Eli shrugged and exhaled. 'Well, in the absence of any better ideas, Fintan, I think you're right to give it a try.'

He got in his car and drove home, but before he did, he examined his left hand once again. Not a sign of arthritis remained, and all he'd done was exactly as Vera Slattery had said. He wasn't ready to proclaim his belief in witchcraft and sorcery just yet, but the facts were the facts. And her solution had succeeded where all of his had failed. Not only that, but Thirteen, who used to take ten minutes to get out of her basket, so stiff and sore was she, the poor thing, had had a new lease on life as well; there was no denying it.

If only he could find his wedding ring now, he'd be thrilled. He'd taken it off that day with Vera, but there must have been a hole in his trouser pocket – it came of overstuffing them with things – and it was looking like he was going to have to buy a replacement.

# CHAPTER 16

*Dear Nellie,*

*I've put aside a project on fascinating but complicated mechanical engineering to devote the next hour to writing to you. I hope you appreciate it!*

*Malachy says you are very welcome to stay here, so California here you come! Auntie Em and Uncle Blackie will be distraught seeing you off, I know, but I can't wait for you to be here.*

*I'm so excited. You'll love it here.*

*This weekend Malachy and I are going to Santa Cruz. There's a beach and a whole boardwalk of restaurants and fun fair rides and loads of huge sea lions that lie around barking apparently. I told him I need to check out some fun things for you because you are much livelier than either of us. Malachy is nice – you'll like him. He's very generous and really glad I'm here. But during the days at least, we'll have the place to ourselves because he's always working. He never married or had other children. I think losing Mam actually broke his heart, but he would never say it. I don't know. Listen to me going on about broken hearts. That's more your area than mine!*

*We also had dinner in Fisherman's Wharf and took a tour of Alcatraz – you know, where they kept Al Capone and all the really bad criminals? The hotel porter where we were staying used to deliver stuff out to the island, 'the Rock' as they call it, and he told me that the police were so scared that the crime gangs would attack the transport bringing the likes of Capone to the Rock that they made special railroad cars that looked normal on the outside but where the prisoners and guards were inside, chained, with guns and everything. And when they'd arrive in San Francisco from Chicago or New York or wherever, they'd move the railway car onto another track and take it all the way to the water's edge. Then they'd lift the carriage onto a boat, never letting the prisoners out, and transport them over. It wasn't until they were inside Alcatraz that they were let out. They were greeted by the governor, who said, 'Welcome to Alcatraz. Good luck escaping from here.'*

*It was a place for the worst of the worst. It's spooky looking, and you can see the prison clearly from the city. Every window on the Rock has a view of San Francisco, and this man said if the wind was right, the prisoners could hear the noise of the streets sometimes. They say those who break the rules here go to prison, but if you break the prison rules, you go to Alcatraz. I'll take you to see it when you come, and we'll go to Ghirardelli's for chocolate, and eat Dungeness crab rolls, and have clam chowder out of a sourdough bread roll, and walk across the Golden Gate Bridge – you'll love it, Nell. A million miles from home in every way.*

*Anyway, if all goes well with your parents, you'll soon see for yourself. I know flying might be scary, but it's fun really. The air hostesses are very nice, and they'll look after you if you say it's your first time. You'll have to change planes in Atlanta – that's in Georgia on the East Coast – but it's easy and they'll explain everything as you go. And then I'll be there to collect you in San Francisco when you land. We'll have to take Malachy's car because mine has no luggage space at all.*

*So the next time we speak, you will be here, Nell. Baby Aidan will be happy as Larry in Kilteegan Bridge with everyone making a big fuss of him, and you and me will be over here having the time of our lives.*

*Take care, cousin.*

*Emmet xx*

Even though it had only come two days ago, the letter was worn on the creases. She'd read it so often and was clinging to what he said. The light at the end of the long dark tunnel. She would escape, and nobody there would know anything about her. The baby would be safe and loved, and she would be free. She couldn't wait.

* * *

*Dear Emily and Blackie,*

*Just a short note to say how pleased I am you are letting Nellie come over for a while to help Emmet settle in. His happiness is very important to me, and I will make it a priority to ensure your daughter is happy as well. Emmet is already planning all the trips he wants to take her on. I understand Nellie has been unwell, and although Emmet tells me she is now on the mend, I want you to know that the health care here is excellent, and I will ensure that if she requires medical attention, she will have the best doctors available. Apart from that, she can relax and enjoy everything the house has to offer. My housekeeper, Juanita, is very maternal and is already looking forward to waiting on your daughter hand and foot. If Nellie wants to stay for the whole summer, that is no trouble. I expect she'll be bored once Emmet goes to college, and we'll return her to you then.*

*Congratulations on your new baby boy, Emily. I was delighted to hear you and Blackie are parents again. You must be very proud.*

*All the best,*

*Malachy Berger*

The letter had come two days ago, addressed to their hotel. Emily folded it away after she'd shown it to Blackie, and they'd had a little weep in each other's arms.

* * *

The matron was waiting for them as they arrived to collect Aidan and Nellie, who had both been pronounced well enough to leave.

'Can you come with me please, Mr and Mrs Crean?' she said with a professional smile, leading them to her office. 'Please, have a seat.'

Emily was worried. She knew the nursing home assumed Nellie was taking her baby home today, with the help of her parents. Was something wrong?

The matron smiled at them from behind a desk as they sat on two tubular steel chairs. 'First, congratulations again on the birth of your grandson. He's a beautiful boy and thriving.'

'He is,' Blackie confirmed proudly.

'However, while I know you're planning to take Ellen and Aidan home with you today, the social worker is very concerned that Nellie has still not wanted to see her child or feed him since birth, and she asked me to ask you if you'd ever discussed adoption with Ellen? There are many families who are suitable, and we can easily arrange –'

'No. Absolutely not.' Emily's heart was pounding and she felt sick, but she tried to look calm and smiled as hard as she could. 'No, our daughter doesn't want Aidan adopted. She's feeling a little overwhelmed, I think. The labour was very difficult for her, and she's going to need time to recover.'

'Yes, when the mothers are very young, it can be particularly difficult.' The matron checked a file. 'And I understand she and the baby are going to live at home with you in…' – she paused to read – 'Kilteegan Bridge, in Ireland. Is that correct?'

'That's right, yes.' Emily prayed she sounded convincing, prayed Aidan wouldn't be taken off them even at this late stage. What powers did social workers have in this country?

'Given that Ellen is so unwilling to care for Aidan, can we be sure you yourself will be at home with him and ensure he gets all the necessary care?'

'I will. We will. Of course.'

The woman began writing in a file, and Emily didn't dare even look at Blackie. The silence in the room was deafening; the only sound was the matron's hand on the sheet of paper, writing quickly. Emily longed to know what she was putting there but was too afraid to say anything.

What would she and Blackie do if they refused to allow them to take him? If they thought Nellie was so reluctant that it would end badly for Aidan? A fleeting thought of telling the truth crossed her mind, but she dismissed it. Her heart thumped painfully in her chest, and her throat felt constricted. A cold bead of sweat rolled down her back, between her shoulders, and she gave an involuntary shudder. The woman looked up then and eyed her, her face inscrutable.

After what felt like an age, she spoke. 'Well, then.' The matron closed the file. 'That's that box ticked for the social workers. I'm sorry, but they said I had to ask, even though Ireland is of course outside their jurisdiction. Thank you very much, Mr and Mrs Crean. Now the other thing is that the registrar normally visits on a Friday and a Tuesday to register all the new births, but he was taken ill with the flu this week, so I'm afraid you'll have to register the baby yourselves. But perhaps it would be easier on you to do all that in Ireland anyway. We can give you all the necessary paperwork to fill out the forms when you get home?'

'Of course,' Emily said in bewilderment. She couldn't believe this was so easy.

'Well, unless you have any questions, I would think it would be all right for you to leave this morning. We can give you a supply of bottles and nappies if you wish?'

'Not at all. We already have what we need.'

'Marvellous.' She stood up and ushered Emily and Blackie out the door. 'The paperwork you'll need will be available for you here at the office when you're ready to go.'

And she was gone.

'Is that it? We just walk out the door with both of them?' Blackie whispered as soon as she was out of earshot.

'Looks like it,' Emily said, equally stunned.

LATER, in Suncroft, with Nellie hiding away upstairs in her own room feasting on Candice's *gizzada* and reading a magazine, Emily sat in the window of her and Blackie's room gazing out across the road at the wide black expanse of the Thames and all the twinkling lights on the river. If she'd not been there at such a difficult time for her family, she would have loved to see all the tourist sights – Westminster Abbey, the Parliament buildings, St Paul's.

'Would we come back here for a holiday, you and me and the baby sometime?' she asked.

Blackie, sprawled on the bed with Aidan lying like a starfish on his chest, turned his head on the pillow and looked at her like she had five heads.

'To London?'

'Yes, to London.'

'Why?'

She tried not to sound frustrated. 'Why not? Lena and Eli go to Wales on their holidays.'

'Yes, but Eli's family live in Wales. That's why they visit them obviously,' Blackie replied, as if explaining it to someone who was a bit confused. 'But here in London, we don't know a soul.'

'I know that, Blackie,' she said patiently, 'but there's so much to see. Don't you think it's all fascinating? All the different people from all over the world, the Crown Jewels in the Tower of London, Big Ben. There's so much to experience. I'd love to come back and watch the changing of the guard at Buckingham Palace.'

As she spoke, her husband's face lost its look of confusion. 'My darling wife, if you want to come here and bring the baby and myself and show us the queen of England's fancy baubles, then that's what we'll do.' His eyes shone. 'I'd take the sun out of the sky for you, Emily, I really would. You're the reason I'm a happy man. You're the reason I have that girl in the next room, and the reason my poor old mother isn't slaving away day in, day out in the shop. You're the reason for everything, and anything I can ever do to make you happy, then you need only say it.'

Blackie wasn't one for big speeches normally, and Emily was so touched. She knew he had never taken a holiday in his life before and couldn't really see the point of it, but he'd do it for her and that was enough.

Aidan was a serene little lad who fed and slept. If he was hungry, he'd let them know, but other than that, he hardly cried. They had a little Moses basket for him, but he was almost always in one of their arms. Both she and Blackie loved the solid feel of him, his little body on their chest, snuffling and mewing happily. They were besotted.

Nellie assiduously ignored him, never looking at him or touching him, but other than that, she seemed all right. She was healing well physically, the doctors said before she left the nursing home, and her spirits were fairly good. She was excited at the prospect of going to America, and it was the safest topic of conversation.

It still hurt to think of her so far away, but Malachy Berger's reassurances that he would take care of her went a long way to ease their worries.

They'd known him growing up, although not very well. He was a different class and had gone away to boarding school aged twelve. But what they knew of him was good, and Lena seemed to trust him, despite all their history, so they would have to be happy with that.

They were booked on the boat the following night, and Nellie was due to fly in the morning. Their new life was about to begin.

# CHAPTER 17

'Aw, Em, he's a little dote.' Lena gazed at her new nephew three days later sleeping in his Moses basket, his shock of black hair poking up in a sort of peak.

'He really is. Everyone that sees him says it. He's so cute, isn't he? I spend hours just looking at him. Between Peggy, me and Blackie, he's never put down. I think this is the first time he's been in the basket for more than three minutes.' Emily laughed.

'I can't wait till he wakes up so I can hold him as well,' Lena said, leaning in. 'Eli warned me not to get broody as I was coming over here.'

'Would you want another at your age even?' asked Emily, smiling.

'Hey! I'm two years younger than you, and if you can, I can,' Lena shot back, and both women giggled.

Nobody had questioned the arrival of Emily and Blackie back from Dublin with their baby boy. Enquiries were made as to the nature of the complications by a few nosy parkers, but both Blackie and Emily had agreed to say the conversation-stopping, 'Ah, you know yourself, women are more complicated machinery than men.' And that always worked. Nobody wanted to hear about uteruses or ovaries. All they needed to know was both mother and baby were fit as trout, and everyone was thrilled.

'Nellie will be dying to get home from London to see her little brother, I'm sure.' It was the loud, piercing voice of Maureen Parker rising from the shop below. The door at the top of the stairs was open, and Emily and Lena lifted their heads, listening.

'Well, he'll have to wait for that, I'm afraid, Mrs Parker.' Peggy's voice carried up to them from out of sight. 'Because our Nellie has been lured by the bright lights of America, would you believe?'

Maureen Parker's voice conveyed her excitement at hearing this juicy titbit. 'I thought she was working in a hotel in London?'

'Oh, she was, but sure didn't young Emmet Kogan go to California to university. Malachy Berger is an old friend of the family, as you know. Remember Malachy, whose family used to live in Kilteegan House before Lena and Dr Kogan bought it?'

'I do indeed.'

'Are you buying those balls of yarn, Maureen?'

'I am. If you would wrap them for me, Peggy? Anyway, go on.'

'Well, he and the Kogans have remained friends. He was friends with Lena and Emily and Jack when they were all children anyway. Sure Paudie O'Sullivan used to work up there, God be good to him, so they grew up together. Anyway, he suggested young Emmet apply to some fancy university over there, near where he lives in California, and sure being Dr Kogan's son Emmet is as bright as a button, so he applied and got in and he's having a wonderful time. And sure himself and Nellie are thick as thieves, as you know, so he invited her over for the summer.'

'And Blackie and Emily let her go?' Maureen was shocked. 'With a little brother she should be helping to care for?'

'Well, they weren't right keen, but Malachy Berger is putting herself and Emmet up and she's going to do a course over there, don't ask me now in what. Sure you know the young ones. Emily told me, but sure in one ear, out the other. Hopefully it's something that will be useful to the shop when she comes back.'

Emily glanced at Lena with a grin. Her mother-in-law didn't know the truth about the new baby, but she did know about Malachy being Emmet's biological father, so it was an Oscar-winning performance she was putting on.

'Oh, sure I do,' Maureen said smugly. 'My grandson is studying zoology, would you believe, above in Dublin. Did you ever hear the like? Like you'd have to spend three years learning about how to work in a zoo.'

''Tis far from universities we were reared, that's for sure,' Peggy agreed, and there was a rustle as she wrapped the balls of wool in brown paper.

Emily stood up and quietly closed the kitchen door. 'And just like that, the story will spread. Nellie is in America with Emmet, Malachy Berger is an old friend taking care of them both, and she'll be home to see the baby before too long.'

Lena shook her head in admiration. 'I feared you'd never pull it off, Em. It seemed such a complicated thing to do, but here you are. And here is this little man, happy as a bug in a rug, aren't you?' She cooed at the baby, giving in to the urge to pick him up. He stirred for a moment, then settled in her arms.

'I know. I was so scared there would be questions over there, but they just let us go, like they didn't much care now he was born safe. Nellie stayed with us in the hotel for a few days. She had one room, and we stayed in another with Aidan – it was too cold to go out. Once she was able, Blackie bought her a flight to San Francisco, even though Malachy offered to do it.'

'Was it awful? Watching her go? I thought Eli was going to try to stop me clinging to Emmet's ankles when he went.'

Emily nodded, her eyes bright with tears. 'Awful. She didn't want a big thing, so she said she'd get a taxi to the airport, but Blackie insisted on going too. I stayed with Aidan, and he left her to the plane. I think a bit of his heart left with Nellie that day, but she was so brave, Lena, so well able for it all. It's like she became an adult over there, in the home, having him, like all of it made her grow up. She's so brave.'

'I was on tenterhooks till Malachy rang to say she'd arrived safely, at least that,' Lena replied. 'Imagine, we're entrusting our children into the care of Malachy Berger. Life is so strange, isn't it?'

'It really is, but you know what, Lena? I'll always be grateful to him for taking her and looking out for her. I couldn't have allowed her to stay in London, which was what she wanted at first, but knowing she's over there with Emmet and Malachy, well… I didn't like it at first and I still don't love it, but in some way, it feels like a relief.'

'It is, and they'll have a great time. Emmet is forever sending postcards of beaches and fairground rides and sunsets – it's driving Sarah wild with jealousy.' She laughed. Aidan let out a little squeak, and she bounced him.

'He might need changing…' Emily held out her arms.

'Not at all. You make the tea, and I'll see to this little bundle.' Lena expertly changed his nappy, and soon Aidan was dressed and comfortable again. His dark eyes were open a lot now, and he gazed at her, a funny serious expression on his face. 'I think his eyes will be brown like Blackie's,' she said, stroking his head. 'I can't believe how like Blackie he is. Like, I know, but still, it's amazing.'

'He looks very like the Crean side, though hopefully more like Blackie than Jingo or Dick.'

'You look nothing like either of those villains,' Lena crooned at Aidan. 'You look like your daddy.' She caught Emily's eye. 'The spitting image of your father,' she added decisively.

# CHAPTER 18

Nellie rolled over onto her tummy and luxuriated in the Californian sun that was roasting her back. Copper-headed, pale-skinned Malachy had laughed at her this morning when he saw her heading up the stairs to the infinity pool on the roof. He'd mentioned something about 'mad dogs and Englishmen', but she didn't care. She just lathered herself in suntan cream and gave way to the free feeling of sun on her bare skin. Luckily she had her dad's skin tone, so different from her mother's Irish whiteness, and had gone brown very quickly.

She had decided to relax for the whole day. There was no trip planned, no excitement, nothing to do. Malachy was out supervising a project, and Emmet had made a start on his summer reading list, prepping himself for his first term now that he'd been accepted. He was below in the air-conditioned living room; he'd declined her offer to join her upstairs in the sun. 'Are you mad? I'd be boiled alive.' He'd grinned at her. 'I'll come out after dark, like a vampire.'

Slipping into the pool, she swum a few strokes, marvelling at the sensation of floating in the sky. The water poured over the lip of the pool, being continuously recycled, so there appeared to be no barrier between her and the heavens. She loved this place. To be free again after she'd carried a baby for nine months felt good, and she loved how the water made her feel cleaner and better, washing away her shame. She no longer felt connected to the baby in an upsetting way. Mam and Dad were mad about him, and they'd sent Emmet some pictures to show to her if she wanted to see them. She wasn't sure at first, but she did in the end and was glad she did. He was a sweet little baby, almost two months old now. He had dark hair and he looked so like her dad – *his* dad – it was incredible. Nothing like his biological father, Gerard, she was relieved to note. It would make her seeing him all the harder if he did.

Despite what her parents thought, she had no plans to return to Ireland, at least until Emmet went to college in September, and Malachy seemed happy for her to stay as long as she wanted. She suspected he was so delighted to have Emmet there – he adored him – and if Nellie was there too, then Emmet was less likely to feel homesick and go back. She didn't think Malachy had anything to worry about in reality; life in West Cork was no match for California.

Emmet was every inch the budding scholar now, even though he hadn't even started at Stanford yet. He kept his hair cut short and wore chinos and button-down shirts, with loafers on his feet. Nothing like what people wore back at home. If he walked down the street in Kilteegan Bridge dressed like that, he'd have the entire place nudging each other and making eyes. Nellie sighed to herself. It was so good to be gone from there, where everyone had an opinion about the doings of everyone else. She missed her mam and dad, of course she did, and they were so good sending her money and everything, but she wasn't ready to go back just yet, not for a while.

Her body had returned to her pre-nightmare shape, which was a relief. She'd been horrified after she gave birth to see her tummy was almost as round as it was when Aidan was still inside her, but Mam assured her it would go back to normal, and it had. The first few weeks here were embarrassing, living in a house in a strange country with two men, when so many of her issues were too intimate to explain to them. But Malachy seemed to sense it and had introduced her to a friend of his, a lady called Carolyn, who took her to a female doctor, who in turn was very discreet and promised she wouldn't tell anyone about Nellie having recently given birth.

After that, things got better.

Carolyn was divorced, the first divorced person Nellie had ever met if you didn't count Mrs Weldon, who was getting her marriage annulled. Carolyn was from Texas but worked here in Palo Alto. She was scarily thin, with dead-straight blond hair. She had two daughters around Nellie's age and said that once Nellie was feeling better, she'd introduce them and maybe they could hang out. Nellie didn't really know what 'hanging out' meant, but Emmet explained it was what Americans called being friends.

He already had his own friends from the neighbourhood, kids he'd met when he was here before. They were the children of Malachy's rich social circle, and a few of them were heading to Stanford in September. There was a guy called Kenneth – he was from New York but his parents were from Hong Kong – and another one called George, from Texas, and then two girls, Wei from Singapore and Morgan from Connecticut. They'd all gone to the cinema one night and to eat some pizza afterwards, the most delicious thing Nellie had ever tasted in her life. They were nice to her and very friendly, but super-brainy and wanted to know what she was doing in terms of her career.

They assumed she had graduated from high school, as they called it, but the reality of course was that, thanks to getting pregnant, she had not a single exam or qualification to her name. She'd been too embarrassed to admit that, so she mumbled something about getting her grades transferred from Ireland rather than taking the exams here like Emmet had done, and they seemed happy enough. The assumption was she too would go to Stanford once things were worked out. As if. The only way she'd get in there was washing floors or making the tea, she thought glumly.

Carolyn hadn't been around for the last month, so the offer of 'hanging out' with her two daughters seemed to be off the table as well. Emmet seemed to think Carolyn had designs on Malachy, but Malachy wasn't interested. Nellie suspected her daughters wouldn't have been any less intimidating than Emmet's friends, though, probably off to college as well to study rocket science or something.

If she'd been born brainy like Emmet, she could have done something with her life, not fallen for a faithless married man and ruined everything before she'd even got started. What a fool she'd been. She'd thought she was so clever and wordly-wise just because she was popular and good-looking. She'd been so impressed with herself for having a grown-up lover, and doing that silly little make-up course in Cork, dreaming of owning a chain of beauty shops one day. Now she was going to have to slink home to Kilteegan Bridge and probably work in the hardware shop forever and stay a spinster because her heart was broken and her body had been all used up and no one nice would ever want her again.

She mentally ticked off everyone in her former class at school. Everyone else had a plan. Finish school and get a job or go on to do a course, or else leave to go farming or into the family business. None of them had been as stupid as her.

*None of them are sunning themselves beside a private pool in California either, though,* a little voice in her head said, and she smiled. That much was true.

She spent the morning lying there, thinking her thoughts, until the midday sun finally forced her inside. She took a long cold shower in the luxurious bathroom attached to her bedroom, then spent ages ironing her hair as she'd read about in a magazine. Everyone here had poker-straight hair, parted in the middle, and wore either very short skirts or bell-bottom jeans. She ringed her eyes with kohl and applied her make-up and realised she was beginning to look like her old self, even if she didn't feel like her. She'd done a bit of shopping, since all her clothes were from Ireland and she didn't want to look like some kind of country hick, and now she selected a tiny mini skirt and a vest top with spaghetti straps. She put on a bra under it, but then changed her mind and decided to do as the local girls did and go without. Her mother would have been appalled to see her exposing so much flesh, but that was there and this was here. Things were different in California, and she'd be different too. She pulled on some platform-heeled sandals that made her look about six feet tall, which she loved, and appraised herself in the mirror. A new and much improved Nellie Crean, she thought.

Malachy had given her a key of her own to come and go, so she slung a brown leather handbag over her shoulder, grabbed her denim jacket, another new purchase, called, 'See ya later, Emmet, I'm just going for a walk,' through the living room door to Emmet, where he was poring over his boring books, and let herself out of the house.

It was the first time she'd been out further than the nearest shop without her cousin or Malachy. She had a poor idea of where she was going, but she walked on around the streets of the neighbourhood, past cafés and shops and people going about their business. She loved hearing their accents and equally loved how hers was such a novelty to them. She strolled aimlessly until she found herself at a railway station.

The next train was to San Francisco. She'd been there to the tourist areas with Malachy and Emmet, of course, but she'd never just walked around the ordinary streets on her own. It was only about an hour by car, so it might be even quicker by train. She could go, take a look around and be back before Malachy came home. Would that be dangerous? She mentally shook herself – how could it be?

The train was due in four minutes; she had to make up her mind. She was a grown-up – well, almost – and she had nobody to tell her what to do. She was her own boss, and San Francisco was on her doorstep.

There were a few others on the platform, a woman who looked amazing in what looked like a man's suit but tailored for a woman and a few boring-looking businessmen. But there was also a group of long-haired girls and boys not much older than her, so she tentatively approached them.

'Excuse me, I was just wondering…'

They all turned to look at her, three boys and two girls. One of the boys, with a beard and beads in his long hair as well as around his neck, was smoking what looked like a homemade cigarette.

'Do I buy a ticket in an office, or can I get one on the train?'

The bearded boy passed his cigarette to one of the girls and stepped forward. She noticed a smell off him, not unpleasant, a sweet kind of smell not unlike the smell in Cork from the brewery roasting the hops for beer, but it was more earthy or something.

'You can buy one over there, or you can ride with us for free. We got a system so that if the inspector gets on, we can warn each other and avoid him.' He grinned, displaying a set of the whitest teeth Nellie had ever seen.

'All right,' Nellie agreed, feeling a bit better about travelling if this friendly boy and his group were going too.

'You've got such a cute accent. Where you from?' the girl who was now smoking the cigarette asked. She was in bell-bottoms and what looked like a bra instead of a top – Nellie could see her bare midriff – and on her feet she had sandals that looked like leather laces criss-crossed over her feet.

'Ireland. I'm Irish,' Nellie said, blushing at being suddenly the centre of attention.

'You're a long way from home, pretty little Irish…' drawled another of the boys. He had blond hair and was lying on his back on the only bench.

Nellie hesitated. She could say she was visiting her cousin, but that sounded a bit childish, so instead she just said, 'Yeah, just travelling around, you know, seeing the sights.'

'You been to the Bay Area before?' asked the blond boy with a slow smile, taking the cigarette from the girl in bell-bottoms but stubbing it out on the bench with a grimace after one puff.

'Yes, but only to do touristy stuff,' she admitted.

Before she had time to say anything else, the train arrived, and she found herself bundled helpfully into one of the carriages.

She and her new five friends sat down on two sets of seats facing each other, and the others introduced themselves.

'I'm Dex, and that's Cokie,' said the blond-haired boy, pointing to the one with the white teeth, 'and that other guy is Johnny.' A short, dark-haired, tanned, brown-eyed fella with a wispy beard and hair in a ponytail gave her a one-handed wave.

'And that's Crystal,' he added, pointing at the girl who'd asked Nellie about her accent. She had white-blond hair and big blue eyes and looked like an innocent flower. 'And last but not least, Naomi.'

Naomi was a tall, wide-shouldered Black girl, wearing what looked like a large purple curtain. On anyone else it might look ridiculous, but on her it was gorgeous. She looked so compelling, with her almost luminescent skin and dark eyes, that Nellie had to try hard not to stare. Her hair was so short it was almost shaved, and she had the most enormous gold earrings. Unlike the others, she didn't seem friendly. Her eyes kept darting from the boys' faces to Nellie's like she was wondering what the lads had been thinking of, bringing this random girl along with them.

'So what's your name?' Crystal asked.

'I'm…' But Nellie paused. She didn't want to be Nellie from Kilteegan Bridge any more, not here, not with these sophisticated people; she wanted to leave that unsuccessful girl far behind her. Her real name was Ellen, which her mother loved but Nellie hated. It was such an old woman's name, and it was what they called her in that place where the nightmare happened. She had overheard two girls in a restaurant in Santa Cruz and one was called Danielle, and she remembered thinking what a cool name it was. 'I'm Danielle.'

'Hey, Danielle, nice to meet you.' Dex gave that slow smile again, rolling another cigarette with some odd-looking tobacco from a pouch. Everything was different here.

'And how old are you?' asked Naomi suspiciously.

This time she didn't hesitate. 'Seventeen.' She would have preferred to say eighteen, but she didn't dare. She knew she looked very young, even for her age, and Naomi gave her a doubtful enough look as it was.

Cokie acquired the cigarette, took a long puff and passed it to Naomi, who did the same. They continued to share the thing, and Nellie guessed they maybe were not that wealthy, not like Emmet's friends, but it was strange. Even the old lads at home who were scrimping for a few pennies for a pint smoked their own cigarettes.

'Hey, that's my J.' Dex punched Johnny in the arm as Johnny took a final puff and threw it out the window.

'Make us another, Dex.' Crystal sidled up to him.

Nellie watched, fascinated, as Dex tore a tiny piece of cardboard and folded it into a concertina shape, then smoothed out a cigarette paper and placed the little cardboard concertina onto one end. He next took some of the tobacco kind of stuff that looked more like dried leaves and placed it on the paper, rolling it between his thumb and fingers to even it out. Then he licked all along the edge and made it into a cigarette, but not like any Nellie had ever seen. It was much fatter at the end, and he poked at it with a match, pushing the tobacco down before he pinched it closed.

He handed the finished product to Crystal, who rewarded him with a passionate kiss. Nellie immediately looked away, but she caught a reflection in the window of Crystal still kissing him with an open mouth, on and on. Nellie didn't know where to put herself as, oh God, Crystal's hand strayed to his crotch... Dex slapped her hand and moved it away, and Crystal pouted but laughed and passed the cigarette to Naomi, who lit it with a flare of flame and began sharing it around.

'You want a drag?' Dex asked Nellie.

'I...I don't really...' Nellie had smoked a bit before the nightmare, as she mentally called the pregnancy, but had felt a bit sick when she'd tried a cigarette afterwards, and these definitely smelled funny.

'I'll share it with you,' Dex said, moving seats to sit beside her. He really was handsome, in a cool, scruffy American way. Her father would regard them as bums who would never do a day's work, but she liked them and they were being so friendly. Well, everyone except Naomi. These were much more her kind of people than Emmet's friends.

'All right.' She took a puff. The smoke was hot and rough on her throat, and she coughed and handed it straight back. 'Thanks.'

'Any time.' He winked at her, and it felt good to have a boy be nice to her, though this time she'd not be so stupid as to trust a man on face value. No, this time she would have her wits about her.

As the journey continued, her new friends talked mostly about music. They were on their way to a gig, which she took to mean a concert, of a band called the Grateful Dead, who she'd never heard of but pretended she had. Soon the entire carriage smelled of their odd cigarettes, but she was enjoying herself around her new friends and feeling more relaxed than she had for a long, long time.

# CHAPTER 19

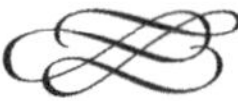

'Well, what do you think?' Skipper smiled.

'And how many acres is it again, did you say?' Ted asked, with a quick glance at Gwenda, who had gone very silent.

'Eighty, give or take. Mostly good. Some of it's a bit boggy, and there's a bit of high ground as well, but good for the mountain sheep.'

'And Bill and Deirdre are ready to sell?' Again, Ted looked at his wife, trying to gauge her reaction. The four of them sat around the farmhouse table having a beer each. The evening was drawing in, but the girls and Sarah were still out at the stables, which gave the adults time for this quiet, possibly life-changing conversation.

Skipper had spoken to Ted earlier about the idea of buying the Madden farm, but Ted had said the most important thing was what Gwenda thought about it. And now the three men were about to find out.

'They do want to sell, yeah,' said Skipper, leaning back in his chair, one thumb in his huge belt. 'They'd offered it to the twins, but that might have been just 'cause they were so sorry to see them go. But it turns out Bill's doctors want him to take it easy because he's got diabetes and angina – he's sixty-five this year – and their daughter, Lucy, has got a big number with the council in Cork, so she ain't comin' back here to go farmin'. Jack and me, we've helped out as much as we can, but with the twins gone, it's a lot of work. Isn't that right, Jack?'

Jack, startled out of his usual silence, nodded. 'Well, there is a kind of problem – they want to stay in their house. 'Tis just the land they want to sell. But we were thinking that maybe if you were interested, you could build a house on the land for yourselves, and we'd farm side by side and help each other out. The girls can work with Skipper in the holidays and...' He fell silent, blushing, having said a lot more than was customary for him, and Skipper took over the conversation again, pushing another couple of beers across the table.

'Look, it's just a suggestion. You guys definitely don't have to – we'll be OK either way. You might not even care for the place. Bill will sell his farm to someone else without a problem, house or not, but if you were thinking of going back into farming, it might be nice, for us and for y'all, if we're neighbours. I know you might think it's crazy, and y'all might be wanting to go back to Australia in the end, but if you wanted to stay here, make a life here, then it might be how you could do it. Gwenda, what do you think? You've gone very quiet there.'

Silence fell in the kitchen. The shouts of the girls' voices rang out from the direction of the riding stables, and the dogs were barking joyously.

Gwenda looked at Ted over her bottle of beer. She usually had a very tough, no-nonsense attitude to life, but now she looked vulnerable. 'Well, I don't know. It's...' Then her voice grew firmer. 'It's a wonderful idea, but we can't, can we, Ted? I mean, we can't justify that kind of money when we already have a fine place to live in Cork that you and Maria have spent so much time and money getting ready for us, and the girls are settled and –'

'The house doesn't matter. We can sell it easily, and it's where their cousins are. But would you prefer it, is the thing?' Ted asked her gently.

Her eyes flickered but her voice remained steady. 'But you must be tired of the land, Ted. It was never what you meant to do. Being a drover was a cover story concocted by the British secret service so you could get away safely after the war, and then you met me –'

'The happiest day of my life,' he said softly.

'And the next thing, I was working you day and night. Now here in Ireland, you can finally have the rest you deserve, and you have an income, and all you have to do is enjoy your life.'

He stroked the back of her hand with his thumb. 'Gwenda,' he said, 'I love being home. Getting Maria's letter, coming here, finding my family, seeing our girls relax into Irish life, well… I can't say it's a dream come true because I could never have dreamed of anything like this, but it…well…it's very special. But this is my place, not yours, and I want more than anything for you to be happy. The house on Wellington Road is a fine one, and I know it has a big garden, but it's just not the same for you, is it, not having the open fields and the endless sky and being outside all day?'

'Oh, Ted…' Her tough exterior was cracking.

'Would you like to own a farm again, Gwenda? I know it's not much I'm offering you. It's not a ranch half the size of Ireland, not like your dad's place, and it's often rainy here and sometimes cold…'

'Not much?' A drop of water swelled on her lower lid, and she wiped it hastily away. 'These beautiful green fields, and the ocean, the chance to farm again, and this time not fighting drought and bush fires? Oh, Ted, I'd love it, but…'

'Then let's talk to Bill and Deirdre tomorrow.'

'But the girls'…'

'It's not like they won't know anyone this time around. We won't say anything to them yet until we've a deal, and if they hate the idea, we'll think again. But you know they're going to be thrilled. They're like fish out of water in the city.'

Her face lit up with hope, but then she came back to the money again. 'But the inheritance your father left you – it will eat it all up.'

'Well, Bill Madden seems like a reasonable man. I'll tell him what we have, see if we can do a deal.'

'Oh, Ted, I don't know what to say…'

'Well, I think you start by saying "howdy, neighbours",' Skipper suggested cheerfully, clinking his bottle of beer off Ted's and then Jack's and then holding it out to Gwenda.

Gwenda took a deep breath, slowly raised her beer, clinked it off Skipper's and, for the first time in her life, dissolved into tears.

* * *

LATER, as they walked the boundary of the O'Sullivan and Madden farms, Skipper explained how they and Bill always co-operated, which made the farms much more economical to run.

'Since the time of Jack's daddy, Bill and Deirdre Madden have been here – they're second cousins. And Jack's grandparents farmed beside Bill's parents, so it goes way back. We help each other out, share machinery, renting one combine harvester, for example, saving all the hay together, and then a baler for baling it all, stuff like that. And if one of us needs to be away from the farm, the other takes care of things.'

The scheme had worked for decades, and Ted and Gwenda agreed they saw no reason for it not to continue with Jack and Skipper.

'So we'll come back tomorrow to have that talk with Bill,' said Ted, 'see if we can make the money work. And of course we'd need to look into building a house too.'

Skipper nodded. 'If you get the materials, we don't mind helping you, and we'd have a place up and liveable in no time.'

They paused at a gate looking over the green valley, and Skipper pointed to the opposite bracken-covered hillside, which was blazing golden in the setting sun. 'Over there, there's a German guy who built a round house of logs and clay, not a stone in it, and a straw roof. We were worried he'd freeze to death in the winter, weren't we, Jack? But it's right cosy. He's got a big old wood-burnin' stove in there. You'd think the place would burn down around him, but it don't – he's snug as a bug in there. Reckon the whole thing cost him less than a thousand pounds.'

'Seriously? That sounds incredible.' Gwenda's eyes shone with enthusiasm. 'And would we need permission to build, from the council or whatever?'

Skipper glanced enquiringly at Jack, who said shyly, 'I doubt it. I mean, they brought in a law about ten years ago, but out here, on your own land, I'd say build away and worry about that if it happens. So long as you don't put in or out on anyone here, nobody will care.'

'Then it's just a question of finding where to build.' She was getting more and more excited as the idea took hold.

'If you pass by Bill's place – we'll take y'all up there tomorrow – you'll see further on, the lane comes to a halt. There's a nice flat lot up above, great views overlookin' the pastures as far as the sea – it might be a nice spot. You wouldn't be overlookin' anyone and nobody could see you, but you'd be near enough to us and Bill if you needed anything, within hollerin' distance.' He chuckled. 'How 'bout you go talk to that guy, the German, and see what he did? Maybe it would suit you guys?'

'What are you all talking about?' Annamaria had come to meet them with Sophie and Sarah, all of them flushed-cheeked and beaming, the three sheepdogs at their heels. Without waiting for an answer, she rushed on. 'Mum, can we stay with Sarah tonight? There's a spare room now Emmet's in America, and Soph and I can bunk in together.'

Ted looked at his wife, who shrugged and nodded. 'Well, if Lena agrees. I mean, we've got to be back here tomorrow morning anyway.'

'What for?' asked Annamaria, looking curiously from one to the other, clearly picking up that something was going on. 'What are you all looking so happy about?'

'Just enjoying the evening air,' said Ted with a grin. 'Now if the boys here don't mind, why don't you go use the phone in the kitchen to give your cousin Lena a call and make sure it's all right to stay over.'

'OK, thanks, Dad.'

'I've got an idea,' said Sarah. 'If you and Auntie Gwenda have to come back tomorrow morning anyway, why don't you spend the night in Molly and May's little house? Don't you think, Uncle Jack and Skipper? It's the cutest little place if you don't mind the odd spider.'

Gwenda laughed at that, a big jolly laugh, her shoulders shaking.

'Spiders? What are you talking about, spiders? You lot don't have spiders in Ireland, not what I'd call a real spider anyway, not like a huntsman that can drag a mouse up a wall to its lair, or a redback that can kill you with a bite, or a deadly funnel-web.'

Sarah giggled and shuddered. 'Well, you must all miss a lot about Australia, but not the creepy-crawlies, I'll bet.'

Sophie grinned, throwing her arm around her cousin's shoulders. 'I sure don't miss the spiders, for one, or the snakes, though I love the kangaroos bouncing all over the place, koalas in the gum trees. We had a possum in our attic before we left. Echidnas, wallabies, wombats… They're my favourite – I love wombats.'

'I'd love to go there. It sounds amazing.' Sarah sighed. 'We just have foxes and badgers and hares and deer and a few wild goats, things like that, nothing so exciting.'

'Of course it's exciting here. You're just too used to it.' Sophie smiled. 'I love your country. It's so green and beautiful. I love the crimson flowers in the hedges, and the way it's raining one minute and the sun's shining the next, and the rainbows all the time. It's like a fairyland.'

'Yeah, I wish I lived out here in Kilteegan Bridge like you do,' added Annamaria. 'I would get up every morning and think I was living in a dream.'

'Right then, dreamers, go and get Lena's permission to stay there tonight.'

And the three girls ran off to call, followed by the dogs.

'Well, I think that settles it, if everything works out with Bill,' said Ted, with a wink at Gwenda, as the four of them strolled back towards the farmhouse. But she didn't answer; she was too busy staring in puzzlement after the girls. 'What is it, Gwen? What's the matter?'

'Those dogs… Wasn't one of them too crippled with arthritis to run?'

'You mean Thirteen,' said Skipper, overhearing her. 'I know, it sure is somethin', ain't it? It's a strange story, to do with a woman called Vera Slattery and this special potion she gave to Eli, which is also to do with spiders in a sort of way. Which reminds me, if you see a wedding ring lying around anywhere, it's Eli's. He had it in his pocket, and it's fallen out somewhere. He doesn't know where he left it, but it's like it disappeared into thin air.'

'We wondered did a magpie find it on the ground and pick it up,' said Jack, 'but we've knocked down every old nest we know of round here and can't find it.'

'Maybe it was the fairies that took it.' Skipper grinned.

Jack rolled his eyes. 'Now, Skipper, don't be mocking the Good People. Look what they did for your silver mare. She was a demon and now she's an angel, and you never lifted a finger to do anything with her in between because your shoulder was so bad.'

'Oh, I ain't sayin' nothin' bad about the little people. Which reminds me, Gwenda, there's things you need to know if you buy Bill's land. Whatever you do, never cut down a hawthorn tree or all your cattle will dry up and your sheep will die, and if you come by a bottle of poitín, be sure to leave a glass out for the fairies – that way you'll have a good crop of potatoes. Isn't that right, Ted?'

'It is indeed,' agreed Ted very seriously, and his Australian wife looked from him to Jack and Skipper in astonishment.

'Well, I thought I knew all there was to know about farming,' she said, 'but it sure sounds like I've a lot more to learn about how to do it in the west of Ireland. So Jack and Skipper, maybe we'd better start with you telling me the story of Vera Slattery and what that's got to do with the fairies.'

# CHAPTER 20

'Nellie, please, don't take advantage of Malachy being away. It's not fair on him, and it's not fair on me.' Emmet stood in the doorway of her bedroom, while she sat at the dressing table elaborately making herself up.

'Emmet, go away. You're not the boss of me,' she snapped, applying a strong slash of crimson to her lips. She'd only told her cousin she was going to San Francisco for the day because she hadn't wanted him to worry, plus she thought he'd cover for her if Malachy called, and now here he was, kicking up a right fuss.

'Well, who are these friends of yours? Where did you meet them and why don't I know them?'

He obviously thought he was in charge of her just because Malachy was away on business overnight and Juanita, the elderly Mexican housekeeper, was at her grandson's wedding, so that left just her and him at home. Malachy had made them promise to be sensible, and she *was* being sensible. There was no reason for her not to go out and see her friends. Emmet was going out to see his; she knew for a fact he was meeting Wei for lunch.

'I met them when I was going for a walk, Emmet. In the Baylands Nature Preserve. I go there a lot. It's cool.'

Emmet looked at her hard, and she dropped her eyes.

The truth was, she'd only been to the nature preserve once. In reality, she went at least once a week to the squat in San Francisco in which Dex and his friends had decided to live for a while.

If Emmet found out who she was really seeing, she knew he'd have a canary, but she still felt her hippy friends were a lot more interesting than the buttoned-up squares her cousin hung out with. She loved when they all smoked joints and played peace songs on their guitars in the public squares and ate hot dogs and drank Coca-Cola. They went to the beach once, up to Santa Cruz, and had even gone skinny-dipping; they were so high, they didn't care how cold it was. It wasn't until the cops arrived and blew their whistles that they all had to run out of the sea naked and dive for cover. She thought she'd collapse laughing that day.

The only thing she didn't really like was the notion of 'free love', which seemed to mean nobody had a girlfriend or boyfriend and everyone slept with everyone else. Johnny made a pass at her early on and got annoyed when Nellie didn't want to sleep with him. He'd said she wasn't a real feminist because she wasn't into sexual liberation, which made her feel stupid and old-fashioned, until surprisingly the sometimes-dour Naomi took her aside for a few words of advice.

'Don't listen to him, Danielle. All these guys try it on the same way, pretending sexual liberation means every girl has to sleep with them whether they want to or not. That's why radical feminists are cutting loose politically. The white boys in the civil rights movement just want us women around to sleep with them and make coffee while they lie around smoking and talking about how they're going to change the world.'

Dex had also tried it on one time, but although she quite liked him, the consequences of sex for a girl were still fresh in her mind. Her body felt rotten and dirty and vile and somehow not hers, so she said no. Unlike Johnny, he didn't complain or try to push her, and she liked him for that.

Their group had been changing recently, less about peace songs and more about drugs. Johnny and Cokie had gone to work picking fruit in the Salinas Valley to make a bit of money, and Naomi and Crystal had declared they were lesbians and moved to someplace called Baja in Mexico.

It wasn't as fun without the girls and Cokie, though she'd been glad to see the back of Johnny. Dex wasn't as interested in doing fun things with just Nellie for company; he only wanted to lie around and smoke. There were new people in the squat who didn't only smoke dope; they also took acid and even heroin. The place was filthier than ever. Nobody ever tidied up or washed themselves as far as she could see, but smoking dope with Dex took the edge off her bad feelings about herself, and besides, she felt sorry for him. Today she'd been hoping to get him to come out with her for a walk and have a decent meal for once, which she would buy because he never had any money. She'd been intending to catch the train back at eight, instead of six as she did when Malachy was around – he liked them to be home for dinner – but she was damned if she was going to tell Emmet that now that he was objecting to her going at all.

'Emmet, I'm seventeen, and I'm just going into the city for three or four hours, OK? Lighten up. I'll be home by seven.' She still didn't mean to be back until nine, but she'd call him and pretend she'd missed the train.

'Look, Nellie, I'm having lunch with Wei – why don't you come along? And then there's an art exhibition that we want to see, and a concert in the evening. It'll be fun, and Wei really likes you, Nellie.'

'She does not. She's only nice to me because I'm your cousin.' Nellie felt a pang of guilt as she said this. She knew it wasn't true. Wei was one of the most straightforward people she'd ever met. She always spoke her mind, which was rather terrifying to Nellie. Nellie was used to Irish people, who talked around and around a subject long before they got to the point, if they ever got to the point at all. If Wei hadn't liked her, she'd have said so long before now. 'Anyway, she's your friend, not mine.'

'Oh, for pity's sake, Nell…' Emmet sighed heavily, like she was being nothing but a nuisance. 'All right, fine, but if you want me to cover for you with Malachy, you have to tell me exactly where you're going.'

With an annoyed hiss, she scribbled out the address of the squat – 9 Frederick Street – on the notepad Malachy had given her to write home on, and which had gone unused until now because she preferred sending postcards. 'There.' She ripped off the page and shoved it at Emmet crossly. Even so, though she wouldn't ever admit it to him, she was a tiny bit pleased that he cared this much about her safety. 'Satisfied now?'

He took the note and scanned it, and his expression hardened. 'No, I'm not.'

'But you said if I gave you the address…' Her voice was shrill with outrage.

'That's before I knew where it was. Frederick Street is in Haight-Ashbury, and it's a really rough street. It's full of squats and junkies. Who are you going to see there?'

She could have kicked herself; she hadn't realised he knew San Francisco that well. 'Friends, OK? The ones I met in the park. Be cool.'

'What are their names?'

'None of your business!'

'It *is* my business, Nellie,' he said firmly. 'Malachy's not here, so he'd expect me to make sure you're all right.'

'No he wouldn't, and I'm going whether you like it or not, *so there*.'

'Fine. I'll cancel Wei and come with you.'

She seethed with a mixture of fury and fright. 'Emmet, don't be such an eejit. You're not my father.'

'Well, maybe I should call Uncle Blackie and Auntie Em and see what they say about it.'

Nellie gasped. She felt like he'd punched her in the gut. All their life she and her cousin had had each other's backs, never telling tales on each other to the adults. 'Emmet, you wouldn't…'

'Wouldn't I?' he said grimly. 'I still regret not going to your parents when you told me about going all the way with that…that…' He paused, then burst out in frustration. 'My God, Nellie, have you learnt absolutely nothing from what happened with Gerard? Is some other ancient creep taking advantage of you? Is that why you won't give me any names?'

She thought of Johnny trying to kiss her and squeezing her breast till it hurt and felt herself go bright red. 'Don't say that, Emmet…'

'Is there a man?'

'I said don't –'

His green eyes burnt with anger. 'There is, isn't there? For God's sake, Nellie, have you got no self-respect?'

She stared at her cousin. She felt sick and her heart was pounding. '*What* did you say to me?'

He brushed his hands back through his coppery hair, struggling to contain himself. 'Look, I'm sorry, but –'

'You think I've got *no self-respect*? Like I'm some kind of…*street walker* or something?'

His temper flashed again. 'I didn't say that, Nellie. Those are your words, not mine. But all right, I admit it, you're frightening me. This is just like when you were sneaking off to Cork and Bandon and wherever, only a million times more dangerous. You were thinking you were in love, when really you were giving yourself away to some… I should have done something…' He stopped, clenching his fists so hard, his knuckles were white.

She couldn't speak; she could hardly get her breath. So this was what he thought of her, deep down. The one person she'd imagined she could rely on, the one person she thought liked her the way she was in fact despised her. He'd only been pretending to be her friend. He didn't think of her as an equal, or clever, or someone who should go back to school, which was what he kept saying to her. No, he looked down on her for what had happened to her. He thought she was a worthless cheap girl with no morals.

Unable even to look at him, she grabbed her bag and jacket and shoved roughly past him, leaping down the stairs so fast she nearly fell.

'Nellie, I didn't mean it! Come back!' he shouted, coming after her.

She slammed out of the house into the California sun and immediately hid behind the corner of the house, where a huge purple bush flowered forcefully out of the gravel. Seconds later he emerged, calling her name.

'Nellie…'

He looked desperately around him as she cowered behind the bush, then he ran off down the street.

'Nellie! *Nellie*!'

On tiptoe, she slunk the other way, sprinted across the garden and then the neighbour's yard, climbed over a fence and headed down the sun-drenched street between square white buildings, taking a roundabout way to the train station.

# CHAPTER 21

Emily sat in the beautifully upholstered rocking chair that Blackie had bought her as a present, feeding Aidan his bottle.

The ease with which this baby had become her child scared her sometimes. She looked down at him, half dozing as he sucked enthusiastically. So far he was a dream, eating, sleeping and just beginning to smile now. Everyone remarked how like Blackie he was – and he was – and Emily just adored him.

He slept in his big Silver Cross pram in the shop when she had to do the books, and everyone admired him. As they did, she felt her heart swell with pride, just as when Nellie had been born. There was much talk of miracles, and various saints were credited with the successful conception and birth of a new baby for her and Blackie after so much heartache. People grumbled sometimes about the gossip any slight occurrence generated in a small town, but in the glow of motherhood, Emily had to concede she would not like to live anywhere else. This was her place, her home, her family's home, and the genuine outpouring of goodwill for her and Blackie was so touching.

Phone calls to America were prohibitively expensive, but she wrote to Nellie every few days and sent some pictures of Aidan, which her daughter had declared were 'sweet', but that was all; she didn't enquire after his health or anything. Nellie wrote only very sporadically, just funny postcards with a line or two about how she was having a great time, and sometimes Emily envied Lena, who got long missives from Emmet each week detailing his whole life.

She was happy her daughter was having fun. The poor girl deserved it; she had been through so much. But she worried as well, though Lena told her not to be anxious and reminded her that Emmet and Malachy were both there to keep an eye on Nellie. Nellie had surely learnt her lesson and was over her 'wild child' period.

Aidan finished his bottle, then did an enormous burp, followed by a grin. She loved the milky, warm, baby powder smell of him and could spend hours just cuddling him, smelling his neck, kissing the folds of fat on his chubby little legs.

She changed his nappy and dressed him in the sweetest little outfit Gwenda and Ted had bought him; they'd had someone send it from Australia, and it had a little koala on the front.

Blackie came up the stairs then, and she smiled up at him as he stood gazing down at her and Aidan, just as he had used to do at her and Nellie.

'What?' she asked.

'Nothing,' he said. 'I'm just admiring you there.' He took Aidan from her and gave him a cuddle.

'I thought you had a load of deliveries this morning?' she said, with pretend disapproval.

'I do.' Blackie crooned at the baby, who smiled. 'But Daddy needed a cuddle, so in between the coal and the cement trucks, he rushed upstairs to see his little man.'

At night, if Aidan stirred, it was always Blackie who went to him. He was awake before Emily even heard the baby, and she often got up to find them both asleep on the sofa, a crochet blanket over them as Aidan slept happily on her husband's chest.

'Blackie, has Fergus been yet? Was there anything from Nellie?' she asked. Fergus was the postman in Kilteegan Bridge, a bone-idle man with a 'bad back', who rarely delivered before lunchtime.

'Yes, he came before lunchtime for a change – he must be wanting to get off early for something. And no, nothing from Nellie.'

'I hope she's all right.'

He leant down to kiss her anxious face. 'Don't go worrying about our Nellie now, Em. She's having a wonderful time over there, I'm sure of it.'

'I suppose so.' She sighed. She heard the lorry draw up outside. 'That's the cement now. You'd best go down.'

'I will, but don't you be fretting up here all afternoon, do you hear me? It's a lovely day. Why not take himself for a stroll and have the whole parish ooh and aah over him? I'll have to do something with that fuse board in the storeroom – there's a loose connection or something. It's buzzing, and there was a spark came out of it yesterday. I was trying to get ahold of Pat Leahy, but it would be easier to get an audience with the pope.'

'Well, whatever you do, don't electrocute yourself. I'll walk up to the Leahy's if you want, see if Colette can get him to call in. I'll carry on up to the farm after. Ted and Gwenda have started on their timber house already. The German man is showing them how, and apparently, they're all working on it, Ted and Jack and Skipper, and Gwenda as well, mixing clay and chopping logs like a mad thing according to Biddy Lambert.' Emily laughed. The parish had been all agog at the idea of a house built without brick or stone, and people were finding all kinds of reasons to be strolling up the Maddens' lane these days for a look.

'Do that.' Blackie kissed her cheek again. 'If one more person suggests I should be put out that they're using free materials from the land around them instead of buying blocks and slates and cement and everything else from us, I'll be arrested for assault. Tell them I'm dying to see it, and I'll be up to give a hand on Saturday. Mam says she can mind the shop.'

'Eli offered too, but I think they politely declined.' Emily chuckled. 'He's not the manual labour kind.'

'I know. Soft hands are the mark of a man with brains to burn,'

Blackie retorted, examining his own calloused hands, 'and 'tis far from mixing cement or chopping trees he was reared.'

'Speaking of hands, he's still not found his wedding ring. He's more upset about it than Lena is. She said they'd get him another one, but he loves it, and it was engraved with their names and the date of their marriage inside.'

Blackie nodded. 'I know. He's been looking everywhere it might be. Jack even wondered if the magpie had it, but they've pulled down every nest in the area and nothing.'

At that moment, Peggy called him from downstairs to warn him the driver had finished his smoke and was anxious to be off. Emily had told Peggy time and again there was no need for her to come into the shop every day, but since Aidan arrived, she'd started coming in full time again, and to be honest, it was very useful.

Blackie handed her the baby. 'I'd better see to the cement, otherwise that fella will land the bags at the door and I'll have to give the day hulking it to the back.' He headed for the door to the stairs.

'See you later, love.' Emily waved Aidan's little hand. 'Bye-bye, Daddy.'

'Bye-bye, son.' Blackie grinned.

# CHAPTER 22

Nellie wished she had the strength to save Dex from himself. He was such a nice boy underneath, so handsome too and so sensitive, but the drugs were destroying him. She'd managed to get him out for a walk that afternoon, and then she'd taken him for a meal in an expensive restaurant, but he'd left his enormous steak almost untouched. And now he was tripping badly on LSD. Since Naomi and Crystal and Cokie had left, nobody in the squat seemed to care a damn if he lived or died.

Dex's twin, Dylan, had already died, over in Vietnam. He'd told her about it in floods of tears one night, how his mother had stuck the US Marines sticker in the window when Dylan went because she was so proud of her son. Dex was refused because he'd had a collapsed lung in his teens, so he was saved going to war, but Dylan wasn't so lucky. When his twin was killed, his mother replaced the sticker with a gold star they sent her and still said she was proud. Dex had just upped sticks from Portland, Oregon, and drove to San Francisco, leaving his college education, his parents, his life, for this existence of drugs, music and casual relationships.

He was so angry about the war, about the waste of life, the sickening need of men who would never have to hold a gun to wage war in a place most Americans couldn't find on a map. On and on he'd rant about it, and Nellie felt so sorry for him; he and his twin had been very close. Nellie thought that if she could only get Dex away from his current crowd, he'd have a chance to get out of this self-destruct mode. He'd even smoked heroin a few times. She'd talked and talked to him about doing less drugs during their walk, and talked some more over the meal that he had been too sick to eat, and he agreed with her and said he would give up everything but marijuana. But as soon as they got back to the squat, someone gave him a tablet of acid and he took it.

Now as she sat and watched him scream at someone who wasn't there, and a girl who wandered by throw up in a corner of the already stinking room, her sense of self-preservation, or maybe what Emmet called self-respect, finally kicked in. Nellie knew she had to get out of there.

She peeled herself off the sticky sofa, stepped over a couple deep in a passionate moment and let herself out.

Out on the street, leaving the squat suddenly didn't seem such a good idea. It was after eleven, so the last train back to Palo Alto was probably gone even if she did want to go home, which she didn't; she was still too angry with her cousin. She would have to stay in a cheap hotel. But then she remembered she hadn't enough money for that; the steak that Dex had refused to eat had cost a lot more than she'd bargained for.

She thought about what else she could do. Malachy had an office in Union Square, and there was a night doorman there, she knew, because Malachy had taken them to the theatre one night and they'd parked his fancy car in the office car park and the doorman greeted them and had a few words. If he was still there, he'd surely help. Maybe she could telephone the house from there and Emmet could book her a room in the city – Malachy seemed to have accounts everywhere – and she could stay overnight and go back in the morning; she had enough left for the train. It would be sickening to have to ask him for help after the way he'd spoken to her, but she had no choice.

She started walking down Fell Street and into Alamo Square. She was proud of how well she could get around the city, which had seemed enormous and intimidating at first but now was manageable. As she walked towards the Western Addition, she began to feel a bit more vulnerable. She skirted around the Tenderloin, an area she had heard horror stories about, sticking to the Nob Hill side where the rich people lived.

Malachy's office overlooked the fanciest square in San Francisco, where all the expensive shops were. As she arrived at the front door, a feeling of dread descended. The place was in darkness, no doorman or anyone to be seen. The night they'd gone to the theatre was a Saturday and today was Tuesday; perhaps there was only somebody there at weekends.

A policeman was standing on the other side of the Dewey Monument that honoured some American general or something – she'd forgotten what Emmet told her about it – but she didn't dare approach him. Every encounter with police in this city had been bad so far, parties getting busted and people like her friends seeming to be at the root of all the police's suspicions. Since someone attempted to assassinate President Ford in the city last year, they were on high alert. If she dressed like Emmet's female friends, she might not alert the suspicion of the cops, but she knew her outfit would be enough to have her arrested probably. She'd had a lucky escape earlier in the day when she'd been questioned on the street with Dex, who stuffed his acid into her bag as he was searched. It was a canvas bag with a peace sign painted on it, and she was carrying it now. Crystal made them and had given her one as a parting gift.

She was getting cold, the midnight mist rolling in off the bay chilling her, even though it was summer. She was only wearing a black bra top, which exposed her midriff and her back – it was tied with a string around her neck and another around under her shoulder blades – and electric-blue satin hot pants, so short you could see the cheeks of her bum. Stupidly, she'd left the squat in such a hurry that she'd left her red jacket hanging on the back of the bathroom door. She was cross about that because it was a favourite; her Nana Peggy had given her the money to buy it last December when they were in Cork doing Christmas shopping.

Tears sprung to her eyes thinking about her Nana Peggy. She wished she was at home so fervently, it was like a physical pain.

She walked on without knowing where she was heading, or why. Her knee-high boots with the platform heels were really uncomfortable now.

*Don't panic,* she warned herself. She would figure this out somehow. A tear formed in the corner of her eye, and she felt such a pang of loneliness. What was she doing here? So far from home, so far from her parents and her nana. She'd been on the run from how dirty she felt, but she seemed to have brought it all with her, the stupidness and the hurt, and her dirty, used-up body.

In that instant she would have given anything to be in her bed at home in Kilteegan Bridge, to hear her dad snoring down the hall, the squeak of the bus stop sign outside the shop swinging on its metal pole, the night stars twinkling all the way out to sea that she would watch from her bed if she kept the curtains open. How she longed for the comfort of someone older and wiser to take charge. If only her dad was here this exact minute. Her mother would be cross with her for getting herself into such a dangerous situation, but Daddy would just hug her and protect her and make everything all right.

'Hi there. I'm sorry, I didn't mean to startle you, but are you all right?'

Nellie spun around to see who'd spoken. It was a girl, a little older than her, in a pair of jeans and a turtleneck sweater with a coat over it. Nellie envied her cosy outfit.

'Ah yes, I'm fine.' Nellie knew enough about the city to know it was best not to engage strangers in chat.

The girl smiled. She had big brown eyes and dark-brown hair tied up in a ponytail. 'It's just you don't look very OK, and it's quite late.'

'I just, em… I lost my purse and I live in Palo Alto, so I'm trying to find a way to contact my cousin.'

'Here, let me help. My name is Aria, by the way. Take my coat.' She removed her woollen knee-length coat and put it around Nellie's shoulders. The warmth was delicious, and Nellie felt a wave of relief pass through her. This girl was nice; she'd help.

'I... Thanks.' Nellie smiled through her tears. 'I wouldn't ask, only I'm desperate, but could you lend me a dime to make a phone call?'

'Sure. How about you come with me? We'll go get a hot cup of coffee, maybe something to eat. I know a place just two blocks away, and we can get warm and make a plan?'

Nellie looked warily at her. Maybe this girl wasn't the guardian angel she desperately needed, but on the other hand, she was all she had. Men weren't to be trusted and she would never go with a man who approached her like this, but Aria was a girl like herself – surely it would be safer with her than being out on the street.

Deciding she would risk it, she fell into step beside the other girl. Aria really was very chatty and friendly; it was going to be fine.

# CHAPTER 23

Emmet had fallen asleep on the sofa waiting for her to call him, ask him for money or something.

He'd met Wei for lunch and told her how worried he was, and about their row, though not the full story because the baby was a secret. Wei had told him not to be such a mother hen, that Nellie was seventeen and had a perfectly good head on her shoulders.

Even so, he'd gone back to the house instead of to the art gallery in case Nellie rang, looking for help. Then he'd spent the rest of the day seething and staring at the phone that didn't ring and wondering who Wei was 'hanging out' with instead. Probably Kenneth – she'd said she was going to call him to see if he was free to come to the gallery and the concert afterwards. She and Emmet were dating, but apparently, they weren't exclusive. This was a new concept to Emmet, and he wasn't sure he loved it. At home if you so much as danced with a girl, the whole parish was expecting you up to the priest to have the banns read, which was a bit too much, but he would have liked a bit more commitment from Wei.

He wasn't short of girls to flirt with if he'd wanted; they all loved his Irish looks and accent in California. They were very different from Irish girls. They were all tall, very thin, tanned and polished, with long straight blond hair, and it seemed like their fathers were all millionaires. They went skiing at Lake Tahoe in the winter, spent summers at 'their place in Santa Barbara', and one had Burt Reynolds for her godfather. They were like beings from another planet. But there was something about Singaporean Wei that intrigued him. She was tiny, barely five feet, with shiny black hair, golden-brown eyes and a handspan waist. She was so driven in her wish to succeed in America, she made him look like a slouch. He'd never met anyone like her. She was fun and fascinating but also kind of terrifying.

Torn between wondering about Wei and worrying about Nellie, he'd fallen asleep, and now it was eight in the morning, with the sun shining in. He ran up to her bedroom, hoping against hope.

Her bed was unslept in.

He tried not to panic. She'd given him the address, 9 Frederick Street, so he could go there and yank her out by her collar if necessary, get her away from these so-called friends of hers, whoever they were. Though she would raise all holy hell at him, especially after he'd practically accused her of being…he didn't know, a loose woman or something. He must have sounded like Monsignor Collins. He wished he could go back in time and unsay what he'd said.

The truth was, he'd assumed when Nellie joined him in California that she would be all meek and grieving and glad to be rescued from her life, but it hadn't worked out like that. She'd rebuffed any efforts at friendliness from Wei or the other girls in his group, preferring instead to keep herself to herself. Or so he'd thought. But in reality, she'd been making friends with…who? Some total lowlife, judging by the address. And he hadn't even noticed.

The telephone rang in the hall. If it was Malachy, should he lie about Nellie having stayed out overnight?

'Hey, Emmet.' It was Wei. 'Any sign of her yet?'

'No, and I'm really worried now.' He was lying. He wasn't just really worried; he was sick with dread. Supposing she got herself in trouble again? Maybe he should call Malachy for help… But Malachy would call Emily and Blackie in Ireland, all hell would break loose, and meanwhile Nellie would probably stroll back in any minute, speaking in her newfound American accent, telling him to be cool and lighten up, then have a meltdown when she found out what he'd done. 'I think I'm going to have to go and find her.'

'Well, if you're that worried, then let's do it,' Wei said cheerfully. 'I'm sure she's fine and all that, but maybe she's run out of money to get home. She did give you the address, so she can't really complain if you turn up.'

Wei was eminently sensible. Her father was the chief of police in Singapore, and she was an only child. Her mother had died of a heart attack when she was ten, so she and her father had managed alone.

'You're right.' Emmet made up his mind. 'She'll be furious, probably never speak to me again if she's even still speaking to me anyway, but if anything happens to her, I'll never forgive myself and my family will never forgive me either.'

'Pick me up by the Hoover Tower. I'll be there in twenty minutes.'

He was surprised and pleased. 'You want to come along?'

'Why not? To be honest, Kenneth was pretty boring company yesterday at the gallery and at the concert. Kept analysing stuff instead of just looking and listening. Even going on a wild goose chase through squatland might be more fun.' And she hung up.

Smiling, Emmet fetched his car keys.

When he picked her up in his Corvette, he was amused to see she was wearing a leather jacket despite the blazing sunshine. Being from Singapore, on the equator, Wei was always cold. He told her once that she must promise to never go to Ireland – she'd freeze to death. Still, he'd like to bring her home one day. The idea of the beautiful Asian girl strolling down the main street of Kilteegan Bridge made him smile. She'd turn heads, that was for sure.

On the drive to San Francisco, she studied a map of the city. 'So this place is in Haight-Ashbury, right? That's a dump.'

Emmet nodded. 'I know. I think she's been there before on the sly. She says they're her friends, but when I said I'd come with her to meet them, she said I wasn't her father and I'd want to lighten up.'

Wei smiled. 'In Singapore, girls are expected to behave a certain way, with decorum, you know, being respectful and obedient, I suppose. That way a girl might catch the eye of a wealthy husband and make a good marriage. It's very restricting. Coming here, where everyone is their own person and can do as they please more or less, it's exhilarating. I find it so anyway, and I'm sure Nellie is finding that too.'

If only Wei knew about Gerard and the baby, thought Emmet. Aloud, he said, 'The difference is you are a mature, sensible adult, and she's a stupid kid that hasn't the sense of a sparrow.'

Wei laughed. 'Maybe she's right, Emmet.'

'About what?' He glanced at her as he eased onto the freeway.

'Maybe you should lighten up.'

Her teasing tone took the sting out of her words, but it made him think. If studious, serious Wei thought he was too uptight, maybe he was? Though not about Nellie; he was right about her. And he still didn't like this weird, unserious dating he and Wei were doing, where she seemed to think it was all right to take Kenneth to the gallery and concert hall instead of him.

'I'm not boring like Kenneth, am I?' he asked, a bit anxious.

'I didn't say you were boring. You're just not that relaxed.'

'You're pretty focused yourself.'

'Sure, in my work. But not in my social life. We don't all have to be the same, though. That's OK. Maybe you find me annoying.'

'You're not annoying. You're sweet.' He smiled.

'Ah, a compliment from the mighty Irishman. Praise indeed.'

'What's that supposed to mean?' He shot her a look of surprise.

'You know very well.' She flicked back her thick black hair and slipped a band around it to make a ponytail. 'You're handsome and clever and that accent melts girls' resolve, but you're mean with your affections. Everyone wants to get to know you, but you don't let them in, not even me.'

'That's rubbish.' He was genuinely taken aback. 'I let you in a lot, whatever that means. I'm Irish, Wei. We don't go in for all that deep and meaningful connection the Americans seem to love so much.'

'And that just adds to your allure, but don't think I don't know what you're up to.'

'And what might that be, oh wise one?'

'Making yourself so mysterious, the rugged Irish man, with the wild Celtic soul, that if only a girl could tame it, he would be hers forever, but his hard exterior repels all but the most valiant or determined.'

Emmet guffawed. 'Are you sure you're not taking English literature instead of engineering? Mysterious and rugged – yeah, right.' He winked at her as he drove. Something about her intrigued and delighted him. She was so forthright, she could be considered rude sometimes, but he loved it about her. With her hair in a ponytail, the sharp corner of her jaw was visible as she mapped their route.

He said, 'Your hair is nice like that. It shows your face better.'

'Buttering me up now to prove you're an emotional being?' Her right eyebrow rose sceptically. 'You'll be trying to get me into bed next.'

'No I won't.' Emmet was slightly hurt but didn't want to show it. She had him all wrong. 'I'm not like that. Forget I said anything.' He concentrated on the road ahead. He could feel his cheeks burning.

'Can't do that, I'm afraid, Mr Kogan. I forget nothing.' She punched him playfully on the shoulder as he drove, and he relaxed and laughed.

They parked in Malachy's building's car park and continued on foot towards Frederick Street. The city wasn't huge, and if Nellie was out and about, they might see her easier if they walked. In the centre of Union Square, a bunch of young people were gathered, playing guitars and singing peace songs. It was a rally of some kind. They stood on the edge of the circle and scanned the crowd, who were crooning, 'Give peace a chance,' but Nellie wasn't there and they walked on.

The address in Frederick Street proved to be a flat over a shop called Fun Rides that sold bicycles painted all sorts of colours and decorated with flower stickers.

The shop was closed, but there was a door beside it slightly ajar. The smell of weed was overwhelming, even from where they were standing on the pavement outside, so it was clearly a hippy hangout. Emmet felt suddenly very conscious of being dressed in a buttoned-up white shirt and formal trousers; he guessed the very sight of him would be anathema to Nellie's friends, just as they would be to him. Wei was in jeans and a light-blue t-shirt under her leather jacket, and while she was in no way a hippy, at least she looked less conservative than he did. As they stood at the door, she pulled her sleek dark hair out of the ponytail, messing it around her face. Instantly she looked cooler and more likely to fit in. Then she pushed at the door and went up the stairs inside, and Emmet followed her.

There was a door at the top of the stairs, and Wei pushed that open too. It led into a large room that had once been opulent but now was filthy. Even over the aroma of weed, the place smelled awful. The large windows looked onto the street, and the carpet was strewn with hot dog wrappers and empty beer bottles. In one corner were several mattresses on the floor with a variety of quilts and blankets balled up over them. There was a large table constructed out of wood planks resting on trestles, and ashtrays overflowed on every surface.

A girl was lolling on the pile of mattresses, a long-legged Black girl in a tie-dyed t-shirt that barely covered her crotch.

'Hello?' said Emmet. The girl rolled her head towards him.

'Hello,' she slurred, eyeing him up. 'I'm Lorraine.'

'Do you know a girl called Nellie?'

'S'no Nellie here, never has been.'

'Oh…' He felt sick, and not just from the stink. 'Are you sure?'

'Sure I'm sure,' she mumbled. 'No Nellie here. Ask Dex if you like. He's the only other one here now. Everyone else moved on today after the cops came. He's asleep in the bath.'

In the bathroom, which stunk and had scraps of torn-up newspaper by the toilet instead of a loo roll, a blond-haired boy was curled up asleep in the brown-stained bathtub. Emmet leant over him, shaking him hard. There was no response, but as Emmet straightened up, he caught a distinct whiff of Charlie by Revlon, Nellie's favourite perfume. He knew the name because she'd asked him to buy her a bottle when she first arrived – she said it reminded her of better times – and she splashed it all over herself every day. He turned with a smile, thinking she must be about to walk in.

The scent was coming from a grubby towel hanging on the back of the door, under which was her red suede jacket. 'That's Nellie's.' He checked the label. 'St Bernard – that's a brand at a shop at home. This is definitely hers.' He drew it to his nose, breathing in her scent. 'She can't have gone far. She wouldn't have left it here – she loves this jacket. Her nana gave it to her. Lorraine was lying.'

'Or maybe knows her by a different name?' suggested Wei reasonably. 'Let's go ask.'

They went back to Lorraine, who was sitting up, looking sick, and Emmet held the jacket in front of her. 'Do you know the owner of this?'

'Yeah, yeah, Danielle. Can you get me a glass of water?'

'Danielle? Did she have long fair hair and –'

'Bright-blue eyes. Yeah. Water.'

'Where is she now?'

'Water…' She wouldn't say anything else until they'd coaxed a rusty dribble of water from the sink on the wall, washing out an empty beer bottle and filling it. After Lorraine gulped it back, her eyes cleared a bit and she grinned at them. 'Poor little Danielle, she's gone. We'll never see her again.'

Wei crouched down beside Lorraine. 'Gone where? With who?'

'The flower girls, pretty little things… Two of them came here this morning to pick up this jacket, but they couldn't find it. They had a couple of super-straight guys with them who accused Dex of selling the jacket, but he took a big extra drag of his joint and whited out while they were shouting at him, so they just picked him up and dumped him in the bath.' She seemed to think this was quite a funny story, but then she gave Emmet a suspicious look. 'Hey, are you one of them?'

'One of who?' He was in shock.

Lorraine glared at him. 'The men who run the flower girls. Make them stand on street corners selling flowers to make money, tell them they're doing God's work, pull all sorts of tricks to control their minds.'

'Emmet's Danielle's cousin. We're worried about her,' explained

Wei gently, still crouching beside Lorraine. 'Emmet, fill her bottle up again, would you? So, Lorraine, where can we find these flower girls?'

Lorraine waited until Emmet returned with the water, drained it, and said, 'Selling flowers of course. Don't join 'em. Worse than drugs. Hey, I gotta go…' She glanced around, as if suddenly realising where she was, and stood then, and on only slightly wobbly legs, made for the door.

* * *

EMMET SAT STARING at the telephone, summoning up the strength to ring Malachy and tell him he'd lost Nellie to some sort of weird cult. They were in Malachy's office in San Francisco, where the doorman had recognised Emmet and kindly let him in to use the phone. He'd known nothing about such groups, but Wei explained they were kind of a feature of life here.

Wei watched him, puzzled. 'Look, don't freak out. She's under eighteen, so we can involve the police if necessary. We'll get her out easily enough if we move quickly, and they're not going to kill her or anything in the meantime. They might be all religious, but they look after their own, so it's not like it's the end of the world. At least they don't take drugs and stuff, and they eat healthy food.'

'I don't know. She's already been through enough…' He pulled himself up short; he hadn't said anything to Wei about Nellie's troubles.

'Emmet.' Wei said his name slowly, as if she was deliberating. 'Tell me to mind my own business if you want to, but why are you so anxious about ringing your father? I've never ever seen him get mad at you. So why do I feel like you walk on eggshells around him?'

He sighed. 'I don't know. It just feels complicated.'

Wei knew that Malachy was his father. Her parents were friends of his, and Malachy in America had never made a secret of Emmet; in fact he liked to show off his son. He had a large photograph of him in the living room, sitting on his pony when he was seven, with Lena holding Ollie's bridle. So Wei was right to ask. Why was he worried about ringing Malachy? His biological father had always been kind, generous and accommodating, he provided him with unlimited pocket money, and he talked of Emmet as his heir. He never shouted at him to tidy up like Eli sometimes did, though at the same time, he never gave Emmet a sudden hug, not like his real dad. It was hard to explain, but everything was a bit more formal with Malachy. It was like they were kind of dancing around each other, like they were in a play or something, Malachy starring as the proud parent, Emmet the golden son.

That's why it was so hard to call Malachy, he realised. Losing Nellie was not just a disaster – it was a failure. And he didn't want Malachy to think badly of his cousin. Much as he liked Malachy and was grateful, Malachy wasn't family.

'Besides, she's not a complete idiot,' continued Wei. 'She'll soon realise what she's got herself into and want to get out again.'

'I don't think it's as simple as that with Nellie,' he said quietly.

Wei sighed, lolling on the velvet sofa in the office while Emmet sat in Malachy's red leather swivel chair behind the enormous mahogany desk. 'OK, here's another question. Why are you so worried about Nellie? She seems pretty confident and capable. What's the deal with her that makes you treat her like she's made of china or something?'

'I…' He stopped.

'Well?' Wei was looking at him with her golden eyes.

He felt a sudden huge wish to confide in her. But could he trust this girl? Right now she seemed to see the disappearance of Nellie as being as much her problem as his, but maybe that was only in passing. Maybe she had as casual an attitude to secrets as she did to relationships.

'You can trust me, Emmet,' she said, as if she could read his mind. 'I won't tell anyone.'

He sighed, resting his elbows on the desk. 'But it's not really my secret. I haven't even told Malachy, and I'm not about to either. Nellie hasn't even told her own parents the half of it. If it got out in our home town in Ireland, she would never be able to hold her head up there again, and if she thought you knew about it, she'd be mortified.

Probably you'd think it was stupid to worry about it if you knew what it was, but Ireland's a long way from California and people talk –'

Wei interrupted him, her voice unusually soft. 'You don't need to explain about social pressure to me, Emmet. I'm Singaporean, and what people do and say, how they behave, is very closely monitored there.' She inhaled. 'And just so you know you can trust me, I'm going to tell you my secret first. My mother didn't die of a heart condition as I said she did. She killed herself. And my father was informed by the officers who were his subordinates that she had been found. It was incredibly hard for us, and deeply personally humiliating for him. My mother was unfaithful to him. He was and is difficult, cold or something, and when she left my father and went to her lover, the man rejected her, so she shot herself. She wrote it all down in a letter, full of self-pity and not a mention of me in the whole thing.' Her tone became hard then, like scar tissue over a deep wound that had never healed. 'It was read in court at her inquest. My father had to stand and listen as men who he'd surpassed professionally, and who were bitter about his success, heard the sordid details of his home life. But he did it. And never discussed it again after that.'

'I'm so sorry –'

She cut him off with a sharp chopping movement of her hand. 'I didn't tell you for sympathy, and I don't want to talk about it. I just wanted to give you something so you know you can trust me. Now shoot. Explain what the problem is.'

Emmet nodded. 'Nellie had a baby – that's why she's here. The father was a much, much older married man, and she had to give the baby up for adoption.' That was enough betrayal for now; the true story of Aidan's new parentage belonged to his aunt and uncle. 'That's why I'm so worried. I'm not sure, but I think she's hurting really badly inside, and she's maybe vulnerable to anyone who shows her what she thinks is love right now. I let her down really badly yesterday. I didn't tell you the whole thing about the row, but I basically panicked and asked her if she was sleeping with some other man and told her she had no self-respect. She was really, really hurt, so this is all my fault.'

He waited for Wei to be furious with him, and she did roll her eyes a bit, but then she said, 'Well, we'll just have to track her down and rescue her, and then you can apologise and I'm sure she'll forgive you. Now call your father. Get it over with.'

He dialled the number and got through to Malachy's secretary, and after a series of clicks she put him through.

Without any small talk, he told Malachy that he and Nellie had had a fight and that she'd stormed off and now he'd found out she had joined some weird cult in San Francisco and had to be got out straight away. He said he was so sorry, that it was all his fault, that he hadn't realised how vulnerable she was feeling.

Brushing aside his apologies, Malachy said calmly, 'I'll be on the first flight I can get back. Just go home and wait by the phone. I'll make some calls.'

'To who?' Emmet panicked. Was Malachy planning to call Kilteegan Bridge?

'I know the chief of police and the city mayor. I'll get this prioritised. These cults are a nuisance, but mainly they prey on girls no one cares about. Not this time.'

Emmet breathed again. 'OK, so we won't say anything in Ireland for now?'

Malachy exhaled as well, and there was a long pause. 'No,' he decided eventually. 'Emily and Blackie don't need to hear half a story when they're so far away, and we'll get this sorted quickly enough. Stay there and I'll see you soon.'

'He wants me to go home and wait by the phone,' Emmet told Wei, pale with relief. 'He says he's going to sort it all out, get the police and the mayor on it.' Never had he been more grateful for Malachy's connections.

'I've an idea as well, which might help,' Wei said, reclining with her arms behind her head.

'What is it?' He was ready to grasp at any straw.

'Well, if they're looking for vulnerable girls, why don't I just go wandering up to one of these girls selling flowers and act like I'm lost and alone?'

Emmet laughed grimly. 'Yes, great idea. So you get abducted too, better and better. So not only would my Auntie Emily string me up and then my Uncle Blackie, I'll have the head of Singaporean police after me as well.'

Wei grinned. 'No, seriously, I bet I can get them to invite me to join. I've heard plenty about these cults. There were lots of warnings all over campus. One of them got a real grip in Berkeley, so the authorities in Stanford did a big campaign, mainly aimed at girls, I think. Anyway, how they work is they're all sweetness and light at the start, luring people in, especially very young, lost girls. And I don't even look my age, I'm so small. Then I can maybe find her and get us both away, or at the very least, discover where they're holding her and let you know.'

Emmet shook his head. 'No way. That's much too risky. That girl Lorraine said these guys were more dangerous than drugs. I don't want you tangled up with them. I'm not sending you in there.'

Wei gave him one of her looks, the one that said, *Please, are you serious?*

'Firstly, Emmet, you could not send me anywhere, so let's get that clear from the off. Secondly, I am a cop's daughter. Americans and Irish might think that you have the monopoly on bad guys, but growing up with my father in Singapore, I can assure you I can look after myself.'

'Wei, no. Just no. What if someone attacked you? Or...I don't know...' Emmet stood and shoved his hands in the pockets of his trousers, staring out the plate-glass window looking over the square.

Next thing he knew, he was flat on his back, Wei's knee in his chest, both his hands trapped beneath his body. 'Ahh...' He gasped and wheezed, winded.

Grinning, she jumped up and pulled him to his feet as he choked down air, getting his breath back.

'What? What was that for? And how did...' He had his hand to his chest, where her knee had applied much more pressure than any person of her size should be able to exert.

'I told you, and I wanted to demonstrate. I can handle myself. My father made me learn Krav Maga, the deadliest form of martial arts in the world. He was responsible for the locking up or execution of some of Asia's most dangerous people, so as his only child, I was always at risk, and so he had me become proficient in self-defence in case anyone ever attacked me or tried to kidnap me or anything like that. So, as I say, I can handle myself.'

'But how did you… I mean, you're tiny…'

She laughed at his open-mouthed incredulity. 'It's not about size – it's about strategy. Anyway, it doesn't matter now. I just wanted you to see I'll be all right. So are we going?'

He felt very far out of his depth. 'Shouldn't we wait for Malachy? He said to go home and wait.'

Wei shook her head decisively. 'No, just call Juanita and ask her to stay near the phone and take any messages. If the police and city officials start sniffing around and asking questions after Malachy calls them, these guys will realise someone is looking for her and maybe whisk her away, then we'll have to start over, looking for her in some other city where your father's not so well-connected. So we need to do it now, in case they move on. We'll find one of these girls, and I'll go up to them. You can watch from a distance, and if they take me off somewhere, you can follow, and hopefully they'll lead us to wherever they're living in the city. Even if they have more than one house, and I end up in the wrong one, I can keep my ear to the ground and get news of her.' She patted him on his painful chest, which would be bruised tomorrow. 'This is a good idea, Emmet. Trust me.'

'Do I have a choice?' he groaned.

'No.' She winked. 'Now are you coming or not?'

'You are a genius, Wei, you know that, but absolutely terrifying too,' he said ruefully.

'Oh, you've no idea, Irish boy, none.' She grabbed her leather jacket and bag and strode out of the office, leaving him to follow her.

# CHAPTER 24

It was her second or even third week out selling flowers on the street, maybe more; she'd lost track of the days and nights after being taken to her wonderful new home by Aria, the girl she'd met after leaving the squat. And she had a new name as well as a new life. She was Eleanor now. She had been born again as a different person, one who wasn't a dope smoking waste of space like Danielle, and who didn't have to carry the sins of Nellie Crean.

Nellie had been in so much pain and hurt that she'd told Aria everything that first night, about the older married man, the baby. The whole sordid story had come tumbling out, right up to her time in the squat spent smoking weed. But Aria and several other girls had clustered around her and hugged her and made her welcome in her new home. Apparently nobody there had a family but the one in the Mother House, as they called it, and that family loved her despite her sins in the past. They said she was run down from the life she was living, not enough nutrition, too much alcohol, drugs, and she needed them to build her up again. They gave her hot food and vitamin pills and a bed to sleep in, and much of the time after that had passed in a warm blur.

Sometimes she wondered whether Emmet was looking for her,

but Aria said if he hadn't noticed she was hanging out with drug addicts, he obviously didn't care that much about her. And his life was going in a different direction from hers anyway. He was putting his faith in the wrong kind of God – money – and his friends were all wrongdoers, college-educated people who thought science had all the answers, who had lost their way. She'd been a different person back then when she knew her cousin, a sinner, someone who had strayed off the path of righteousness, but she was forgiven now, the slate wiped clean, and she was better off among friends who would watch over her night and day and keep her safe.

At other times, she worried her parents might wonder why she was no longer sending them postcards, or expect her home at the end of the summer, but again Aria urged her to leave it all behind. She'd found a better, more caring family, and she was doing a kind thing by leaving her past-life mam and dad to live their lives with their new baby. She might miss her original family, but as Aria said, they were getting on without her. They had a baby to love, and that little boy would fill any space Nellie's absence might create. And she could always pray for them if she wanted to feel close.

As well as that, the nightly lectures she'd been attending often gave harrowing accounts of people who made contact with their families, who in turn contacted the police. This led to long prison sentences for everyone, because the judiciary and the politicians wanted to silence the truth speakers, to stop them shining a light on the corruption and sin these people were involved in.

There were about twenty other girls in the Mother House, which was one of three in San Francisco and one of a hundred nationwide, and Aria was her most constant, closest friend. It was like being at a boarding school, all of them sleeping on tiny metal cots in a huge white-painted attic room that stretched the length and width of the house. There were some men around as well as the girls, but they tended to be older and were distant and aloof and never even acknowledged her existence, which suited her fine. The men lived separately, in their own private rooms in a modern one-story annex. Aria explained the separation was for the sake of modesty; often they had girls who were too flirty. So the only time Nellie saw the few men at all was in the lecture room on the ground floor, or when everyone was in the refectory at big long tables, eating bland, vegetarian food, the same thing every day, rice and what looked like a kind of stew but with beans and tomatoes in it.

She was still given vitamin tablets with her meals to build up her strength, and she'd been provided with warm and comfortable clothes. There were two different outfits. When selling flowers on the street, the girls wore conservative but normal clothes like the ones in Maureen's Fashions back in Kilteegan Bridge – skirts to the knee, jumpers that Americans called sweaters, blouses, tights that they called pantyhose and plain flat shoes. But in the Mother House, everyone wore what were really just white pyjamas – wide-legged trousers and a tunic.

Nobody owned any of these white outfits personally, so when you washed in the evening, you put your street clothes away and changed into the home clothing, which was all folded on shelves outside the shower room. The trousers had elasticated waists, so they more or less fit everyone, though one of the girls, Angelica, was a bit overweight so she was only allowed half rations of food until she fit more comfortably in the home clothes. Nellie had to tighten the drawstring on hers to stop them falling down.

She'd seen Angelica go into a store one day when they were out selling and buy a cake, but although Nellie said nothing, Angelica got found out. There was a paddle, and she was beaten. Nellie hated to hear her cry, but afterwards they were so kind to her, soothing her and hugging her and telling her how lucky she was to have finally found the road to happiness. Aria explained to Nellie that the punishment was so Angelica would understand that gluttony was a sin. Eating too much food, and especially too much food with fat and sugar in it, meant the person's willpower was weak, and that was no good. It was vital to have willpower in order to keep to the right path and find the unlimited love waiting for you.

Everywhere Nellie turned, people explained to her about the unlimited love in store, about God, about a man in some country far away called the Messiah, and about how it was necessary to follow the Messiah's rules of life, which seemed fine to her, especially as chastity featured heavily. They also needed to wash day and night. Cleanliness was next to godliness, and just as Jesus washed the dust off his feet, all the girls must wash the dirt off their bodies as well as out of their souls.

These friends were so much better for her than her last lot of so-called friends. They talked about her sins, sins of the flesh, and how the path to enlightenment could not be seen through the dark murk of her past. Luckily for her, they said, she'd been saved. Dex and the others hadn't understood how dirty she was inside; they'd talked about sex like it was a good thing. She hadn't even dared tell them she knew about sex already, or about the baby and Gerard; they'd have just taken that to mean she was happy to sleep with anybody. This new group of friends understood and sympathised with how she felt used up and filthy, and they promised to make her whole again. It was like she was being reborn, fresh and new and innocent.

There were still times, if she woke in the night, that she forgot where she was. She'd wait to hear the rumble of her dad's rhythmic snoring from down the hall, or the birds' dawn chorus in the tree behind the shop where she and Emmet had a treehouse, or she'd imagine she got a whiff of her nana's apple tart, or heard a snatch of her mam singing tunelessly as she washed the ware in the sink. A deep longing for home would threaten to overtake her, and sometimes she cried. Then Aria or one of the others would give her some extra vitamin pills and tell her again about the wisdom of the Messiah, the love of God, and she'd go to sleep again. And in the morning, she would decide that it was quite nice just to exist, not to have to make decisions or take responsibility for anything, just be told what was good for her by people she trusted. It was so much better than being Nellie or Danielle, who both thought they could make decisions for themselves and so made terrible ones.

Aria was right – she was safer in here. And what's more, she was part of something good and noble. Her new friends were working hard towards a wonderful future, a world with no war, where people just loved each other, though it could only happen if this Leader man was elevated to a position from where his wisdom and goodness could be spread to the whole world. And of course he needed money to fight all the corruption, all the evil warmongering politicians who wanted the destruction of mankind.

That's where she and the other girls came in. All she had to do was sell these flowers on the street. The money would go towards the Leader winning power and changing the world for the better. Power where, or what the money was actually for, was a bit hazy. They did explain, but she didn't really understand. She assumed it was because she was a bit stupid, unlike Emmet and Wei and the others back at Stanford.

When she wasn't too sleepy, she enjoyed the travelling to different cities up and down the coast, beautiful places like Santa Cruz and Solvang and Carmel. She loved looking at the ocean; it reminded her of West Cork. Standing on the street hour after hour was hard work, but everyone was so happy with her when she sold loads of flowers. Men liked to buy them from her mostly. She felt awkward when a man was talkative and got her into conversation, but Aria had told her always to smile and make the customer feel as if she liked him, and it was nice to come back home with lots of money and feel so appreciated.

Today she was in San Francisco, but yesterday she'd been selling flowers in a seaside town called Monterey, and on the way home, driven in a van by one of the aloof, distant men of the Mother House, they'd passed through the town of Salinas. All around the town was a lush green valley, where workers, mainly from Mexico she was told, worked in the fields harvesting fruit and vegetables. She remembered some people in the squat getting work there, picking vegetables and fruit. It looked like paradise. She saw a sign that said 'Welcome to the Home of Steinbeck'. A memory flashed of a book they'd read in school called *Of Mice and Men* by someone called Steinbeck, and she wondered if it was the same person. It was one of the few books she'd liked. It was about friendship and how far people were willing to go to protect a friend.

'Is that the Steinbeck that wrote *Of Mice and Men*?' she asked Aria, who always sat beside her. She noticed that each new recruit always had the same person with them all the time, acting as their 'mentor'. It was how they looked out for each other, she supposed.

'It is. Did you read it?'

Nellie nodded. 'I did, at school, back in Ireland. I liked it.'

'Me too. I liked how George and Lenny looked out for each other, how they stuck together even when the whole world seemed to be against them, and how they were right but the world was wrong. It's a bit like us, isn't it?'

Aria gave her one of her wide, warm smiles. She was, Nellie had learnt, twenty-four, but she looked younger. She was from Nebraska originally, which was in the middle of the country, but now the group was her home. Wherever they were, that's where she belonged. It was the secret to happiness, she often explained, working side by side for a better future with people you loved and who loved you. She painted such a beautiful picture.

'It is like us,' Nellie agreed, and smiled back.

Now, here on the streets of San Francisco, the evening was drawing in. Her bucket was very heavy. She'd been there for hours, since early morning, and even the late-night shops were closing and the other girls had gone; they'd been called away by their mentors. Had Aria forgotten her? She couldn't leave her post until she was called home – she had to show her commitment. And anyway God was always watching over her, protecting her, and she didn't have to be afraid.

A policeman approached her and asked her name. She told him Eleanor Crean, the name she went by now.

'And where are you from?' the officer asked, writing her name down.

'Palo Alto,' she said, adopting her best Californian accent. She was a good, quick mimic, and she really felt American now. The past was over, back there. Her parents had a new child, a better one, one that wouldn't cause them heartache like she had. They were better off that way.

'Palo Alto?' The policeman made a note of that as well. 'But you're from Ireland originally? And might you be called Nellie sometimes, for short?'

Nellie's brain had been kind of foggy – she needed to sleep and was really hungry too – but now she went on full alert. She needed to get rid of this officer. He seemed to know who she was. He must have been spying on her. He was on the side of the wrongdoers, like all the cops were in America. The wrongdoers profited from sin, evil, drugs, alcohol, casual sexual relationships, and they wanted people like her and Aria to stop fighting for a better, kinder world. They hated how people like Nellie shone a light on their sins, showed people a better way. Out in the world, the authorities were not to be trusted. They might say they were for your good, but they never were; it was only a way to trap you in the wrongdoers' sinful ways. So she had to be careful, tell them nothing. They were in the darkness, and she was in the light.

'Irish?' She laughed, and her voice sounded strange to her own ears. 'No, officer, no, not at all Irish. And why would I be called Nellie?' She laughed shrilly again.

He moved closer, smiling. 'Now, miss, I think you'd better come with me.'

'Eleanor!' Aria jumped out of a car, grabbed Nellie's hand and pulled her away. 'Quick, get in.'

'Hey! Hey! Nellie!' The officer tried to stop her, but Aria bundled her into the back seat of the car and jumped in beside her, and within minutes they were back at the Mother House.

Both of them were having a hot shower as Aria apologised over and over for leaving Nellie too long while she looked after another girl who had taken ill; she'd called a car from the Mother House to bring the sick girl home before coming back for Nellie.

'Imagine, they could have kidnapped you! I'd never forgive myself. Oh, Eleanor, there are such evil men out there. If we'd been a moment longer…'

Once they'd finished showering, Aria brought her down to the ref and found some food for her. It felt so good to be rescued. The leftover dinner was vegetarian, as all their food was – it was inhumane to eat animals, as Aria had explained to her – but it was still warm and tasty enough, and she was happy to eat it. Two of the purple vitamin tablets were beside her water glass, and she swallowed them down gratefully. She was home.

# CHAPTER 25

Eli opened the door, to find Emily and Blackie smiling on his doorstep, along with little Aidan wrapped in a big fluffy blanket in his carrycot.

'Pat Leahy has had to cut off the electricity to do a quick fix on the wiring, so we're here begging our dinner.' Emily laughed as she kissed her brother-in-law's cheek.

'You're more than welcome – there's plenty. Sarah's at the farm, and Pádraig has gone to a friend's for the night. How are things, Blackie?' Eli shook his brother-in-law's hand.

'Grand altogether, Eli, only that we've not had a card from our wild daughter in a couple of weeks. What she's doing over there on a daily basis, we don't know, but if she doesn't get in touch soon, we'll be having to go over there and find her ourselves, won't we little man?' Blackie cooed at Aidan.

'Ah sure, they're probably having too much fun. Emmet's as bad. We haven't heard from him for a couple of weeks either,' Eli said cheerfully.

'I know I'm probably being like a clucking hen.' Blackie sighed. 'And you're right, she's probably having a great time. But to send the odd postcard wouldn't kill her, surely.'

Lena was delighted to see her sister and brother-in-law and got down two more plates for the dinner of bacon, cabbage and boiled potatoes mashed with butter and cream. The whole thing was covered in delicious parsley sauce, all the ingredients from Jack's farm. They sat around the table, chatting about the goings-on in Kilteegan Bridge. The subject of Fintan Slattery's leg came up of course; the fairy curse was the talk of the place since the old farmer had appeared in the Donkey's Ears with his leg perfectly healed and admitted to everyone how he'd propitiated himself to the hawthorn tree back in May.

Eli laughed. 'For once the gossip is right. He did exactly as Vera told him to do, went down to the tree on May Day, said a prayer down there of abject contrition and then left some poitín and some cream and butter and things like that. And lo and behold, his leg was on the mend before the week was out. It was a slow recovery but steady, and the last time I looked, there wasn't even a scar left behind.'

'And Eli believes in the Good People now, don't you, Eli?' Lena teased him, offering everyone more bacon.

'I don't know, but I'll tell you something, Lena – it wasn't anything I did. I failed miserably and was all out of ideas, so fairies, his wife, the power of prayer, sheer luck, I've no idea, but whatever he did, it worked, so I'm not going to be the one to say it wasn't the Good People. See, I even try to call them the name Vera told me, the Good People, not fairies.'

'Well, I don't know.' Emily smiled. 'But our father would never have touched a fairy tree and neither would Jack. So it's not nothing, but I'm glad he's getting better. The poor man was in an awful way.'

'Did you hear what the Monsignor had to say about it, though?' Blackie grinned.

'No?' Eli was intrigued. His dealings with Monsignor Collins had been very rocky in the past due to their differing views on contraception, to put it mildly, though the priest had quietened down since Dr White had been struck off.

'Well, apparently someone mentioned to Monsignor Collins that Fintan had been healed up at the fairy tree, and he said it was total nonsense and that they were not to believe a word of all the old heathen codswallop, that it was Dr Kogan cured him with antibiotics and that was all there was to it.'

Lena pealed with laughter. 'Well, what do you know, Eli? You were public enemy number one, but at least you're better than the fairies, is that it?'

'So it would seem.' Eli's laugh resonated in his chest. 'Vera fixed my left hand, though,' he added, helping himself to more potatoes. 'I tried everything and nothing worked, but she rolled some spiders' webs over my skin and told me to wash my hands in water from a holy well, and don't ask me how, but it worked. And I tried the same on Thirteen, and look at her now, bounding around with the two new dogs like she's young again.'

Blackie finished eating, placing his knife and fork together. 'I'll tell you something, Eli. You'll not find a person around here that doesn't believe that Vera Slattery has some skill.'

'Lena told me about you being cured of whooping cough by being passed under the belly of a donkey when you were a boy?' Eli grinned.

'Yes indeed, and it worked a treat along with the turnip and the brown sugar. But no, that was Madge Kelly, the mother – Madge Farrell was her married name – but I'm talking about Vera herself. The other day, she told my mother to look in the pocket of an old bag of my father's, just thrown on a shelf in the storage room behind the shop. Era, I'd say 'twas there these fifteen years, covered with cobwebs and the whole lot. But anyway, my mother did it, and sure enough wasn't there a hundred pounds in the pocket, just rolled up, no explanation.'

'Really?' Lena was fascinated. 'Peggy never told me that. That's like my story about the key, isn't it, Eli?'

He nodded. 'It is.'

'Peggy couldn't believe it,' Emily said, 'because Dick never had a shilling to his name, but there it was. He might have won it on a horse or something and got so drunk he forgot. She was almost ashamed of how it was found, through fairy magic. She wanted to put it in the church poorbox, but I talked her out of it. I told her to buy herself a really nice set of paintbrushes and art supplies. She's always scrimping and saving, but we went to Cork with the money and she got loads of stuff. She was like a child in a sweetshop in the art supply place.'

'Ah, that's great.' Lena smiled. 'And I can't get over how talented she is. The painting she did of Second Chance for Emmet to take to America with him is incredible. She's amazing.'

Blackie beamed with pride. His mother had been dealt a poor hand in life: an abusive father; sold into marriage to Dick Crean, a total waste of space; and one of her two sons turned out to be just like his father and had to be got rid of permanently last year. She'd slaved in the hardware shop all her life, and what little profit there was, Dick put over the bar in the Donkey's Ears. But now Dick was dead and Jingo was gone, never to return if he knew what was good for him, and she finally had peace.

In that environment, her talent for art had blossomed even further. She'd done two more courses after the night class in the school, and now she was rarely seen without paintbrushes or canvas.

'Speaking of Peggy's pictures,' said Eli, 'I hear she has one done of how Ted and Gwenda's new house will look based on the plans, which is like the eighth Wonder of the World according to Kilteegan Bridge. I met Jack and Skipper earlier when I was coming back from checking on Mrs Lenihan and her new baby. They're delighted with Gwenda, she's a marvel by all accounts, making a great job of Maddens already. It's turning into a great relationship between the two farms.'

'Yes, he told me the same when he came in for sheep nuts.' Blackie nodded. 'Apparently Ted knows his stuff too and the two girls are up to their elbows in it, no bother to them, and sure they're horse mad, so they're delighted to be here.'

'And is Bill managing not to follow Gwenda around, telling her what to do?' Eli joked. Bill Madden's addiction to his farm and his belief that nobody else could do it right were legendary in the family.

'Well, he is, I think, but Gwenda is well able for him. He told her she was setting up the crush for the bull calves all wrong, and she asked him what was the biggest number of beef cattle he'd ever owned. He said fifteen or something like that, and quick as you like, she replies, she says, "Talk to me, mate, when you've castrated five *hundred* bull calves in one day."'

Everyone laughed.

Blackie helped Eli clear the table and wash the pots and plates, then took the doctor outside to show off the new-to-him car he'd bought last week.

Happy, her belly full of her sister's excellent cooking, Emily stood and warmed up Aidan's bottle in a hot pan on the range.

'So what's up with the electrics?' Lena called to her from the scullery as she stored away the leftover bacon.

'Oh, I don't know.' Emily sat back down to feed Aidan his bottle. 'Pat Leahy says the whole place needs rewiring. It's the original that was put in years ago, and then was done on the cheap, but it's going to cost a fortune.'

Lena came back into the kitchen, looking concerned. 'Are you stuck for it?' she asked.

Emily shrugged. 'Well, we're just in a bit of a tight spot. Nothing we can't manage, but opening the two other shops so close together and all the costs of fitting them out and stocking them, not to mention paying for Nellie in the nursing home – not that I regret it – has left cashflow a bit tight, as they say. We'll manage, just about, and the new shops are doing well, but it will be a long time before they're in the black. Luckily the shop here kind of funds the whole operation.'

'So when will you go for the full rewiring job?' Lena asked.

'Soon enough. We'll just postpone it for a few months, and once the two other shops are paying for themselves, we'll do it then.'

'Is it dangerous?'

'Ah sure, I suppose if we were to leave it, eventually it would be, but we've survived this long.'

'Well, we could probably...' her sister offered.

Emily smiled at her warmly. 'Ah, you're very good, but no, we'll be fine. As I say, just a bit of a cashflow thing. I decided I'm going to do a whole lot of Christmas stuff this year, decorations and things like that, but I had to pay for them at the trade fair last March, so that's all just sitting there as stock I can't put out until November.'

'Well, don't be stuck. If you need it quicker than that, we can find it somewhere.' Lena took Aidan from her arms to burp him. 'I'd say ask Mam, but she's helped Ted out with the cost of the farm this year out of her own half of the inheritance, so she might not have it until he pays her back.'

The telephone in the hall pealed, and Lena gave Aidan back to Emily and went to answer it.

Emily listened with half an ear while she continued to burp the baby, gently rubbing his back. She couldn't hear Lena saying much, and she wondered who it was. After a couple of minutes, she heard her sister put down the receiver, not on its cradle by the sound of it but with a clunk on the wooden phone tabletop, then go to the front door and open it. *It must be a patient for Eli,* Emily thought. But instead of calling for the doctor, Lena called for Blackie.

'Now who is looking for your Daddy?' Emily cooed at little Aidan, who was nodding off against her shoulder. 'Is it Nana Peggy, do you think?' Peggy sometimes telephoned of an evening, just for a chat, when she was too settled in front of her own fire to bother to leave the house and pop round instead.

She heard Blackie come into the house and the murmur of voices in the hall, Eli's voice as well, then Blackie picking up the phone. A few moments later, Lena came back into the kitchen. Emily smiled up at her, then froze inside. Her sister's face was so pale. 'What? What is it?'

Lena opened her mouth, but no words came out.

'Lena, tell me, what's the matter? Who is that on the phone talking to Blackie?' Emily was terrified, though she kept her voice to a whisper so as not to wake the baby. 'Tell me it's not the fire brigade. Oh, Lena, has the shop… Have I jinxed it by talking about it?'

'No, no, nothing like that,' said her sister quickly.

'Then what?' A worse thought struck her. 'Has something happened to Peggy?'

'No, Emily, and please don't panic. Everything's going to be all right. It's being sorted out. But that's Malachy on the phone.'

'Malachy Berger? Is it Nellie?'

'Look, don't panic, Em. Nellie's fine. She was seen only yesterday…'

'Seen?'

'I don't know the whole story, but Malachy's just explaining it to Blackie now. Let's wait until he –'

'No. Tell me what you know.' Emily forgot to whisper this time, and Aidan gave a little wail. 'Shh, shh, shh,' she soothed him, then begged in low anguish, 'Lena, tell me.'

Lena hesitated, with a glance at the door.

'Lena, please, my heart can't take this.'

'All right, Em.' Her sister sat down and took her hand, still pale. 'Try to stay calm, but it seems Nellie has fallen in with some sort of… um…religious people…in San Francisco.'

'Some…what?' Emily was confused; this didn't sound too bad. 'Religious people? You mean ones who aren't Catholics?'

'No, that's right, they're not Catholic. It seems to be some sort of religious organisation that recruits young girls to sell flowers…'

'Flowers?' repeated Emily, bewildered.

'And they seem to get them thinking about religion in a way I suppose they wouldn't normally do, like they teach them their ways and they all live together and –'

'Are you telling me my daughter has joined a cult?' Emily struggled to keep her voice down; she felt like she might faint. Like everyone in Kilteegan Bridge, she was in horror of cults. The Monsignor had a particular terror of them and often preached about how no gurus should be allowed into Ireland, bringing their satanic, heathen ways with them and kidnapping Irish teenagers and moving them to bolt-holes all over the US and into South America, Canada and even further afield to Africa or Asia.

Lena squeezed her hand soothingly. 'That's how it looks, yes.'

'How long has this been going on?' Emily whispered.

'Three weeks.'

'Nellie is in a cult for three weeks, and I'm only hearing about it now? How could Malachy not have told us she's been missing?' It was hard not to scream with fury, she felt so distraught. Only the baby in her arms stopped her.

'She's not missing, Em, I told you that. They know where she is, and she's fine and healthy. The police have been keeping an eye on her, ready to pick her up as soon as they can get her alone, but it seems these people keep her carefully monitored. Also the police are hoping to launch a big case against them, so they don't want to undo months of work by going in after Nellie or something – I'm not too sure. It's part of a bigger investigation, I think. Malachy's very well-connected, and they have a lot of officers on the case. She ran away when one of them talked to her, but they'll get her the next time, or it might have to end up in a raid to get her out. That's why Malachy rang – he wanted you to know that everything's all right in case it gets in the papers.'

'Oh God, oh God.' She felt herself trembling like a leaf. If she could leave the baby... But she couldn't; he was too young... 'Blackie will have to go over there.'

Lena frowned slightly. 'That's not a good idea, Em. Malachy says the police say close family are often the worst ones to try and get their loved one back.'

Emily bristled at the insult to her husband. 'A lot he'd know about close family. Of course she'll want to see Blackie. Nellie adores him –'

Her husband came bursting into the kitchen at that point, and his face told of the terror he felt. 'Oh, Emily, what will we do? Malachy's after telling me –'

'I know,' said Emily, suddenly feeling much calmer. When her husband was in a panic, it was her job to be the steady one. 'Lena's told me – our daughter's joined a cult. What we're going to do is, you're going to go and get her out. You just need to explain to those guru types that Nellie's not one of them. She won't want to be. She hates going to Mass, let alone living in a cult, and she'll be so happy to see you, she'll come right away.'

He looked hugely relieved to have a ready-made plan laid out for him. 'Right. You're right, Em. I'm going over there. I'll get her back, don't you worry. There's nobody – and I don't care who they are – going to stop me going in there and getting her.'

'Blackie, I understand you want to go,' said Lena patiently. 'I'd be the same. But Malachy is friendly with someone high up in the police, and they know what they're doing, so maybe we should just wait and let them do their job.'

To Emily's relief, her husband shook his head adamantly. 'Lena, I don't care what the American police say. I'm going to get our daughter. I'll take all the help any policeman or anyone else is willing to offer, but she's ours and I'll get her back myself.'

Lena opened her mouth to protest again, but Eli, who had come in behind Blackie, shot his wife a warning glance and said, 'Sure, Blackie, it's your and Emily's call to make.'

'Could I telephone the airport from here, see if I can book a plane?' Blackie asked his brother-in-law nervously. 'Is that how you do it?'

'Of course, Blackie, and I'll come with you to do it.' Eli put his hand on Blackie's shoulder. 'The operator will put us through, and we'll sort you out.'

As soon as Blackie had left the room, Emily stopped feeling calm and sank into a chair and started crying, her tears dripping onto Aidan's tuft of black hair. Lena fetched her a small brandy and took Aidan, whose eyelids flickered, and returned him to his carrycot, where he settled and closed his eyes again.

'Lena, where is she?' Her tears were falling in earnest now. She pushed the brandy away; her sister had forgotten she hated spirits. 'Why can't things be simple? What did we do wrong, Blackie and I, that Nellie turned out like this? We should never have let her go over there in the first place. She was too young and too upset by everything. And it wasn't right to put the responsibility for her on Emmet, or Malachy Berger, who barely knows her. We're her parents, she's ours to mind...'

'You didn't do anything wrong, Em.' Lena knelt beside her chair and took both her hands in hers. 'You've supported Nellie all the way, but she must have been more damaged than we realised by everything that had happened and she's acting out.'

'She kept saying she was fine,' sobbed Emily. 'I should have known.'

'You can't read people's minds, Emily, not even if they're your own flesh and blood. I never know what Jack is thinking for instance.'

'But she's my daughter. She's a physical part of me…'

Eli and Blackie came back in, and Emily's husband was looking much happier. 'There's a flight from Dublin first thing,' he told her. 'I'll have to go to London and from there to New York and then get a connecting flight to San Francisco, but it can be done. I don't care what I have to do, or who I have to batter, I'll be bringing her home with me, Em, I promise you that.'

'I know you will, Blackie.' She smiled up at her big, strong, but unworldly, husband, wiping the recent tears from her eyes. Apart from the ferry trip to London, he'd never left Ireland, and he'd certainly never flown in an airplane, but here he was, prepared to make this long trip all alone. She'd always taken the lead in their marriage, but Blackie was clearly determined to do this, and she was impressed with how solid and strong and determined he was being.

He looked anxious again. 'Though it's going to cost almost seven hundred pounds, Em, because it was all last minute. Do we have it?'

Her heart sank. They didn't have that much, or she would have already spent it on getting the wiring fixed. Before she could decide how to break it to Blackie that he wouldn't be going after all, Eli stepped in.

'If you don't have it as cash right now, we can lend it to you. No rush to get it back to us,' he said, with a glance at Lena, who nodded. 'We have enough cash in the safe because I was going to pay the pharmacy bill tomorrow, but they won't mind waiting till next month. They bill me every quarter, so I got the cash out of the bank yesterday. I'll just go and get it.'

'Thanks, Eli. That would be a great help, just till we can rearrange some things,' said Emily gratefully, and Blackie shook his hand warmly.

'Thanks, Eli, thanks very much.'

'You'd do the same for me,' said Eli. 'I feel like I should come with you, Blackie, or someone should.'

'Not at all. I'll be fine, and sure Malachy Berger will be there at the other end, and your Emmet, together we'll get her back.'

Emily, who had been thinking like Eli, made a quick decision. She couldn't let Blackie navigate his first flight all alone without her with him to make sure he at least got on the right plane in Dublin with all his tickets and his passport – luckily he had one for going to England – and his travel itinerary and maps and Malachy's phone number and everything else he would need. 'Could you mind Aidan tonight, Lena? I'll go with Blackie to Dublin and see him on the plane, and I'll drive back tomorrow. Peggy can open the shop, and I'll be back in the afternoon.'

'Ah, Em, there's no need to,' Blackie protested.

'No, love, I'm going with you.'

'And there's no problem minding Aidan,' Lena said. 'And let me make you a picnic for the road before you go, a flask and some sandwiches. There'll be nowhere open at this time of night.'

'Thanks, Lena. Right, Blackie, we'll go home, get a bag together, so that'll be fine, and Aidan's things, nappies, his bottles and his baby formula and everything he needs. And I'll ring Peggy to open the shop early in the morning – there are several deliveries.'

'I've a much better idea,' said Lena as she quickly fetched down a loaf of bread and started slicing the remains of the ham they'd had for dinner. 'Sarah is up at the farm tonight – Skipper and herself and Ted's girls are going to see a horse in the morning – and Pádraig is sleeping at his friend Cormac's house, so how about Eli and I come with you now and stay at your place? Pat will have the power back on by now. Aidan can have his own cot and everything and all his stuff is there, so he'll be more settled, and I can open up the shop early in the morning.'

'That's a much better plan.' Emily nodded. 'Thanks, Lena, you're just... Well, I don't know what we'd do without you.'

'You'll never have to find out.' Lena smiled at her. 'And everything will be all right, Em. Blackie will have her back to you in no time. I'd say she'll be rescued before he even arrives, but it's great he'll be there to bring her home safe.'

Emily nodded bravely. 'I know he will,' she said firmly, though she wished she felt as confident as Lena about this.

As it happened, Lena was no more confident than Emily, and was at that very moment offering up a silent prayer to her dad and Doc to watch over Nellie and protect her until she could be restored to her family.

# CHAPTER 26

Nellie sat with about twenty other girls in a lecture room listening to the new Master speaking about the need for obedience, the need to comply with the rules of his house for the greater good, not just for themselves but for the whole sinful world. People disregarding the rules of their Master were really disregarding the rules of the Leader, and that was what had the world in the mess it was in.

It reminded her a bit of Monsignor Collins, with his passion for the pope, and she felt a stab of unease at the thought of him. The priest would be less than impressed if he could see her now. He would probably call this a cult, but it wasn't – it was just a group of like-minded people worshipping the Supreme Being by living lives of purity.

She let her gaze drift to the Master, and to her surprise, she found he was looking straight at her. The Master of the last house had been tall, bony and dark-skinned. This one was of middle height, slightly plump, clean-shaven with pink and white cheeks, a big nose, large teeth between thin red lips, and small pale-blue eyes. He smiled at her, and she smiled back, startled, then dropped her gaze. All the other girls had their eyes on their laps. The girls weren't supposed to look at the men of the house under any circumstances, though the Master hadn't seemed to mind. Maybe it was different for him because he was like a saint; he couldn't spoil anyone's purity nor have his own disturbed.

Her mind wandered again, wondering how Aria was getting on without her. There had been a big panic in the Mother House when the policeman tried to kidnap her, and she'd been moved to this other, stricter house on the outskirts of the city. It was her first day here today, and it felt like a punishment. Her new mentor, a woman of nearly thirty called Heidi, wasn't anything like as nice as Aria. She pinched and poked at Nellie, and the rules were a lot more strictly enforced. No talking to anyone except your mentor. No looking at the men at all if you didn't want to spend your whole day meditating on your knees on the tiled floor of your cubicle.

A wave of excited gasps brought her attention back to the present; the Master must have said something of interest. He was leaving the room now, and the girls were standing up, ready to go to the refectory to eat, each of them murmuring to their mentor.

'What did he say?' Nellie whispered to Heidi.

'You should pay attention,' Heidi whispered back with a disapproving frown.

'I'm sorry, I just didn't catch it...'

Heidi sighed coldly. 'Ten of our girls are to move to a new city. They're going to the East Coast, all the way across the country. The Master hasn't said where exactly, but they'll go by bus later this week. Isn't that exciting for them?'

'Oh...yes...' It seemed like a big scary thing to her to leave San Francisco. 'Do I have to go?'

Heidi looked at Nellie like she was something nasty on her shoe. 'No, the ones who are to be elevated are virtuous girls who pay attention and who are ready for the next step.'

Despite Heidi's implication that Nellie was neither attention-keeping nor virtuous, she felt a rush of relief, and she decided not to question what 'the next step' might mean. Everyone kind of spoke in riddles here, but she didn't want to appear foolish. Heidi seemed to know exactly what the things she said meant, so Nellie just nodded.

As she made her way to the ref for a meal, she did a double take. A girl she recognised had just passed her in the corridor, in the direction of the lecture room. This house had twice the number of girls living in it than the last one, and they ate and studied in shifts so there were enough benches and tables for them in the ref. Later, as she ate her bowl of rice and beans, she racked her brain to remember where she'd seen that girl before. They had her on three of the purple vitamin pills here for some reason. She thought her brain felt a bit fuzzy or something, but she wasn't sleeping well, and when she mentioned the fuzzy feeling to Heidi, the other girl said she was probably just tired. The young woman she thought she recognised was Asian, with silky dark hair that reached just above her shoulders. She had a fringe – or bangs as they were called in America – and golden-brown eyes. Could it have been...? No, impossible. She had to be wrong.

She would have liked to ask Heidi what the girl was called, but it would have to wait. In this house it was required to eat in silence; eating was a meditation in and of itself.

After the meal, she was taken to a different meeting room, without Heidi, for a special reflection. The leader of the reflection was an older man with brown age spots on his face. He spoke in a dull shaky drone, and she had to fight the urge to fall fast asleep as he went on and on to the ten or so girls in the room about marriage and how important it was. It was how the movement would grow and prosper, and they should all be grateful to be chosen for a suitable husband, because with marriage came the production of children, and those children would be unsullied by the sins of the past and faithful to the teachings of the Leader, and they and their mothers would be a cause of celebration.

The other girls seemed excited by this, but Nellie knew she'd never marry and certainly she never wanted another child, so it was hard to stay interested. She did her best to sit upright, however, her spine not touching the back of the hard plastic chair, as she'd been instructed by Heidi. No slouching was allowed. Her eyelids began to droop...

Then she was wide awake. Sitting two rows in front of her was that girl again, and it really was Wei, Emmet's friend, the one he was crazy about even though he tried to act all cool around her. But it was still impossible to believe, despite the evidence seen with her own eyes. Wei was so driven, so focused on her education, so happy about going to Stanford. Was it likely she had realised the error of her ways? That she had turned back from the dark and been saved? Surely not…

Then Nellie pinched herself for doubting the power of the Supreme Being to touch anyone He chose. The light of God was for everyone. All that remained for her was to be glad for Wei. And of course she was glad, and she wished she could speak to Wei, congratulate her, but Heidi had explained it wasn't allowed to approach the other girls in this house. They were much less huggy here, and the girls weren't encouraged to mix or chat. People slept in tiny partitioned cubicles instead of open dorms, and there were no group showers. Each person was on their own spiritual path, and it was nobody's business where they were on that journey, just as hers was unique to her.

The talk came to an end, and as they filed out of the room, Wei bumped shoulders with her and slipped a note into her hand without even glancing in her direction. Nellie's heart missed a beat. She should tell Heidi at once…but she didn't. She was lonely here without Aria. She would like to have a friend.

Later, showered and alone in the tiny cubicle that was her room – although really it was just plywood partitions on each side with a nylon curtain on a string for a door – she unfolded the scrap of paper.

*Emmet and Malachy are working with the police to get you free from here. Just be ready to run when I say. W.*

Panic flooded through her veins. What was this? What was Wei doing, trying to get her to leave? Was Wei still a wrongdoer? She should find Heidi at once. She had strict instructions to make her mentor aware if anyone from the wrongdoing world tried to suck her back into her past life, like that policeman had tried to do.

But something stopped her.

She didn't want to go back, to experience again that terrible ache inside of self-loathing, of loneliness, of emptiness that couldn't be filled by beer or cigarettes or weed. That was all behind her, she was saved, and the outside world was wicked and evil and would drag her back down into the muck as quickly as she let it. But the Master talking about marriage had frightened her. They wouldn't make her marry someone, would they? She didn't think so.

But she still didn't tell Heidi.

# CHAPTER 27

Nellie woke groggily to someone shaking her by the shoulder, their breath on her cheek. She was disorientated, and it was still dark. Heidi had made her a cocoa earlier and given her a cookie, something they hardly ever had. It was horribly sweet, sickly, probably because it was weeks since she'd tasted anything with sugar in it, and besides, sugar was bad for your soul. She'd wanted to spit it out, but Heidi had stood over her, tight-lipped and with her hands on her hips, while Nellie forced the cocoa and cookie down. She didn't remember much after that. She must have gone to bed – she thought she remembered going – and then she had bad dreams and tossed and turned. A baby crying…fire…Gerard as the devil, threatening to spear her with the prongs of his fork.

'Wha…?' she asked the dark figure bending over her. 'Is…Heid…?'

'No, it's me, Wei. We need to go,' the girl murmured in her ear. 'There's a window in the bathroom that I've managed to unscrew. You'll have to hang and drop – it's about six feet. Do you think you can manage that?'

'Wha…?' She knew she should scream for help, but her throat was too dry to do anything but croak. She struggled into a sitting position, her head spinning, her brain a painful fog. 'I don't want to go anywhere,' she managed to say.

'Nellie, listen to me. There's no time to argue. These people are a cult. They kidnap girls and pretend to marry them and use them for sex, then the girls have babies for the cult. I posed as someone vulnerable and they took me in, but you were in a different house. All I could do was find out where you were and let Emmet and Malachy know. They've had you watched to make sure you were safe, but now I can get you out…'

'Wei, please, go away,' Nellie said weakly. 'The wrongdoers have lied to you. This is my family. We serve the Supreme Being. I don't want to leave.'

'Oh, for goodness' sake! Love it enough to fake-marry the Master and have his babies?'

She felt sick. 'The devil has been talking to you. The Master is purity and goodness.' She tried to summon the strength to scream for Heidi.

'It wasn't the devil, it was Heidi. I heard her talking to my own mentor earlier. There's a mass marriage going on. They've been planning it these last two months. There's ten girls going from this house alone – or it *was* ten. There's eleven since you caught the Master's eye today.'

The scream died in Nellie's throat. The image of the new Master, his pink and white cheeks and pale-blue piggy eyes flashed in front of her. 'No,' she whispered hoarsely. 'You're lying. Heidi said I wasn't going anywhere.'

'Listen, Nellie, this is a load of crap and you know it. You're a smart girl, so let's just get out of here now, will we?'

'What's going on up there? Who's whispering?' called a loud voice. It was Heidi, her footsteps ringing up the aisle between the cubicles. Without a word, Wei dived under Nellie's cot bed. It was very low to the ground, and only someone as tiny as Wei could have disappeared under it so fast and so completely.

Nellie heard Heidi throw open a couple of curtains and bark

something about 'no talking', and then she opened Nellie's with a snap.

Nellie lay on her back with her eyes tightly shut, doing her best to breathe evenly like she was asleep. She was horribly conscious of Wei hidden under the cot and didn't know why she didn't betray her then and there. But Wei would get in trouble, probably get the paddle, and Emmet was in love with Wei, and Nellie and Emmet always looked out for each other, so she had to look after his girlfriend...

She shouldn't be thinking like this. She was supposed to have left her old family behind, and anyway Emmet despised her.

Heidi came and sat beside her and pinched her cheeks until she 'woke up'.

'Heidi?' Nellie pretended to yawn.

'Hurry, you need to get ready. I've such exciting news. You're going be travelling east like the other girls – isn't that fabulous? And the Master was able to get you a train ticket, so you don't have to go by bus with the others. The train is so much more comfortable and so much faster, and the Master thought he'd give you a treat and let you travel with him. Isn't that wonderful? I'm so, so happy for you, Eleanor.' Heidi didn't sound happy at all; she sounded bitter and jealous.

'I'm going to travel with the Master?' Nellie was bewildered. That pink and white face flashed in her head again. She knew she should love the Master – it was the best way of loving the Leader – but there was no getting away from the fact that he looked like a pig.

'Yes, you are. Aren't you the luckiest girl ever?' Heidi said in her harsh voice. 'Stand up.' She pulled Nellie's nightie roughly over her head, then forced her into her workday skirt and blouse and zipped and buttoned her up. 'But the train goes in an hour, so we need to get you ready right away. You'll have to shower on the train – it's a sleeper so it has bathrooms. Make sure you don't go anywhere near the Master until you are perfectly clean from head to toe.'

'But...but...where is the Master taking me?'

'To the next step, of course, remember? You're to be elevated. Extraordinary.'

'Will I come back again?' Did this mean she would never see Emmet again? Malachy? Her mam and dad?

'I don't know, Eleanor. Stop asking pointless questions. Now put your shoes on. Oh!'

'Oh' was the last thing Nellie ever heard Heidi say. The mentor had knelt to tie Nellie's shoelaces, and the next moment the woman was flat on her back, Wei straddling her chest. There was a struggle for a second or two, but then Heidi was unconscious. Was she dead? Nellie tried to focus, but it was so hard. She was so tired, and her limbs felt so heavy and unwieldly. Wei flipped Heidi's limp body over and pushed her out of sight under the cot. It all seemed to take less than a second.

'Come on.' The Asian girl was already on her feet again, holding out her hand to Nellie, who was staring at the bed, her hands to her mouth.

'Is...is she dead?'

'No, just knocked out. She'll be fine. Now come on, before anyone else comes to find you.'

'But...' Her feet felt like concrete blocks; she was unable to move.

'Nellie, come on!' hissed Wei.

It was awful. It was all awful. So many lies. Gerard said he loved her and was going to marry her, the matron at the nursing home said birth didn't hurt if you just relaxed, Dex said he was giving up acid, Emmet had pretended he thought she was clever and good... That's why she was here, that awful row with Emmet, his contempt for her. He'd obviously sent his girlfriend to drag her back, and now Wei was lying about the Master wanting her to have his babies. It was ridiculous. Horrible. Yet the way that blue-eyed piggy had smiled at her... She shuddered.

'Nellie!' Wei grabbed her shoulders. 'Trust me, it will be fine, just do as I say, please.'

Every time she'd trusted someone, they let her down. Gerard told her she should trust him, that nothing bad would happen if she let him take her to bed. Gerard, the start of all this horror. The end of her innocence. She remembered that flirty smile, which she'd mistaken for love... But then a voice from somewhere inside reminded her that real love – her mam and dad, Emmet, Nana Peggy was true and good. She wanted so much to go home. Her real home, in Ireland. No matter what anyone said, they were not evil. They were good and they loved her.

She made her decision. Something of the old, brave, impetuous Nellie came to the fore. 'All right, let's go.'

They moved softly together down the shadowy corridor, between the silent rows of curtained beds, into the shower room, then into one of the toilet cubicles at the end. After locking the door behind them, Wei climbed onto the seat and pushed open the tiny window. She beckoned Nellie to climb up beside her. 'Stand up on the cistern now, put your feet out the window – I'll hold you. Wriggle around onto your front, then slip slowly down and drop.'

Nellie's legs were like jelly; she needed all the support Wei could give. The landing in the yard hurt her right ankle, and a dog barked furiously from somewhere around the front. As Wei landed beside her, a big black Doberman pinscher came tearing around the corner and hurled itself at them. Wei kicked it neatly in the throat, cutting off the bark, and then in the testicles, leaving it writhing on the ground. 'Come on, let's go.' Another dog was barking, getting nearer in the dark, and suddenly there were spotlights illuminating the yard and a man shouted, 'Hey, who's there? Stop!' And as Wei half-dragged Nellie, they heard the sound of a man's feet pounding towards them.

'Run, run,' begged Wei, pulling Nellie with her, but Nellie was still so weak. Her legs were wobbling, and her ankle was screaming in pain. There was a large locked gate ahead of them, the street behind. Did Wei expect her to climb it?

'Gotcha.' A man's strong arms passed around her waist. He lifted her off her feet and ran with her back towards the building, her chin jarring on his shoulder. She struggled weakly and realised she was sobbing, so frightened. But maybe it was for the best. It *was* for the best; she was being rescued for her own good...

More men, none of whom she recognised, went running by and

pulled Wei down from the gates where she was climbing. Wei spun around, kicking, punching, and then fell to the ground, tackled by three men, one of whom picked her up and came running after Nellie and her captor, Wei slung over his shoulder like a doll.

'Wei...' sobbed Nellie.

'Be quiet! She's a wrongdoer,' snapped her captor as he hurried up the stone steps of the building.

On the far side of the gates across the yard, cars suddenly came screeching to a halt, flashing blue lights, sirens, uniformed figures leaping out of the cars, more men's voices, different voices. Then a megaphone.

'This is the police! Open the gates and come out. Every person in the building is to come out with their hands up.'

The man carrying Nellie cursed and threw her aside against the white-painted brick wall just inside the door, then went tearing off down the corridor into the bowels of the building. The next man dumped Wei beside Nellie like a sack of potatoes and hared off after the other one. Dizzy and sick, Nellie pushed herself into a sitting position and tried to arrange herself against the wall. Wei was lying on her back beside her. Nellie eased the girl's head onto her lap and stroked her shoulder-length black hair. Wei's face was as white as snow, her lips blue. Blood trickled from her temple.

The person with the megaphone outside the gates kept repeating the message, over and over again. 'This building is surrounded. Come out with your hands up. This building is surrounded. Come out with your hands up.'

People poured out of side rooms and down the main stairs, and there was increasing chaos everywhere. Girls wandered around bewildered in their white robes as one of the male leaders, the older man who had given the lecture about marriage, stood on a chair and ordered them all to stay strong.

'Remain calm. We have done nothing wrong. This is to be expected. Say nothing if they interview you – tell them nothing of our life here. Remember they are of the sinful world and don't understand what danger they are in. They believe it is we who are deluded, but we know better. Say nothing, and you will have to be released. This is so important everyone – just say nothing. They'll try…' His voice was drowned out by the roaring of the megaphone and girls screaming and crying. 'They'll try…' he shouted, 'to be kind, to say you've been abused, but you know the truth, you know what we are, what we do here. Don't let them into your minds…'

'This is the police,' boomed the person on the megaphone from outside the gates. 'Come out with your hands up. This is your last opportunity. We have a warrant to search the property and will force entry within five minutes if everybody does not emerge with their hands up. Come out with your hands up.'

The crush of people in the hall was increasing. Far more people were in this Mother House than Nellie had realised, and nobody seemed to know in which direction to run.

A girl slumped down against the wall beside Nellie, wailing. 'They are coming for us, the sinners who resent our truth, just as the Leader predicted.'

But another one pulled the girl to her feet. 'Listen to me! We have committed no crime. They can't do anything to us. Refuse to speak to them. The Leader foresaw this and has made plans – don't worry.'

Opposite where she was sitting, a small door flew open, showing a steep, narrow staircase, and more girls appeared, all dressed in the white tunics and wide-legged trousers. Several of them were carrying babies, which were screaming at the upset in the middle of the night. Men were descending behind the young mothers, also dressed in white.

'Nellie?'

Wei's eyes had opened, and she was staring up into Nellie's face.

Nellie's heart turned over. 'Wei, thank God, I thought you were…'

'I'm fine.' The girl rolled over and sat up, wiping the blood from her face and looking at her hand. 'What happened? What's going on?'

'The police are outside…'

'Thank God for that. Let's go hand ourselves in and tell them everything.'

Nellie immediately panicked. 'But they'll imprison us! We'll never be let out.' It was hard to ignore all the advice she'd been given at lecture after lecture about never speaking to the authorities, how they would lock you up and throw away the key.

'They won't, and anyway, Malachy knows the chief of police. They've been keeping a watch on you all this time. There was always someone with you, until that one time you got away. Come on, come with me, Nellie. Everything is going to be OK. You're going to be back with your real family in no time. I wouldn't be surprised if Emmet was outside right now, waiting to see you.'

'Oh...' Did she want to see him? Not if he looked at her that way again, such contempt in his eyes.

'He wants to apologise to you, Nellie. He knows he was horrible to you, and he feels so guilty for what he said. He thinks you're a wonderful person. He cares so much about you.'

Both of them got unsteadily to their feet. Wei gripped Nellie's hand, and without any effort, they became part of the unhappy, jostling crowd, swept along in the melee through the open front doors and into the front yard, where the gates had been forced open and the courtyard was full of police with guns.

Female members of the group were already being led to buses under armed guard, silent and tight-lipped as they'd been instructed. The women who carried babies were being escorted to waiting ambulances, and the men were being held against the side wall, all standing with their hands up, staring ahead, saying nothing.

Then she heard someone calling her name, someone beyond the line of armed officers. 'Nellie! Nellie!'

It was Emmet, standing tall beside Malachy Berger, both men waving and beaming. She and Wei looked at each other, then pushed through the crowd towards the barricade, gripping each other's hand in case they lost each other, but the police moved forward and stopped their progress.

'Go to the right, board a bus,' the policeman commanded, his weapon cocked.

Nellie fought back tears. So the Master had been right and Wei had been wrong. They were going to be in prison until they died.

'It's all right,' Wei assured her. 'We'll do as they say. There are lots of people whose families are looking for them. We'll go and they'll release us.'

'I…I'm afraid to go. What if they…'

The policeman barked at them once again. 'Get on the bus!' But then another officer in a more elaborate uniform broke through the line and approached them.

'What's your name?' he asked Nellie.

'Eleanor –'

'Nellie Crean,' said Wei loudly. 'Her name is Nellie Crean.'

'Nellie from Kilteegan Bridge, Ireland?' His voice turned instantly gentle, and he led them into a quieter corner.

'But…but I'm staying with my cousin – he's over there. I…I just want to go home…please. And this is my friend Wei. We didn't do anything…'

'Oh, your friend Wei did do something, Nellie.' But he was smiling as he said it. 'Without her help we would not have been able to get a warrant to break in here, because as well as keeping track of you, your friend Wei smuggled us out all the evidence of abuse and coercion of young girls that we needed to convince the judge.'

'They never touched me, I swear.' Nellie's cheeks blazed with shame. 'They were very respectful.'

Wei threw an arm around her waist. 'They groom girls, Nellie. They keep them away from everyone. That's why your mentor never left your side, why we weren't allowed to talk. Those babies upstairs? Those were the babies of the girls brought in before you. You would have ended up there too.'

The officer put his hand on Nellie's shoulder, and she shuddered involuntarily at his male touch.

'It's all right. You're safe now,' he said, withdrawing his hand. 'You've caused quite a stir, young lady, but all's well that ends well. We've been after this cult for quite some time, but they're smart and they usually prey on girls with no family in their lives. But you've turned out to have a very powerful family indeed. Mr Berger is your uncle, I understand?'

Nellie was briefly puzzled to hear Malachy described that way, but then she supposed if he was Emmet's father, it made sense. 'Yes… I… He is.'

'And now we have a witness prepared to give evidence against the cult, your friend Wei, and hopefully we'll have a second witness in you as well.'

'Will I have to go to court?' she asked, frightened again.

The officer smiled reassuringly. 'Well, you'll be required to make a statement, and if and when the time comes you're needed as a witness, we'll call you. But for now, I think you should go home, take a bath, have a meal and try to get some rest. You've had quite the ordeal.' He turned and waved his arm over his head, signalling Emmet and Malachy to come through the line of officers.

As Emmet reached her, Nellie saw nothing but love and kindness in his face. 'I'm so sorry, Nell. This is all my fault for shouting at you. It was just I was so frightened for you. Can you forgive me?'

She fell into his arms and cried some more. He soothed her and held her tight.

'Did they hurt you, Nell?'

'I'm so sorry, so sorry…'

'No, I'm sorry, really. Your dad is on the way, Nell. He's getting on a plane right now.'

'My dad?' Nellie cried even harder, this time with joy. 'Coming here?'

'Yes. Malachy decided he had to tell your parents despite the police insisting it was a bad idea, and Uncle Blackie immediately booked a flight from Dublin. Now, do you mind if I pass you over to Malachy to sob on and ruin his expensive shirt while I congratulate the most amazing detective and undercover agent ever to not be in the CIA, at least not yet?'

As Malachy put his arm around Nellie's shoulder, Emmet moved to pull Wei into a powerful, loving embrace, which the girl returned with the same degree of enthusiasm.

'You're my hero,' he murmured into her thick black hair. 'You're amazing.'

'Don't go all soft and emotional on me now, Irish,' she murmured back, but she couldn't help looking pleased, and Nellie and Malachy exchanged an amused glance.

The four of them passed through the barricade as all around them people in white clothing were being shepherded into the buses under the watchful eye of armed officers and the ambulances left, taking the babies and their mothers to hospitals. The blue flashing lights lit up the night as Malachy helped Nellie into the front of his car.

As he opened the passenger door, one of the police buses passed. She looked up and saw Heidi, who glared down at her angrily. Nellie ducked into the car, flooded with different emotions – relief that Heidi had been found and was physically all right, relief to no longer be under her control.

'I've caused so much trouble and worry for everyone. I'm so sorry. I don't know how it happened…'

Emmet and Wei were deep in conversation in the back of the car, but Malachy shot her a smile as he pulled away from the curb. 'All that matters is that you're safe, Nellie. Nothing else. I was glad I was in a position to help. Doug LeBron and I go back a few years now – that's the officer you spoke to – and he understood how important you are and how much your family loves you, so he was glad to help. Besides, it suited him, and it will mean a nice promotion for him too, so there are plenty of silver linings.'

Instead of going straight home to Palo Alto, Malachy stopped at his offices in downtown San Francisco and instructed the porter to order in some food. Then he brought them up to his suite and told them to make themselves comfortable while he disappeared into his inner office to make some calls.

Within moments it seemed, the elevator pinged and the doors opened straight into the apartment, and a nice older woman laid pizza and ice cream and Coke on the glass table. The three young people sat around on the dove-grey sofas and tucked into the food and drink. The pizza was tomatoes, mozzarella and Italian sausage and was delicious, though Nellie felt a bit guilty for eating meat, and the ice cream and Coke still tasted too sweet to her. But she didn't feel sleepy or strange after eating for once, and then she heard Wei explaining to Emmet how the girls were given sedatives masquerading as vitamin tablets, and she nearly died of shame at her own stupidity.

Then, as she took another slice of delicious hot pizza, a question occurred to her. 'Wei, how did you get information out of the house to the police? I mean, I wasn't allowed to speak to anyone on the outside.'

Wei explained she sold flowers like Nellie did. With Emmet's help, the police kept an eye on her, and every day a different man who was always called 'Elvis Jones' would buy flowers and she would conceal a note among the leafy stems. It was pure luck she'd managed to find Nellie's whereabouts, especially as she hadn't known Nellie was going by the name Eleanor; she'd just happened to pass her on the street one day and Heidi had been in an expansive mood, boasting about how the group had three houses in the city, all in expensive locations, which she'd named off proudly. Though in the end, it hadn't mattered, because Nellie turned up at Wei's Mother House anyway, and that was when Wei decided not to wait for the police. 'If we hadn't run when we did, you might have been smuggled out to the train minutes before the police got there, so it's just as well you were brave enough to come with me.'

'It's you who were brave, Wei. I was just lost.'

'And drugged, to be fair,' Wei said matter-of-factly. 'Those purple tablets are tranquillisers.'

'And I was moved from two to three a night when I moved to the second place.'

Nellie still felt woozy but not totally disorientated as she'd done before. The drugs were wearing off.

'Drink more water Nel, get those drugs out of your system.' Emmet said. 'Malachy has arranged for a doctor to see you in the morning, just to check you over.'

. . .

NELLIE SMILED for what felt like the first time in months.

'I'M FINE EMMET, thanks to you and Wei and Malachy, I'm going to be fine.'

# CHAPTER 28

'So they'll get the message at Dublin airport, and your sister will have a happier drive home again.'

Eli smiled as Lena got into Emily and Blackie's bed beside him. It was the early hours of the morning now, they'd been up most of the night, talking and worrying, but Malachy had rung to say Nellie was fine and that they would speak later. Eli had contacted the airline and asked them to pass on the message to Mr and Mrs Crean when they arrived for Blackie's flight. She was after settling Aidan, who was restless and jumpy, not just missing his mother but disturbed by the rain that rattled heavily on the roof and windows and the creak of the trees behind the yard that swayed and bent in the fierce wind, leaves and twigs taking flight through the air. The bedrooms were in the attic on the third storey, above the shop and then above the kitchen and living space, and there was a loose slate banging just over Lena's head. Blackie would have to fix that when he got back from America or the roof would start leaking.

She snuggled up and kissed Eli's neck. 'The relief. Eli, I feel like I haven't exhaled properly since we heard about Nellie running off in the first place. Imagine someone so independent-minded getting involved in a cult.'

'I know. It's mad, isn't it? But you know, a doctor I met at the cystic fibrosis conference in Cork told me one of those cults tried to buy a house up in the country, in Westmeath or Offaly or someplace like that. They already have a place in Dublin.'

'Best of luck to any cult getting past the Monsignor here, though. You'd have to give him credit for that.' She rested her head on his chest, and then jumped and gasped as a brilliant flash of lightning lit up the whole room, followed almost at once by a clap of thunder so loud it sounded like a house was falling down above them, or the tumbling crash of a lorry unloading bricks.

'And you think she'll come home with Blackie?' Eli tightened his arm around her shoulders, offering her safety in the storm.

She listened for a moment to see if Aidan had woken, but there was no cry so she relaxed again. 'She will. I think she needs her parents now. Malachy said she's fairly shaken. You know, without Malachy's influence and help, things could have been a lot worse.'

'He's a good man,' agreed Eli. 'And I wish he'd meet someone, not because I think he still has a thing for you, though I do think that –'

'Ah, Eli, stop.'

'No, no, listen. I just want him to be happy, and being single and childless, well, I don't know. All the money he has, he should have someone special to share it with him, like I have you.'

Lena tickled him playfully. 'Hey now. Just because Jimmy Piper and Mrs Weldon finally got rid of that husband-turned-vicar of hers and are planning to tie the knot next week with you as best man doesn't mean you should take up matchmaking as a job.'

'I don't know. I'm a bit of an expert in the romance stakes,' he murmured, kissing her as the lightning flashed again. The thunder sounded further away this time.

'Eli, we can't. This is Emily's bed! I'd be mortified.' Lena giggled.

'We'll strip the bed in the morning and never tell her…' he mumbled as his lips traced behind her ear, making her squirm with pleasure.

'All right then…' she said, mock weary, as he laughed and drew her close.

* * *

LENA THOUGHT SHE WAS DREAMING. She tried to sit up, and as she did, the coughing started. The room was full of smoke, and her eyes streamed. Eli slept like the dead, naked beside her.

She thumped him until he woke, coughing all the time, then rushed to the bedroom door, dragging on her nightie over her head, opening it to be met by a wall of more smoke, glittering with sparks. 'Eli, the baby!' she screamed in horror.

'Close the door!' Eli shouted. He ran to open the large sash in the gable of the house, but however hard he tugged at it, it wouldn't budge. He grabbed the bedside locker and hurled it at the window. The panes of glass shattered, and he went at it again, using the locker to smash the timber in between.

'The baby! The baby!'

'I know! Get out, get help, and I'll go for him.' He ripped the sheets off the bed, tying them together, coughing all the time, and threw the makeshift rope out of the window. 'Go, Lena! It's too short, but bend your knees as you drop and try to roll onto your side. Go and get help…'

'But I can't leave you here…'

'Go, get help!' Eli shouted again. 'I'll get the baby.'

Lena realised they were wasting precious time and climbed out the window, gulping fresh air and holding onto the sheets, dropping the extra six feet painfully into the alley when the sheets ran out.

'Wake everyone. Run, Lena,' Eli called down to her, pulling the sheets back in, and she did as she was told. Tears of terror flowed down her face as she sprinted down the side of the house, out onto the street.

'Fire! Fire!' she screamed and screamed, and it seemed to take forever, but maybe it was only seconds before people were appearing in their dressing gowns to see what was going on. She shouted at the men to get ladders and the women to get any containers they had, and everyone to make a human chain passing buckets of water across the street. The entire downstairs of the shop suddenly went up in flames, and there was still no sign of Eli with the baby.

She saw him then, at the small window of Aidan's little nursery, looking out onto the main street from the third floor. He was holding a tiny bundle of blankets in one arm and using the tip of a flatiron to smash the window with his free hand.

The men had arrived with ladders, and they laid the tallest against the wall. Sean Kinsella, who'd bought the pub from Twinkle, climbed it, with several men holding the base of the ladder, though the heat from the shop was intense. Just as Sean made it to the top, the men helping had to let go and scatter as the glass window at the front of the shop shattered, spitting shards and burning goods out into the street.

Sean swayed and struggled to keep the ladder stable – it had been knocked slightly askew by the blast – and Eli handed Sean the baby just before the ladder began to slide sideways down the wall. Several men tried to get close enough to catch the falling man and the bundle, but amid the smoke and the flames it was impossible, and the pub landlord and Aidan came crashing down together into the street.

'Jump, Eli, jump!' Lena shouted as she rushed to grab the bundle of blankets that had rolled away from Sean's arms into the street. The baby was whimpering thinly, too shocked to cry, but he was alive and seemed unharmed. She handed him straight to Annie Gallagher, who had just arrived, and ran back towards the shop. Other people were dragging Sean Kinsella away from the flames, pulling his body over the carpet of broken glass, no time to lift him. Eli was still trying to knock out enough of the frame to get his big body through the small window. No one could get near enough to prop the ladder up again, and he was going to have to jump from such a height. He was going to break an arm, maybe a leg… 'Jump, Eli, jump!' she screamed up at him again.

The next few minutes passed in a haze. A bright light, an explosion, screaming. The fire brigade came from Bandon, hoses were deployed, an ambulance, then another and then a third. Neighbours she'd known since she was a child held her back, and eventually she was physically brought away, into the Copper Kettle, where Chrissie made her hot sweet tea.

# CHAPTER 29

The following evening, she was in the small sitting room of Kilteegan House, where she and Eli would sit together as the evening shadows fell, the fire lit, reading or chatting. Wave after wave of people came and went through the door from the library, all her friends and neighbours wanting to see her, to sympathise. Maria was in the armchair on one side of the hearth, speaking softly to those who stopped to talk to her. Jack stood on the other side, shaking hands. Lena just sat on the sofa facing the small fire and said nothing to anyone. She knew she should try to do something, say something, but she couldn't.

Skipper guarded the door, letting in as many as he thought she could take at a time, with occasional breaks of solitude. Peggy, Ted, Gwenda and Klaus were in the kitchen, organising the food and drink, trying to find room for all the casseroles and sandwiches and bottles of whiskey people brought with them.

Emily, who was hysterical with guilt, was at the hospital with Aidan. He was going to be fine, despite having a few cuts and bruises. Sean Kinsella had a burnt hand, a badly broken arm and a dislocated shoulder from protecting the baby as he fell, but he'd be all right too, it seemed.

Lena tried to be happy for Aidan and grateful to Sean. After all, Eli had died for Emily's baby and Sean had helped in the rescue, but she felt nothing. The deep, dark chasm inside her, the pain, the fear, the overwhelming sense of loss forbade her to do or say anything.

Eli's parents, Sarah and Charlie, had been told. They were on the ferry from Cardiff with his brothers and sisters, his Uncle Saul and Aunt Ann as well, and some of Eli's friends. And Emmet, Blackie and Nellie were on their way back from America. The twins were trying to get back from New Zealand in time, though Lena didn't see the point. For some reason people seemed to think the arrangements of who was where were comforting to her. As if the arrival of Eli's mother, or her younger sisters, could somehow touch her, when she knew she would never feel again.

Sarah sat beside her on the sofa, dully thanking people on her mother's behalf as they came to shake hands. Pádraig, on Lena's other side, was pale and robotic; he spoke when spoken to but nothing else. She knew she should put her arms around her children, to comfort them, have them comfort her, but she couldn't. Her Eli was gone. Dead. She repeated the word over and over to have it make more sense, but it didn't. *Dead,* she made herself say in her mind. *Eli is dead.* But still the reality could not penetrate her dark, cold core.

This wasn't like when her dad died, or Doc; this was something entirely different. Their deaths were premature, and she'd been devastated, but she knew on some deep level that the day would come for her to bury them. Eli was different. Eli was her; she was him. They only made sense as a pair, a team. They were a couple, and then a family. He was her reason for living, her rock, the one she'd always turned to when she was unsure or scared or lonely. It was always Eli. He would joke or hug her or come up with a solution. How on earth was she supposed to stay here, in this world, without him?

She couldn't.

Skipper came in and offered her a small plate of sandwiches, but she just shook her head. She hadn't eaten anything since it happened, despite all the entreaties from various people. She couldn't swallow, not while the fireman picked through the wet, smoking ruins of the shop and apartment to find the remains of her husband and the ambulance waited.

The Monsignor's looming presence then filled the room.

'Mrs Kogan, I'm truly sorry for your loss. He was a good man, and this parish will miss him enormously.'

She gazed up at the large black-robed priest, unable to find anything to say.

'I have taken the liberty – and please, if it's inappropriate, then please say so – of contacting Rabbi Bloom at the synagogue in Cork. We thought I could host a simple service in the Kilteegan Bridge church, then I will introduce the rabbi, who will say a few words and then perform the Jewish ceremony at the graveside.'

Something about him was sincere, and though Lena had always known him as a pompous ass, she knew this time he was just trying to help.

'Thank you. I...I'm not sure. His mother and uncle will be here later – they'll know better. Perhaps you can talk to them.'

'Certainly, Mrs Kogan, I'll do that. And again, my deepest sympathies. Several Masses have already been arranged for the repose of his soul. He was respected and admired very much. He and I got off to a bad start, but I came to realise everything your husband did was out of concern and compassion for his patients, who loved him in return.'

'He was loved, Monsignor. My husband was loved,' Lena heard herself say.

'Indeed he was, Mrs Kogan, indeed he was. And I respected him enormously, please understand that.'

He withdrew, and Skipper ushered him with the next wave of sympathisers towards the kitchen and dining room, where everyone was gathering and talking. Then Jack told Maria and Sarah and Pádraig to take a break, go and get something to eat. He closed the door after them and came to sit beside Lena.

'People will understand if you've had enough. You don't need to meet everyone. Would you like to go for a sleep for a while?'

Lena shook her head. 'I won't sleep. I need Eli to be beside me so I can fall asleep, Jack.' She leant against her brother, who wrapped her in his arms. 'What am I going to do, Jack? Please tell me, because I don't know. How am I supposed to live without him?'

'Let it out, Lena, let it all out. There you go, love.' He rubbed her back and held her as she grieved for her husband.

'I don't even have his body. How can I say goodbye if I don't even have his body…'

Eli's remains had finally been taken away in the ambulance, a pitiful, unrecognisable heap of charred bones.

* * *

THE FUNERAL in the Kilteegan church was a crowded blur. The church was packed, the mourners genuinely devastated.

Pat Leahy, the electrician, had not come; he couldn't face it, someone said. The old wiring was surely the cause of the blaze, and he should have realised it needed replacing right away instead of thinking he'd fixed it enough for now. Lena was glad he didn't turn up to sympathise. His carelessness was why she had to live her life without Eli; she wouldn't have been able to bear to look at him.

Emily and Blackie could hardly face her either. Pat had said the place needed rewiring soon enough, and they'd put it on the long finger for money reasons. Would Lena ever be able to forgive them? Nellie had arrived home with Blackie, ashen-faced, and Nellie was blaming herself too. If she hadn't had the baby, and if Eli and Lena hadn't been minding him while her parents came chasing after her…

Lena found it too hard to care about Nellie's feelings, couldn't comfort her or tell her it wasn't her fault.

Malachy had travelled from America with Emmet. Rosa, Eli's cousin from New York, also was there. She was sitting in the pew behind Charlie and Sarah, and Saul and Ann, and Eli's younger brothers and sisters, now young men and women. His fellow doctors from Cardiff, old friends, were sitting across the aisle. Molly and May hadn't made it, something about a cancelled flight, Lena found she didn't care. Nothing and nobody could take away her pain.

The Monsignor spoke warmly from the pulpit about Dr Kogan,

and his care and concern for his patients, and no mention was made of past denunciations. The rabbi was announced and said a few words, then led Eli's last, short journey to the graveyard. The coffin had come straight from the undertaker's. There had been no viewing; her husband hadn't been laid out at home. She knew without being told there was very little of his poor lovely body left. Jack, Ted, Pádraig, Emmet, Klaus and Blackie carried the coffin from the church to the grave. It was an unadorned plain wooden box, as the Jews didn't go in for elaborate caskets.

After the procession, she stood at the graveside, frozen despite the warmth of the day, as the rabbi spoke about Eli, about a dedicated doctor, a kind man, a faithful husband, a loving father. She bit her lip to stop herself screaming at him. She didn't want to hear her beloved Eli's name on the lips of this strange old man who had never met him. He was saying all the right things, of course he was; he'd done his homework, to be fair. But this was her Eli. Hers. He was all of those things they said, but more than that, he was hers. And she was his. If he was gone, who was her person? Whose person was she?

She had her children either side of her, her family all around. Sarah and Charlie, Eli's brothers and sisters, Saul and Ann – they were gathered on the other side of the grave. And all of the Kilteegan Bridge community were there. But she had never in her life felt so alone. If she could have fallen into the grave, laid on top of the box and died, then she would have done.

The rabbi said the burial prayers. They were unfamiliar to her, but Eli's Jewish relatives participated, and Sarah and Pádraig and Emmet followed the Jewish tradition of filling earth into the hole using the back of the shovel. Lena watched them, remembering herself, Emily and Jack at the same ages as her children were now when they lost their father, Paudie. They'd been standing less than twelve feet away from this very spot, feeling the same sense of being bereft. Why couldn't she comfort them?

Afterwards, everyone went back to the house again. They'd asked Lena what she wanted to do after the burial, but she didn't care. Having people, not having people – it was all meaningless. Eli was dead. He was lying, or the burnt remains of him were lying in a hole in the ground in the cemetery of Kilteegan Bridge, and she would never see him again. Never laugh at something he said, never feel his arms around her, never make love to him...never, never, never.

Other people's outpourings should have given her consolation, to hear how well loved he was. Jimmy Piper was inconsolable; he and Mrs Weldon had called off their wedding because they couldn't bear to go ahead without Eli as best man. Annie Gallagher had lost the roses in her cheeks. Margaret, his secretary, was in floods. Young people, mothers, fathers, old people she'd known all her life, they were all distraught. But it didn't help. She knew Eli was loved. He didn't need to die for her to know that.

Slipping away from the crush of mourners, she climbed the stairs to her bedroom for a few minutes of peace. She stood looking out at Eli's pale-blue car parked on the gravel, and the avenue down to the surgery at the gate lodge of Kilteegan House. She had to try to make herself believe that he would never stroll up there again, in his shirt-sleeves, the lovely leather bag Jimmy Piper made for him in his hand. Eli walked like a lion prowled, she'd always thought, gracefully.

There was a light tap on the door, and her heart sunk. Who had come to bother her now? The door opened, and Doc's forthright friend Anthea was there, her perfectly made-up face and maroon-coloured nails coordinating perfectly as always with her elegantly cut coat.

Lena looked at the Dublin doctor but said nothing.

Anthea came in and stood before her. 'I won't bother with the platitudes, Lena. This is awful. I deal with death daily, but this...it's so wrong.'

'Your coat is beautiful,' Lena managed, her voice sounding strange to her own ears.

'Thank you. Lena, I'm not here to annoy you. I'm here just to say one thing. You won't be able to think about practical things like money for a long time, but Mike has asked me to tell you that he will come and run Eli's practise for you as long as you like, and he will make sure you and the children are taken care of. He has no family of his own to care for, so whatever you have to worry about right now, money doesn't have to be a part of it.'

Lena's head ached. 'That's too generous. He doesn't have to…'

'Dearest Lena, take the help when it's offered. We're all your family and we love you. Didn't you think of Doc as a second father?' She picked up the hinged silver frame from Lena's side of the bed, the frame Lena had found in the locked drawer of her godfather's desk, and showed Lena the pictures of herself and Mike as children. 'See? Doc thought of you both as his children, and this is Doc looking after you now, through your godbrother, Mike.'

# CHAPTER 30

Malachy Berger strolled the estate of Kilteegan House, reliving old memories, and wondered if the place was cursed. Behind those walls, his mother had been murdered by his father, all those years ago. Months later, August Berger had shot Paudie O'Sullivan, Lena's father, taking aim from Malachy's bedroom window, the room that now belonged to his own son, Emmet.

Emmet was walking silently beside him, his hands in his pockets, and Malachy glanced at him with a sad smile. 'Old memories,' he said. 'Your mother and I were about your age when our parents died. It felt surreal.'

'When did it stop hurting?' The boy's green eyes were full of pain, and Malachy wished there was something he could say or do but knew there wasn't.

He put his hand on Emmet's shoulder as they stopped at a gate and looked down a valley where the fields rolled emerald to the ocean. 'Truthfully, never, but it gets manageable. When I'm in America, I only have happy memories really, but coming back here…' He felt the boy's shoulders quiver with grief.

'I think I should stay with Mam for a while.'

Malachy nodded. He'd been thinking along the same lines. 'I

understand. And I'd like to stay on for a while myself. I won't get in the way, or bother your mother or anything, but if it would help?'

'It would. Thanks.'

They walked on in companionable silence, surveying the estate they had both called home at different times. Emmet pointed to the next field, which was flat and cropped by sheep. 'He used to play rugby with me there. And we used to pick blackberries for Mrs Shanahan in the corner of it.'

'I'm glad you have such happy memories. They won't help much now, but they will, in time.'

They reached a stile that led over a stone wall into the orchard. As Emmet put his foot on the first step, he said, without looking at Malachy, 'Maybe I should study medicine in Cork, like Dad wanted me to do at first, instead of engineering in Stanford.'

Malachy followed his son over the stile. To his mind, Emmet was a born engineer, not a doctor. 'Well, don't rush into any decisions while you're hurting, Emmet. Doc's godson, Mike, is going to take over the medical side of things here, so you don't have to worry about that. And I know Eli would be supportive of any decision you make.'

Emmet smiled back at him as he hopped down into the orchard. 'He would. He always encouraged me to do my best at anything I tried. I remember the first time I jumped Ollie over that ditch there. We were all having a picnic, and I didn't really mean to do it. I fell off and Mam nearly went mad – I was only about seven – but Dad picked me up, checked me over and put me straight back up on Ollie and told me to try again but not to fall off this time.'

'And did you?' Malachy asked, amused.

Emmet nodded. 'I wanted to impress him, show him how brave I was, but I was terrified. I've jumped it a thousand times since.'

'Sarah has your mare, Second Chance, now?'

'Yes, she's a better horsewoman than me these days – she's absolutely fearless. But she was Daddy's girl. I just don't know how…' The tears pricked his eyes, and he tried to hold them back. Malachy put his arm around his son's shoulders, drawing him in with a strong hug.

'He was a wonderful father to you all.' He stopped there, before he could say what was in his heart. *And God knows, I was jealous of him, so much I could never come back. He had Lena, he had you, my son, raising you as his own...* He looked into Emmet's eyes that reflected his own unusual green, and instead of voicing his personal pain, he said, 'And if any man could raise my boy well, it was Eli Kogan. He was a great husband and father, and I wish with all my heart, for you and Sarah and Pádraig and your mother, that this terrible thing had never happened.'

Emmet turned his head away, overcome by tears, and Malachy passed him a handkerchief without comment. Taking it, the boy wiped his cheeks hard, scrubbing them red. 'I'm going to give Mam the house, properly, legally,' he said hoarsely.

Malachy nodded, pleased. 'I'm glad. I'll be honest, it's what I wanted to do in the first place, but I knew she wouldn't take it from me directly.'

The boy looked at him curiously as he stuffed the damp handkerchief into his pocket. 'Can I ask you something, Malachy? It's personal.'

'Yes?' He wondered what was coming. Maybe a question about how he could possibly have abandoned Lena O'Sullivan, even though they were both so young at the time and he hadn't known she was pregnant.

'How come you never married? There are enough beautiful women who are mad about you. I've even met some of them. Poor Carolyn is all out of ideas.'

Taken by surprise, Malachy laughed and shrugged. 'Oh, you know. Too busy working, I suppose, all the hours. I never stop...'

'You're not working now, so you can stop if you want to.'

'That's because I *need* to be here, with you. If there's any advantage to owning your own business, it's being able to take time off when necessary. I have some great foremen working for me.'

'You still love my mother, don't you?' His son spoke quietly but with the conviction of one who knows for certain that he's right.

'Ah now, Emmet...'

'I don't mean to make you feel bad. I just think it must be hard for you the way things turned out.'

Malachy sighed, weighing up what, if anything, to say. 'It's all irrelevant now anyway, has been for years.' He glanced at his son as they crossed the orchard towards the stables, where Pádraig was kicking his ball dully and repetitively against the gable wall. 'Look, the only important thing right now is, whatever my feelings, past or present, I'm only here to help, not get in the way or upset your mother. I'll do anything, and I mean anything for your family, Emmet, to make this loss easier to bear. I owe it not just to Lena, but to Eli too for all he did in raising you so well.'

As they neared the stables, Pádraig caught the ball off a bounce and came to meet them, looking fed up. 'Where have you two been? Everyone keeps disappearing on me.'

'Isn't Mam here?' asked Emmet.

'Yes, but she's upstairs in bed and doesn't want to see anyone, and it's only Auntie Emily in the kitchen with Aidan, and she keeps crying and feeling guilty about the fire. Sarah's taken Second Chance up to the farm to get away from it all, and Uncle Blackie's down the shop trying to make it safe. I wanted to go with him, but he wouldn't let me – he said it was dangerous.'

Malachy felt a stab of alarm. 'I expect it is dangerous. The last thing we need is your uncle having a beam fall on him. I'll go down there now.'

'I'll come with you,' Emmet said, heading towards Malachy's car.

'Can I come too?' Pádraig trailed them. Malachy had rented a dark-blue two-seater Jaguar this time. 'I can cram in behind the seats.'

'No, Podge, stay and keep Mam and Auntie Emily company,' said Emmet as he got into the passenger seat.

'But they both just keep crying, and not even together. It's awful…'

'I'm sorry, Podge. I'll be as quick as I can.'

'Forget it,' said Pádraig miserably as he went back to kicking the ball fiercely against the high wall.

Malachy turned the ignition but paused before putting the car into gear and looked at his son, who was staring after his younger brother. 'You know what I think you should do, Emmet?'

'Yes, I do,' said Emmet. 'And so do I. I was being stupid. You don't need me, and he does.'

And he got out of the car and went to kick the ball with his little brother, who for the first time since the tragedy brightened up and smiled his old infectious smile.

* * *

Blackie Crean was in the charred remains of his shop and home, filthy from head to toe as he rooted through the loose debris, removing sharp twisted bits of metal that were once kettles and pot stands and picture frames, sweeping up the shards of plate glass.

Never had he thought it was possible to be brought so low. He was bankrupt, his home and business gone, and worse than any of that, much, much worse, he had caused the death of his best friend. He'd never said it out loud, and he felt it might have been presumptuous to do so, a man who left school at twelve being best friends with a doctor, but it was true. Eli had been his best friend, and now he was gone, and his wife's sister had been left widowed, and it was his fault for not fixing the bloody wiring.

He looked up when he heard Malachy crunching towards him over the debris, and he took a handkerchief from his overall pocket and ineffectually tried to wipe his palms.

'Well, Malachy,' he said. 'Here you are. I would say welcome, but I can't in all honesty…' He waved his hand grimly around the smouldering remains of his home and business. 'If you want a cuppa, we'll have to head over to the Copper Kettle, because there's nothing here.'

'Actually, I was going to ask if you would mind if I looked around the building, Blackie?' Malachy asked quietly. 'Just to make sure what's left of it isn't going to tumble down around your ears.'

'I guess I'd only deserve it if it did,' said the humble man miserably. 'I should have paid for Pat Leahy to do the job sooner, but…'

'If anything needs securing, I can do it for you. Is that your own tree that's down in the back?' asked Malachy, looking past him through the tumbled back wall into the yard.

'No, it's an old bit of woodland belonging to the Lamkins. They've left it unminded for years. I built Nellie and Emmet a treehouse there once, when they were small, and it's that one came down in the storm the night that…' His voice cracked. Somehow, it felt like another blow, the way the treehouse had been destroyed as well, with its happy memories of Nellie's childhood. Nellie was down at Peggy's, where they were all staying. She'd been keeping away, unable to stand the sight of her family home in ruins.

'It's a big one.' Malachy began picking his way across the black sludge of burnt debris soaked by rain.

Blackie stretched out a hand in alarm. 'Malachy, don't, come back. It's dangerous over there. I have the electrics turned off at the mains, but I don't know if it's safe by the wall – that's where it looks like it must have started…'

The engineer turned to him with a slight smile. 'Do you know how much I know about calf ration? Or ringworm, or which size tractor tyre would be needed for a Massey Ferguson?'

'Not much, I'd say,' Blackie replied, taken aback.

'Exactly. I know nothing at all because that's your business and I wouldn't have a clue. But buildings are my business, and I happen to be quite good at it. So just let me look around, all right?' Malachy carried on towards the charred back wall, climbing over what was left of the counter.

Blackie followed him, shaking his head. 'Ah sure, this is very good of you, Malachy, but to be honest, there's no money to secure the place properly anyway, not until we have the other shops sold.'

The architect looked at him in surprise. 'You're selling?'

Blackie's shoulders drooped. He'd ruined so much, so completely; he was the lowest of the low. 'Sure we borrowed against this shop here to open the other two, and it would have been fine if this hadn't happened. I owe Lena seven hundred as well. But the insurance won't pay out, you see. The electrician told us we should do the job, and we didn't…'

Malachy seemed surprised. 'I heard Pat Leahy said it was safe enough and could wait? It's himself he's blaming.'

'Ah sure, he knew we were short of money. I'm not going to drag him into court by putting it on him. My business is going down the tubes anyway, and it's my own fault, so I'm not going to bring Pat down with me, and Emily agrees...' Blackie's jaw set in a determined line. 'It's my fault, and mine alone.'

'Really?' Malachy seemed to have lost interest in what Blackie was saying. He had stepped out over the remains of the blackened back wall into the yard behind and was now looking closely at the branches of the tree where they had struck the house. They were charred by fire, like everything else. From there, he looked carefully at the bricks lying under the branches, then tracked back into the house, kicking aside rubbish with the toe of his shoe, burnt rolls of material, a scorched bale of wrapping paper, grunting to himself. 'Well, there's no wiring here, anyway,' he muttered under his breath, then went back out into the yard to inspect the tree again.

Blackie watched him, wondering what on earth Malachy was seeing that interested him so much. All Blackie could see was the devastation of his hopes, his family, his carefully rebuilt reputation.

'You said there was a storm that night?' asked Malachy.

'There was. Myself and Emily had a tough time driving through it. We were trying to get to the airport on time.' Struggling through the wind and rain while the shop burnt down and Eli died saving their little boy. 'A terrible wind, lots of trees down like this one, all across the country. We had to take a few detours.'

'But it was lightning brought this tree down, not the wind,' said Malachy, kicking at the trunk of the mighty chestnut where it had split in half. 'Brought it down in flames. You can see how the fire spread up the trunk and into the branches, and then when the enormous, most likely dead tree fell, it took half of your back wall with it and ignited the material and papers inside behind the counter.'

Blackie stared, bewildered, hardly able to understand what Malachy was saying. 'You mean... You're saying... But the assessor told me it would most likely have been the faulty wiring, and that's negligence, so they won't pay out for that.'

'I'm saying,' said Malachy, 'get your insurance inspector back here straight away and I'll make minced meat of him. Those insurance types are as slippery as eels, but this one isn't going to get away with his nonsense. It wasn't even your tree, so there's not an iota of blame that can be pinned on you. You can stop blaming yourself, and you can take those other shops off the market. I'll see you get your money twice over, Blackie, don't worry. I'll do up a report so detailed it will be watertight, and they'll have not a shred of justification to deny your claim.'

Blackie felt dizzy and weak. He gulped down air and exhaled through his nose. A burden of darkness, of unbearable guilt, was lifting from his shoulders like a black mist. He felt he hardly deserved to be happy. And he wasn't happy – he was still shaken with grief – but at least now he could go to Emily and tell her she could look her sister in the face again. It wasn't their fault.

'Get on to that insurance agent now, Blackie,' said Malachy. 'Tell him I'm your representative now, and he's to deal only with me. You've enough to do, and I eat these fellas for breakfast.'

Blackie nodded, still not trusting himself to speak, and stuck out his hand.

Malachy grasped it.

'Thanks, Malachy,' breathed Blackie faintly. 'Thanks very much.'

# CHAPTER 31

Maria put the apple tart on the window to cool. She had given Annie Gallagher the day off and taken over the cooking.

'Will I whip the cream, Granny?' Nellie asked.

'Do, love, and can you check on the roast chicken as well?'

They were in the kitchen of Kilteegan House preparing lunch for all of Maria's children. Emily and Blackie were coming with Aidan, Jack and Skipper were due any minute, and Molly and May had finally made it back from New Zealand. They'd missed Eli's funeral, but they were staying for a couple of weeks. It was the first time all the O'Sullivans would sit down together since Eli died, and Maria was praying Lena would join them this time. She'd said she would, but she'd said that before and then changed her mind at the last minute.

'Is Rosa or Malachy coming?' Nellie asked, counting places as she set the table.

'No, it's just us today. I did ask them, but they have some business to discuss with each other before Rosa flies back to New York tomorrow. She delayed her flight for a few more days so she could speak to him. He's been great, up and down to Dublin and Cork sorting everything out for the reconstruction of the shop. I'm so glad he was able to prove the fire wasn't your parents' fault. The guilt was eating poor Emily up, and Blackie as well.'

Since Malachy's discovery, Maria felt a dark poisonous weight had been lifted from her whole family. Everyone was still devastated about Eli's death of course, that hadn't changed, but this was one less agony at least. Her lovely son-in-law could be honoured for his noble sacrifice without bitterness or blame.

'But it was someone's fault,' Nellie said in a small voice.

Maria looked at her in surprise. 'No, Nellie, it was the tree got struck by lightning in the storm.'

'But Uncle Eli wouldn't have died if it wasn't for me. If I hadn't run away, then Mam and Dad wouldn't have come after me, and so Uncle Eli and Auntie Lena wouldn't have been in the house minding Aidan.'

They had the kitchen to themselves. Maria led Nellie to the table and sat down with her, holding her hand. The girl was different now, less wild, less gregarious. She never wore make-up these days and was always just dressed in jeans and a t-shirt, her hair pulled up in a ponytail. She spent a bit of time with Ted's girls; she and them and Sarah were often together now, and it was good to see it. She needed her family; they all needed each other.

'Darling Nellie, the world is full of what-ifs. Sure if things had been different, who knows who might have died? One of your own parents maybe, trying to save Aidan.'

'But if Aidan hadn't been born...' Tears filled Nellie's blue eyes.

Maria squeezed her hand. 'Ah, Nellie, you can't blame a wee baby for existing. Babies are meant to be loved, and if your Uncle Eli had his time over, he'd do the same thing again as he did that night. He was a great man, and if there is a good way to die, then surely there's no better way than in saving the life of a child.'

'Auntie Lena is wasting away from sorrow.'

Maria sighed sadly. 'My heart is broken for my darling Lena. She's bereft, and I know how it feels. When your granda died, I honestly prayed my heart would just stop beating, the pain was so intense. I willed it to. I would fall asleep at night and pray that God would take me to him, to put us back together, but he didn't, and every morning, oh Nellie, that split second before you realise what happened, and then the awful gut-churning reality again. I hardly slept in the months after. I was afraid to close my eyes because I'd have to wake up to it again. So I know, and I wouldn't wish that pain on my worst enemy, let alone my beautiful Lena.'

Nellie wiped her streaming eyes with her sleeve. 'I still can't believe it. Uncle Eli...'

'I know, darling. It's so hard to come to terms with, but we will. Even Lena will in time.'

'I've never seen my dad like this. He's just so...despondent or something. Like he could cry at any moment.'

'This is hard on every one of us, and on you too.'

'Ah, Granny, don't sympathise with me. I've caused enough drama.'

'No, love, you've been through an ordeal too, and you need minding and care as well. There's no hierarchy of grief or pain, love – you feel what you feel, and it's yours to have. One thing about spending so much of my life in a psychiatric hospital and talking to so many psychologists and psychiatrists is you learn a bit about human nature. I'm not wired right in the head, you know that.' She smiled to take the sting from her words. 'And sometimes the way I feel isn't right or appropriate. But despite not being a very good mother when my children were young – and I realise now it wasn't my fault, but still – I just want to help them now. Help you too, if I can.'

'Thanks, Granny.'

'So if it ever gets too much, trying to come to terms with what happened to you in America, well, there's always a bed for you at my house. You don't need to ring or ask, just turn up, no questions asked.'

Nellie nodded gratefully. 'America is amazing. It's such a wonderful place with so much to see and do. I think I was just not as grown up as I thought, and other people saw that and tried to exploit it. I didn't see it until it was too late.'

'It wasn't too late, love,' Maria reassured her granddaughter. 'You're a lovely young woman with her whole life ahead of her, and we live and learn. That's all this life is, really, one big lesson. It takes us longer to learn some than others. That's why we keep being given the challenges, over and over, until we learn whatever it is we need to learn.'

'I don't know that I learnt much at all, Granny,' Nellie said ruefully.

'You certainly did.' Maria laughed. She was amused by Nellie thinking she was unchanged, when she was so different from the wild, headstrong child of a year ago. 'You learnt that not everyone can be trusted and that we must live life with our eyes and ears wide open. You learnt that your family loves you and will support you no matter what. You learnt that you are worthy of respect. You've learnt that your love and life are precious and shouldn't be squandered on people who don't deserve it. The list goes on and on. This was the biggest learning year of your life.'

'I suppose so.' Nellie sighed. 'How come Emmet is so sensible and I'm such a disaster, though?'

Maria chuckled. 'Emmet has his lessons to learn too, trust me, but life is funny. He's not just your cousin, Nellie, he's your best friend and will always act in your best interests. He's proved it over and over. And someday he'll need you to do the same, so be sure you're ready for it.'

'I can't see Emmet joining a cult,' said Nellie, smiling slightly.

'Maybe not, but as I say, life is a long lesson and he'll face his too. So just watch out for them.' She smiled. 'They may not be as dramatic as yours, but they will come.'

'He's over at the Lamkins now, saying goodbye to Isobel before she goes off to finishing school. And he's talking about staying here instead of going back to America with Malachy.'

Maria frowned. 'Well, we'll have to see about that…'

The sound of tyres on gravel interrupted their conversation. It was Jack and Skipper, with Sarah and Pádraig, who'd stayed up at the farm last night.

'Nellie, Skipper says he'll drive us all to Bandon to the pictures this evening,' said Sarah, looking brighter than she'd done for a while. '*The Return of the Pink Panther* is on, and I know we probably don't feel like it, but it might cheer us up a little bit?' She glanced at her grandmother for reassurance, and Maria nodded.

'Young people have to enjoy themselves. Your father would have said the same thing. He wouldn't want you all to be housebound on his account – that's not what he brought you up to be, miserable. He only wanted you all to be happy.' She dug in her pocket and pulled out a five-pound note, handing it to Pádraig. 'And get some fish and chips after.'

Normally such a treat would have Pádraig whooping for joy – he loved the pictures and fish and chips – but now he just took the money with a small word of thanks and a slight smile. Still, like Sarah, he looked better than he had in a while.

'Where's Mammy?' Sarah asked. 'Is she really coming down to eat with us?'

'She is, so go on upstairs, love, and tell her it's ready,' Maria said, and Sarah and Pádraig beamed and ran for the stairs.

Moments later they were back, poor Pádraig as pale as he was the day they told him his dad was dead, and Sarah's eyes were red-rimmed.

'She says she's not hungry,' Pádraig said, his voice conveying that he was on the edge of tears. 'So she's not coming down after all.'

Skipper and Jack shared a glance, but before they had time to do or say anything, Maria handed Jack the tea towel. 'Dish up there, and I'll be down in a minute.'

'Er, Mam…' Jack began. Since the O'Sullivans were children, they'd learnt it was best to keep their mother away from emotional situations. They'd learnt to cope by themselves or with each other, and the central tenet of that coping was to keep their mother out of it. Everyone in the family knew it, and though her mental illness was spoken about more openly now, thanks to Eli, the consequences of her erratic behaviours over the years were not. It was too hard for everyone, and the past could not be changed.

'I know, Jack, I know. But I actually can help her, because I was in her shoes. So please, trust me this time. I promise I won't make it worse.'

She turned then and went into the hallway and up the stairs to her broken-hearted daughter.

# CHAPTER 32

Lena sat at the window of their bedroom on a dusty-pink velvet chair she'd bought at an auction when they'd first moved into Kilteegan House. On her lap was a shirt of his she'd taken from the laundry basket; it still smelled faintly of him. The wardrobe was full of his clothes, but they were washed and didn't have the scent of him, only of carbolic soap. She wished so much she'd never washed any of them.

She could never imagine moving from this seat, or letting go of this shirt. Never envisage eating a meal or taking more than a sip of water, or standing up even. She felt like if she stood up now, she would shatter into a million pieces, such was the weight of her grief. Her Eli, the man who had taken her as a scared and pregnant and single Irish girl in a foreign country, and loved her, and kissed her tears away, and got her baby back. People thought she was the strong one, as she made the decisions – Eli joked all the time about being henpecked – but he was the rock. He was her safe place.

When Malachy left her and she was pregnant with Emmet, Doc arranged for her to stay with his friends in Cardiff. He delivered her into the arms of Eli Kogan then, not knowing how it would turn out. When Doc died, Eli held her up. When August Berger breathed his last venomous hate-filled breath, Eli was the light of goodness and truth and love. When Phillippe Decker threatened them, Eli was by her side, every step of the way. Having their babies, raising them, reading stories, going on picnics, rolling around on the floor pretending to be a wild animal, making them hyped up before bed, that was her Eli.

She was so incredibly proud of him. Every family in the parish went to him, and he gave everyone the respect and time they needed. He never gave up.

The outpouring of grief at his funeral – it was genuine, she knew, but she couldn't take comfort from it then. It was as if a large block of ice encased her and kept her away from everyone else. She almost resented the other mourners, wanting to scream, 'You think you're sad? You think you've lost something? You think this is pain, what you feel? You don't know. He wasn't yours. He wasn't the other part of your heart.'

How would she live? Sleep in that huge empty bed every night on her own? Be all her children needed her to be, to be mother and father to them? She hadn't the strength of a sparrow now; she couldn't even stand up. There were no more tears, for now anyway; she was dehydrated from crying.

'Eli,' she whispered into the void of her future. 'Where are you? Please, don't leave me. Please, I need you.'

There was a movement behind her, and she turned, imagining for a stupid moment…

Her heart sank when she saw who it was. The last thing on earth she needed now was Maria. She hadn't the energy or the strength to deal with her unstable mother; she just needed to be alone.

'Can I talk to you, love?'

'Mam, I'll be down later, I promise. I just need…' She stopped. She didn't know what she needed, apart for everyone to leave her alone.

'Lena, I know you don't want to see anyone at all or come downstairs, but would you listen, just for a few minutes, and then I'll leave you alone, I promise.'

Lena gazed at her mother dumbly, through eyes that felt gritty and so very tired.

Maria sat on the end of the bed, facing Lena as the weak sunlight came through the window. Lena lowered her eyes. She could hardly bear to look at the bed, Eli's side to the left, hers to the right. The blanket was one Eli's mother, Sarah, had bought for them when they got married, a gorgeous pink and lilac patchwork quilt. Eli had teased Sarah that it couldn't possibly be a present for him but a gift for Lena alone since he was not a fan of pink.

Beside the bed on his locker was a stack of medical books. Every night he would research something, some new strategy he could use to help a patient, some procedure he could suggest. He was never finished learning. He had reading glasses too, which lay on top of the books, an addition since last year, and she used to tease him that he was too vain to wear them outside of the bedroom. He'd forgotten to bring them to Emily and Blackie's house that fateful night.

'One day,' her mother began, 'about three weeks after Paudie died, I got up, calmly, and got dressed. I brushed my hair and washed my face and came downstairs. You and Emily were out feeding the hens, and Jack was up in the triangle with Thirteen, saving the hay. Molly and May weren't born yet – I was very pregnant. The household was running as it had always done. Somehow meals appeared on the table – you and Emily saw to it – and the farm was running because of Jack.'

Her words washed over Lena, but Lena wished Maria would just go. She didn't want a trip down memory lane.

'And I decided then and there that I would take the car, drive it to the cliffs at Sheep's Head and walk off them, into the churning ocean below. Nobody could survive that. That way, I'd be no more nuisance to you all and I'd be with Paudie again. It seemed like the most sensible option.'

'You weren't a nuisance, Mam,' Lena said wearily.

'Oh, I was, and well you know it, Lena. I was dangerous and exhausting, and I saw no grief but my own. I didn't have any understanding that you three were grieving too, that you'd lost the only parent you'd ever had.'

'Mam, I'm sorry, I just can't...' Lena needed this to stop; it was too much on top of everything else.

Maria ignored her pleas and continued. 'I drove out the gate and down the lane, and then I saw the car had no petrol, so I turned around and went back to get some money. You were there, at the back door, the feed bucket in your hand, and you helped me out of the car. I was huge then. The twins were big girls.' She smiled. 'So you helped me in and made me a cup of tea, talking to me in that soothing voice you all learnt as little ones, the voice that tried to stop me going hysterical.'

Lena closed her eyes and leant her head on the chair; maybe she could just sleep for a few minutes.

'But when you handed me the tea, I put it down and I opened my arms to you. It took you a second or two – you were afraid of me, with good reason – but you let me hug you, and as I did, you started to cry. The last time you'd cried in my arms, you were a baby. You could never have an emotion like that around me in case it set me off, I know.

'But we stood there in the kitchen, and you wept for your daddy, and I didn't disintegrate. I didn't even cry. I just held you tight and let you sob. And then I knew something.'

'What?' Lena asked, her eyes still closed.

'That even if I was not a good mother, even if I was away a lot of the time, and even if the awful demons in my head won more often than I wanted them to, you needed me. And Emily and Jack and my unborn babies needed me. I wasn't ideal. I was more trouble than I was worth most of the time. But I was all you had, and you needed me. So I never drove to the cliffs, and I never considered it ever again, no matter how bad things got, because I could hear his voice, your dad's, saying, "Come on, Maria love, they need you. Our precious babies need you. Now, get up again, try again, have another go at it."'

Lena opened her eyes and gazed at her mother.

Maria crossed the room and knelt before her daughter, taking both her hands in hers. 'Your children need you, Lena, and you're a million times better at being a mother than I was. But I was all you had, and some bit of you needed me, which was enough. So I know – believe me, I know better than any other person in this house or this town or this country – your heart is broken, and Eli took a large chunk of it with him. But Emmet and Sarah and Pádraig need you. We'll all help, but you're their anchor in the strange and scary new world, you're where they feel safe, so you have to do it, for them. And for him. Do this for Eli, for all he did for you. Mind his children. Be all you can be. And there will be days, darling, when the effort seems so much more than what you have, but ask him for the strength. And he'll give it to you. Every day I got into the car to go to St Catherine's, every single time, Paudie was there. I could hear him saying, "Come on, love, they need you. Have another go. Do it for me. Don't give up."'

Only the plop of the tear onto Eli's shirt made Lena realise she was crying again.

'If you listen, pet, you will hear him. In his lovely Welsh accent, his chuckling voice, his constant good humour. Listen and he'll be there, encouraging you, saying how proud he is of you, how proud he is of his children. And he will comfort you when you get into that bed on your own and it seems so big and cold without him. Talk to him, Lena. Ask him to be with you, and he will be. Call on your dad, call on Doc – I know they're not far away.'

Lena nodded, but she wasn't sure she believed any more in the idea that the dead went anywhere. She had no sense of Eli. If he was anywhere, he would make her feel him surely.

Maria stood and pulled Lena to her feet. 'I'm telling you, Lena, he is here. He is watching over you, I promise.'

'Oh, Mam...' She disintegrated into her mother's arms.

'Cry now, love. Cry till you haven't a single tear left, and then come downstairs, eat your dinner, let us love you, let us be around you. Hold your children, and draw his strength from them. Can you do that?'

'I... I'll try...' Her mother was right about the children. She knew she'd upset Pádraig and Sarah when they'd called her for lunch earlier, and that wasn't right.

'Good girl.' Maria linked her arm as they went down the stairs. 'Oh, and Lena, here's a thing. I met Vera Slattery this morning. She was gathering some kind of leaves in the orchard, like Eli said she could. She was asking about you and how you were, and then she said that she had a message for you, to tell you to look in the drain.'

'Look for what?' Lena asked with a faint flicker of attention. Eli had been fascinated by Vera and her potions since he'd been cured, so he'd told the woman to take whatever plants she wanted from around the estate but that he'd love to hear what each thing was for.

'No idea. She said she didn't know.'

They entered the big kitchen where the whole family were gathered, and everyone got to their feet like she was royalty or something. Emily and Blackie with the baby, Jack and Skipper smiling at her, Molly and May looking incredibly tanned and older and wiser.

She nodded at everyone and sat and ate her lunch as her mother instructed. She talked to Sarah about horses and Pádraig about football, and she told Emmet he had to follow his dreams, to not put Stanford on hold, to not worry for her, that she had Mike coming soon to take over the surgery and Eli wouldn't have wanted him to give up his dreams. The chat was subdued. Emily let her hold Aidan for a while, which was lovely. She thanked God the little boy had survived. She didn't say much, but she was there, and she ate, and her children looked relieved at just that much, so that was good.

# EPILOGUE

Malachy Berger was used to dealing with women like Rosa Kogan in business. She was dressed with precision, and her sleek dark hair drawn back from her strong attractive face made her look like someone you would not mess with. No matter what.

'Mr Berger, thank you for coming. I want to tell you my story, if you'll allow me to?' she said, offering him a seat in the sitting room of the pleasant guest house that was run by a German couple three miles outside of Kilteegan Bridge. He remembered being here when it was a private house, at a birthday party he thought, as a child.

'Of course.' Malachy wondered what on earth this was about. This woman was a long-lost cousin of Eli's, younger than Eli by a few years, and presumed dead along with the rest of her Jewish family in Leipzig in 1940. Klaus had found her, and Eli had gone to New York with Lena a few years ago to meet her. She had a very fancy house and a legal practice in Manhattan. They'd been introduced a few days previously, but her invitation to join her for a cup of tea came as a surprise. He had no idea what she wanted.

'So…' began Rosa, 'I know this is not exactly the time, but I'd like to tell you something.'

As the sun turned to rain, dark heavy clouds filled the sky, and soon rivulets of water competed in the race down the glass of the window. Malachy never moved; he just listened. A story of tragedy, of murder, of fear, of abandonment, of beginning again. Not just her personal story but that of members of her extended friends and family, her community.

He listened and did not comment. He allowed her to finish, not just explaining her story but what he had to do with it.

Once an hour had passed and Rosa had said what she wanted to say, she excused him, asking him only to think about what she'd said. He agreed and left her to her packing; she was flying back to New York the next day. He was deep in thought as he returned to his rented car.

The O'Sullivans had invited him for lunch, but he didn't want to intrude; besides, he needed to be alone with his thoughts. Rosa had made it clear. But what would he do?

* * *

AFTER LUNCH, Lena did the washing up as Emily dried. Neither one of them wanted Nellie to think they were watching her as she gave Aidan his bottle and then burped him. It was good to see her pick him up, cuddle him and then set him down in his carrycot with an affectionate pat. It was the cheerful love of a sister for her little brother.

'Skipper is bringing us all to the pictures, and Nana gave us a fiver for fish and chips after. Is that all right, Mam?' Pádraig looked less forlorn at the prospect of a cinema visit now that his mother seemed a little better.

'Of course it is. That's exactly what your dad would suggest.' She turned to Emmet, who was chatting to Molly and May. 'Are you going as well?'

He nodded. 'If you don't mind, Mam. But I can stay if you like?'

'No, go, it's fine.' She would have to send her boy back to his studies and, she suspected, his girlfriend soon. She would have to get used to not having him around.

She gathered the scraps from the table and placed them in the plastic bucket she kept under the sink.

'I can give the hens that if you want?' Emily offered.

Lena shook her head. 'No, I think I'd like some fresh air anyway. Thanks, but I'll do it myself.'

The hens crowded around her feet knowing what was coming, and she scattered the scraps all over the yard, sending them into violent attacks on each piece. When it was empty, she took the bucket to the outside tap to rinse it. As she swirled the clean water around the bucket and threw it down the drain, she saw something gleaming, sitting on its side in the crack where the grid over the drain met the stone surround.

Lena smiled as she reached down and picked it up, knowing exactly what it was. 'We looked here, Eli, you know we did…' She pressed her lips to her husband's wedding ring. 'But yet here it is all the same. Maybe Mam is right. Maybe you're not that far away after all.'

*The End*

# AFTERWORD

I sincerely hope you enjoyed this visit back to Kilteegan Bridge and that you are glad to hear there is one final book in the series to come. It is called *A Silent Understanding* and can be preordered here :

It will be published in March of 2023.

If you would like to see my other books or join my readers club to hear from me now and again about a writer's life in a stone cottage in rural Ireland among other things, just pop over to www.jean grainger.com.

I'll give you a free ebook novel as a welcome gift. My readers club is 100% free and always will be, and I would never give your information to a third party.

If you can't wait till March for your next book, and you'd like to try another of my novels, here is a preview of one of my other books, called The Star and the Shamrock.

This book is based loosely on the fact that the Jewish and Irish communities in Ireland during WW2 leased a farm in Northern

Ireland to accommodate Jewish refugee children from the Kindertransport.

## The Star and the Shamrock

### Prologue

*Belfast, 1938*

The gloomy interior of the bar, with its dark wood booths and frosted glass, suited the meeting perfectly. Though there were a handful of other customers, it was impossible to see them clearly. Outside on Donegal Square, people went about their business, oblivious to the tall man who entered the pub just after lunchtime. Luckily, the barman was distracted with a drunk female customer and served him absentmindedly. He got a drink, sat at the back in a booth as arranged and waited. His contact was late. He checked his watch once more, deciding to give the person ten more minutes. After that, he'd have to assume something had gone wrong.

He had no idea who he was meeting; it was safer that way, everything on a need-to-know basis. He felt a frisson of excitement – it felt good to actually be doing something, and he was ideally placed to make this work. The idea was his and he was proud of it. That should make those in control sit up and take notice.

War was surely now inevitable, no matter what bit of paper old Chamberlain brought back from Munich. If the Brits believed the peace in our time that he promised was on the cards, they'd believe anything. He smiled.

He tried to focus on the newspaper he'd carried in with him, but his mind wandered into the realm of conjecture once more, as it had ever since he'd had the call. If Germany could be given whatever assistance they needed to subjugate Great Britain – and his position meant they could offer that and more – then the Germans would have to make good on their promise. A United Ireland at last. It was all he wanted.

He checked his watch again. Five minutes more, that was all he would stay. It was too dangerous otherwise.

His eyes scanned the racing pages, unseeing. Then a ping as the pub door opened. Someone entered, got a drink and approached his seat. He didn't look up until he heard the agreed-upon code phrase. He raised his eyes, and their gazes met.

He did a double take. Whatever or whomever he was expecting, it wasn't this.

Chapter 1

*Liverpool, England, 1939*

Elizabeth put the envelope down and took off her glasses. The thin paper and the Irish stamps irritated her. Probably that estate agent wanting to sell her mother's house again. She'd told him twice she wasn't selling, though she had no idea why. It wasn't as if she were ever going back to Ireland, her father long dead, her mother gone last year – she was probably up in heaven tormenting the poor saints with her extensive religious knowledge. The letter drew her back to the little Northern Irish village she'd called home...that big old lonely house...her mother.

Margaret Bannon was a pillar of the community back in Ballycreggan, County Down, a devout Catholic in a deeply divided place, but she had a heart of stone.

Elizabeth sighed. She tried not to think about her mother, as it only upset her. Not a word had passed between them in twenty-one years, and then Margaret died alone. She popped the letter behind the clock; she needed to get to school. She'd open it later, or next week... or never.

Rudi's face, in its brown leather frame smiled down at her from the dresser. 'Don't get bitter, don't be like her.' She imagined she heard her late husband admonish her, his boyish face frozen in an old sepia photograph, in his King's Regiment uniform, so proud, so full of excitement, so bloody young. What did he know of the horrors that awaited him out there in Flanders? What did any of them know?

She mentally shook herself. This line of thought wasn't helping. Rudi was dead, and she wasn't her mother. She was her own person. Hadn't she proved that by defying her mother and marrying Rudi? It all seemed so long ago now, but the intensity of the emotions lingered. She'd met, loved and married young Rudi Klein as a girl of eighteen. Margaret Bannon was horrified at the thought of her Catholic daughter marrying a Jew, but Elizabeth could still remember that heady feeling of being young and in love. Rudi could have been a Martian for all she cared. He was young and handsome and funny, and he made her feel loved.

She wondered, if he were to somehow come back from the dead and just walk up the street and into the kitchen of their little terraced house, would he recognise the woman who stood there? Her chestnut hair that used to fall over her shoulders was always now pulled back in a bun, and the girl who loved dresses was now a woman whose clothes were functional and modest. She was thirty-nine, but she knew she could pass for older. She had been pretty once, or at least not too horrifically ugly anyway. Rudi had said he loved her; he'd told her she was beautiful.

She snapped on the wireless, but the talk was of the goings-on in Europe again. She unplugged it; it was too hard to hear first thing in the morning. Surely they wouldn't let it all happen again, not after the last time?

All anyone talked about was the threat of war, what Hitler was going to do. Would there really be peace as Mr Chamberlain promised? It was going to get worse before it got better if the papers were to be believed.

Though she was almost late, she took the photo from the shelf. A smudge of soot obscured his smooth forehead, and she wiped it with the sleeve of her cardigan. She looked into his eyes.

'Goodbye, Rudi darling. See you later.' She kissed the glass, as she did every day.

How different her life could have been…a husband, a family. Instead, she had received a generic telegram just like so many others in that war that was supposed to end all wars. She carried in her heart for twenty years that feeling of despair. She'd taken the telegram from the boy who refused to meet her eyes. He was only a few years younger than she. She opened it there, on the doorstep of that very house, the words expressing regret swimming before her eyes. She remembered the lurch in her abdomen, the baby's reaction mirroring her own. 'My daddy is dead.'

She must have been led inside, comforted – the neighbours were good that way. They knew when the telegram lad turned his bike down their street that someone would need holding up. That day it was her…tomorrow, someone else. She remembered the blood, the sense of dragging downwards, that ended up in a miscarriage at five months. All these years later, the pain had dulled to an ever-present ache.

She placed the photo lovingly on the shelf once more. It was the only one she had. In lots of ways, it wasn't really representative of Rudi; he was not that sleek and well presented. 'The British Army smartened me up,' he used to say. But out of uniform is how she remembered him. Her most powerful memory was of them sitting in that very kitchen the day they got the key. His Uncle Saul had lent them the money to buy the house, and they were going to pay him back.

They'd been married in the registry office in the summer of 1918, when he was home on brief leave because of a broken arm. She could almost hear her mother's wails all the way across the Irish Sea, but she didn't care. It didn't matter that her mother was horrified at her marrying a *Jewman,* as she insisted on calling him, or that she was cut off from all she ever knew – none of it mattered. She loved Rudi and he loved her. That was all there was to it.

She'd worn her only good dress and cardigan – the minuscule pay of a teaching assistant didn't allow for new clothes, but she didn't care. Rudi had picked a bunch of flowers on the way to the registry office, and his cousin Benjamin and Benjamin's wife, Nina, were the witnesses. Ben was killed at the Somme, and Nina went to London, back to her family. They'd lost touch.

Elizabeth swallowed. The lump of grief never left her throat. It was a part of her now. A lump of loss and pain and anger. The grief had given way to fury, if she were honest. Rudi was killed early on the morning of the 11th of November, 1918, in Belgium. The armistice had been signed at five forty five a.m. but the order to end hostilities would not come into effect until eleven a.m. The eleventh hour of the eleventh month. She imagined the generals saw some glorious symmetry in that. But there wasn't. Just more people left in mourning than there had to be. She lost him, her Rudi, because someone wanted the culmination of four long years of slaughter to look nice on a piece of paper.

She shivered. It was cold these mornings, though spring was supposed to be in the air. The children in her class were constantly sniffling and coughing. She remembered the big old fireplace in the national school in Ballycreggan, where each child was expected to bring a sod of turf or a block of timber as fuel for the fire. Master O'Reilly's wife would put the big jug of milk beside the hearth in the mornings so the children could have a warm drink by lunchtime. Elizabeth would have loved to have a fire in her classroom, but the British education system would never countenance such luxuries.

She glanced at the clock. Seven thirty. She should go. Fetching her coat and hat, and her heavy bag of exercise books that she'd marked last night, she let herself out.

The street was quiet. Apart from the postman, doing deliveries on the other side of the street, she was the only person out. She liked it, the sense of solitude, the calm before the storm.

The mile-long walk to Bridge End Primary was her exercise and thinking time. Usually, she mulled over what she would teach that day or how to deal with a problem child – or more frequently, a problem parent. She had been a primary schoolteacher for so long, there was little she had not seen. Coming over to England as a bright sixteen-year-old to a position as a teacher's assistant in a Catholic school was the beginning of a trajectory that had taken her far from Ballycreggan, from her mother, from everything she knew.

She had very little recollection of the studies that transformed her from a lowly teaching assistant to a fully qualified teacher. After Rudi was killed and she'd lost the baby, a kind nun at her school suggested she do the exams to become a teacher, not just an assistant, and because it gave her something to do with her troubled mind, she agreed. She got top marks, so she must have thrown herself into her studies, but she couldn't remember much about those years. They were shrouded in a fog of grief and pain.

Chapter 2

*Berlin, Germany, 1939*

Ariella Bannon waited behind the door, her heart thumping. She'd covered her hair with a headscarf and wore her only remaining coat, a grey one that had been smart once. Though she didn't look at all Jewish with her curly red hair – and being married to Peter Bannon, a Catholic, meant she was in a slightly more privileged position than other Jews – people knew what she was. She took her children to the synagogue, kept a kosher house. She never in her wildest nightmares imagined that the quiet following of her faith would have led to this.

One of the postmen, Herr Krupp, had joined the Brownshirts. She didn't trust him to deliver the post properly, so she had to hope it was Frau Braun that day. She wasn't friendly exactly, but at least she gave you your letters. She was surprised at Krupp; he'd been nice before, but since Kristallnacht, it seemed that everyone was different. She even remembered Peter talking to him a few times about the weather or fishing or something. It was hard to believe that underneath all that, there was such hatred. Neighbours, people on the street, children even, seemed to have turned against all Jews. Liesl and Erich were scared all the time. Liesl tried to put a brave face on it – she was such a wonderful child – but she was only ten. Erich looked up to her so much. At seven, he thought his big sister could fix everything.

It was her daughter's birthday next month but there was no way to celebrate. Ariella thought back to birthdays of the past, cakes and friends and presents, but that was all gone. Everything was gone.

She tried to swallow the by-now-familiar lump of panic. Peter had been picked up because he and his colleague, a Christian, tried to defend an old Jewish lady the Nazi thugs were abusing in the street. Ariella had been told that the uniformed guards beat up the two men and threw them in a truck. That was five months ago. She hoped every day her husband would turn up, but so far, nothing. She considered going to visit his colleague's wife to see if she had heard anything, but nowadays, it was not a good idea for a Jew to approach an Aryan for any reason.

At least she'd spoken to the children in English since they were born. At least that. She did it because she could; she'd had an English governess as a child, a terrifying woman called Mrs Beech who insisted Ariella speak not only German but English, French and Italian as well. Peter smiled to hear his children jabbering away in other languages, and he always said they got that flair for languages from her. He spoke German only, even though his father was Irish. She remembered fondly her father-in-law, Paddy. He'd died when Erich was a baby. Though he spoke fluent German, it was always with a lovely lilting accent. He would tell her tales of growing up in Ireland. He came to Germany to study when he was a young man, and saw and fell instantly in love with Christiana Berger, a beauty from Bavaria. And so in Germany he remained. Peter was their only child because Christiana was killed in a horse-riding accident when Peter was only five years old. How simple those days were, seven short years ago, when she had her daughter toddling about, her newborn son in her arms, a loving husband and a doting father-in-law. Now, she felt so alone.

Relief. It was Frau Braun. But she walked past the building.

Ariella fought the wave of despair. Elizabeth should have received the letter Ariella had posted by now, surely. It was sent three weeks ago. Ariella tried not to dwell on the many possibilities. What if she wasn't at the address? Maybe the family had moved on. Peter had no contact with his only first cousin as far as she knew.

Nathaniel, Peter's best friend, told her he might be able to get Liesl and Erich on the Kindertransport out of Berlin – he had some connections apparently – but she couldn't bear the idea of them going to strangers. If only Elizabeth would say yes. It was the only way she could put her babies on that train. And even then… She dismissed that thought and refused to let her mind go there. She had to get them away until all this madness died down.

She'd tried everything to get them all out. But there was no way.

She'd contacted every single embassy – the United States, Venezuela, Paraguay, places she'd barely heard of – but there was no hope. The lines outside the embassies grew longer every day, and without someone to vouch for you, it was impossible. Ireland was her only chance. Peter's father, the children's grandfather, was an Irish citizen. If she could only get Elizabeth Bannon to agree to take the children, then at least they would be safe.

Sometimes she woke in the night, thinking this must all be a nightmare. Surely this wasn't happening in Germany, a country known for learning and literature, music and art? And yet it was.

Peter and Ariella would have said they were German, their children were German, just the same as everyone else, but not so. Her darling children were considered *Untermensch*, subhuman, because of her Jewish blood in their veins.

If you'd like to read on you can get the book here:

https://geni.us/TheStarandtheShamrocAL

# ABOUT THE AUTHOR

Jean Grainger is a USA Today bestselling Irish author. She writes historical and contemporary Irish fiction and her work has very flatteringly been compared to the late, great Maeve Binchy.

She lives in a stone cottage in Cork with her husband Diarmuid and the youngest two of her four children. The older two come home for a break when adulting gets too exhausting. There are a variety of animals there too, all led by two cute but clueless micro-dogs called Scrappy and Scoobi.

# ALSO BY JEAN GRAINGER

**The Tour Series**

The Tour

Safe at the Edge of the World

The Story of Grenville King

The Homecoming of Bubbles O'Leary

Finding Billie Romano

Kayla's Trick

**The Carmel Sheehan Story**

Letters of Freedom

The Future's Not Ours To See

What Will Be

**The Robinswood Story**

What Once Was True

Return To Robinswood

Trials and Tribulations

**The Star and the Shamrock Series**

The Star and the Shamrock

The Emerald Horizon

The Hard Way Home

The World Starts Anew

**The Queenstown Series**

Last Port of Call

The West's Awake

The Harp and the Rose

Roaring Liberty

**Standalone Books**

So Much Owed

Shadow of a Century

Under Heaven's Shining Stars

Catriona's War

Sisters of the Southern Cross

**The Kilteegan Bridge Series**

The Trouble with Secrets

What Divides Us

More Harm Than Good

When Irish Eyes Are Lying

**The Mags Munroe Story**

The Existential Worries of Mags Munroe

Growing Wild in the Shade

Made in the USA
Las Vegas, NV
13 January 2023